OLD MURDER, NEW MURDER, WHERE ARE THE COWS?

D.B. ELROGG

A MILO RATHKEY MYSTERY

Old Murder, New Murder, Where Are The Cows?
A Milo Rathkey Mystery

Copyright © 2023 Alyce Goldberg, Harvey Goldberg All
Rights Reserved

ISBN 979-8-9856252-7-1 (Paperback)
ISBN 979-8-9856252-5-7 (eBook)
ISBN 979-8-9856252-9-5 (Hardcover)

If you wish to contact the authors, you may email them at authors@ dbelrogg.com

This is a work of fiction. All characters and incidents are totally from the minds of the authors and any resemblance to actual persons, living or dead, or incidents past and present is purely coincidental.

Cover Design by Jera Publishing

Dedicated to Charlie, The Real Blue

SPECIAL THANKS TO

STAN JOHNSON
JODY EVANS
DR. ELENA CABB
DOUG OSELL
NICK GOLDBERG
PIPER GOLDBERG
ROB RAINEY
CONNIE RAJI
KRISTINA CLEMENT

1

The work light on the new barn flickered through the blowing snow as Wally Junior struggled to heave the last case into the aft storage compartment of Eddy Palesko's Piper Cherokee. The howling wind battled with the growing sound of a siren.

"Go!" Wally Junior yelled at Eddy.

"I'm gone, but this is it. I'm out!" Eddy shouted back.

Wally Junior's eyes flashed with anger as he grabbed Eddy by the collar and threw him up against the plane. "You're out when I say you're out."

"Cops are comin'. I can stay and tell 'em what's going on," Eddy threatened.

Wally's smile was evil, menacing. "I can bury you in that field."

Looking into Wally's dead eyes, Eddy flinched. "Kidding. Just kidding."

Wally slapped him hard on the face. "I know Eddy. You and me are pals."

The screaming siren of a rapidly approaching police car was winning the battle with the wind.

"Now go," Wally demanded, throwing Palesko toward the plane's open cockpit.

Eddy scrambled into the pilot's seat and revved the engine. The Piper Cherokee lurched down the dirt road, gaining height, banking to the right, narrowly missing the old barn and silo at the far end of the runway.

Wally slammed the barn doors shut just as Wally Senior limped over from the clapboard farmhouse porch. The old man spat on the ground. "He's gonna be trouble, boy."

"Not for long," Wally Junior smiled. "His plane is never gonna make it."

The old man grabbed his son's arm. "I don't wanna lose that load."

Junior pulled his arm away. "I ain't stupid. Our friends on the Canadian side will make sure Eddy gets bad gas for his trip back."

Wally Senior laughed as a single cop car pulled into the farm. The two men flipped up their parka hoods and stood their ground in the blowing snow as the siren's scream grew louder. The black and white police cruiser slid to a stop at their feet and the siren died. Silence.

The two Schmidts, father and son, did not budge.

The driver, a lanky officer, ordered his partner to stay in the car and took his time exiting the vehicle. Standing against the wind, he yanked down his knit cap and pulled on his black leather gloves, meticulously straightening the seams.

Both Schmidts stood waiting. The cop stepped up to the men, looking from one to the other. "Which one of you is Walter Schmidt Junior?"

Wally Senior sneered. "Well, smart guy, look at us. What do you think?"

The cop's eyes narrowed as he opened and closed his fingers in the leather gloves before moving to the younger man, stopping inches from his face. "Well, Junior, we have reason to believe you're smuggling."

Junior used his six-five height to intimidate. "Yeah, I smuggle snow to Canada."

"Name's Rod Prepinski." The cop put his hand on his holstered gun and turned to walk toward the barn. "This is a fine new barn. Mind if I take a look inside?"

"Got a warrant?"

Pivoting quickly, Peplinski grabbed Wally Junior and attempted to throw him up against the barn door. Wally was a bull of a man. He barely moved.

Trying to save face, Prepinski patted the man's arms and smoothed down invisible wrinkles in this parka. "Solid. Good. I like solid partners. You and I, Junior, are going to be solid partners."

Junior sneered.

"I know that plane that just took off was loaded with boxes of cigarettes heading to Canada. Ten percent off the top will keep you from getting disturbing visits from me, catching you in the act."

Wally Junior sprang, grabbed Peplinski's arm, and slammed him against the barn door. "Crandell, wake up!" Peplinski yelled to his partner. Crandell was slow to open the door. With two steps, Senior was at the passenger's side of the cop car. He kicked the door closed. Senior was gimpy, but fast.

"Now you get this straight, you piece of crap," Wally Junior hissed, holding Peplinski's face tight against the barn door. "This is a dairy farm. We got cows. Hear the cows?" Junior leaned into the cop, his mouth inches from the man's ear. "If I ever see you again, I will end you."

Junior twisted the man's arm behind him. "Do you believe me?"

Peplinski screamed and cried, "Yes! Yes! I believe you."

"Let him go," Senior yelled. "I can't hold this other guy forever."

Wally Junior threw his man down and watched as he scurried to get back into the car and locked it. "A lot of help you were!" Prepinski screamed at his partner, gunning the engine and spraying rocks in Wally Junior's direction.

Father and son stood for a long time, illuminated by the barn light. The cop car had disappeared into the night, leaving only the sound of the wind. "Make sure that plane never makes it back, boy," Senior said.

"It won't."

"Now get to work. Those cows won't feed themselves." The old man spat again.

§

Twenty-five Years Later.

The darkening, gray sky pressed down on the abandoned farm as Kirkland Rafferty Jr. stumbled out of the weatherworn clapboard farmhouse. Catching his balance at the top of the porch, he scoured the empty landscape. Seeing no one, Rafferty raced down the porch steps. His leg broke through the rotting boards of the third step, flinging him to the ground, wrenching his right shoulder. Adrenaline rushed to his heart, sending blood to his brain. Wincing and limping, he yanked himself into the pilot's seat of his Beechcraft Bonanza, which sat waiting near the deserted farmhouse.

"Bad plan, KJ!" He threw the now useless briefcase onto the empty co-pilot's seat.

Nothing was going as planned. Nothing at all. Turning over the engine, not waiting for it to warm up, he forced his twisted arm to pull back on the throttle, powering the aircraft down the rutted dirt runway. The textbook climb in front of the ruin of a barn and silo had him free and clear. As he turned to look back at the old farmhouse, hoping it had disappeared, his arm spasmed.

Without warning, his plane jolted violently and began to lose altitude. There was not enough air between the plane and the ground—nightmare upon nightmare. KJ knew he was going to crash. He leveled the plane as best he could before the nose plowed into the overgrown grassy field. The screaming pain in his shoulder overtook the throb in his right leg and chest. Everything went dark.

§

The McKnights were enjoying the East Village. Sutherland ducked into a doorway to watch Agnes, his tall, charming, auburn-haired wife. She slowed, then stopped, glancing to the right and left.

Spotting him behind her, she put her hands on her hips and chided, "What are you doing, silly boy?"

"Admiring this gorgeous woman," Sutherland said, catching up to her.

"It better be me!" She put her arm through his and gave him a hug.

His weekend surprise trip to New York City was a hit. The pièce de résistance being tickets to MoMa's *Matisse: The Red Studio.* Sutherland was beyond pleased his incredible wife shared his not-widely-advertised love of art. In fact, she was the only one who really knew much about this facet of his life.

They stopped outside McSorley's Old Ale House on 7th Street. Agnes turned to Sutherland. "Are you sure? It looks a little…"

"I know, but I've been told this place is something we need to experience. Let's be brave."

He pushed open one of the worn wooden doors. Stepping through, Agnes looked down at the sawdust which cushioned their steps. Their eyes adjusted to the crowded dark interior with its panel dark wood walls and pictures of celebrities past.

"I would describe it as The Pickwick without the loving care," Agnes said.

Spotting an empty table, Sutherland grabbed Agnes' hand and began racing toward it, beating another couple by a few steps.

"Oh, one of the grab-a-table places!" Agnes exclaimed as she straightened out her dress, having been flung into a chair by her beloved.

"I'm sorry. I called ahead. No reservations allowed," Sutherland said.

Agnes kept her eyes riveted on Sutherland's face, avoiding the angry stares of the couple they had just bested. Sutherland, feeling no shame, read aloud the menu on the chalkboard near the bar.

Agnes buried her head in the McSorley's history card. "Are you kidding? 'Good Ale, Raw Onions and No Ladies!' That was their motto until 1970?"

"I agree that's appalling, but I'm starving. Would you like me to read the menu again?" Sutherland asked.

Agnes peeked up to see the other couple had finally captured an empty table. "I heard liver sausage sandwich."

Sutherland squinted at the menu. "They have a number of tastier…"

"I want a liver sausage sandwich," Agnes announced, cutting him off.

"Liver sausage? You like liver?"

"There's a lot you don't know about me, Mr. McKnight! This creamy liver sausage sandwich with onions, no mustard needed, is just the tip of the iceberg."

"Mysterious lady, eh? Well, maybe I'm mysterious too." Sutherland smiled. "What am I going to order?"

"I don't see humus or salad, so my bet is the burger, extra lettuce, tomatoes, and pickles. You know, salad on a bun."

Denying he was predictable, Sutherland told the waiter he wanted a Feltman's hot dog with extra sauerkraut. "I'm going native!" The waiter was unimpressed. Watching several of McSorley's burgers being served to other patrons gave Sutherland time to rue his pride.

Four ales, two light, two dark, were slung on their table. Agnes stopped hers as they slowed their slide. Sutherland's dark ales bumped and slopped onto his hand. He dabbed up the foamy liquid with a paper table napkin, finishing just in time for the food to be dropped in front of them.

"Two beers?" Agnes questioned.

"They're half pints," Sutherland explained. "I was warned, but I forgot."

Agnes straightened up in her chair while creating a plan to attack her mountain of liver sausage. She scooped her fingers around half the sandwich, then squeezed it, burying the onions in the liver sausage. She carefully bit into it, getting the sausage, the onions, and the rye bread into her mouth with her first bite.

Sutherland watched.

Agnes, eyes closed, made yummy sounds for at least thirty seconds before proclaiming, "This is so good!"

"A third party suggested that we eat here."

"Who?"

"A highly gastronomically respected, and somewhat reluctant, semi-famous third party."

Agnes held her sandwich in midair, contemplating Sutherland's words for a few seconds. "Milo? You took a restaurant suggestion from Milo?" she asked incredulously, referencing the other co-owner of Lakesong, Police Consultant Milo Rathkey. "When was Milo ever in New York City?"

"I don't know, but except for his aversion to anything green, he loves good food, and he was right. This place is not to be missed. Where else can you get a mile-high liverwurst sandwich that could feed a family of ten?"

"Or one hungry wife." Agnes took another bite.

She watched Sutherland enjoy his Feltman's hot dog with extra sauerkraut, including the pickle. When he had finished, she slyly proclaimed, "You know, that was still a salad on a bun. You just substituted cabbage for lettuce."

Sutherland looked perplexedly at his empty plate. "Hmm, you might be right," he agreed. "I do have a style. Care to shop a few more galleries before we return to the airport?"

At the word airport, Agnes' stomach lurched in panic for a moment. *When do we have to be there?*

For once, Sutherland correctly read the situation. "We're not late. We're never late. Our plane waits for us."

Agnes smiled. "Liverwurst with onions and being able to fly on our own schedule really is the height of decadence," Agnes said. "No rushing."

"Or standing in line," Sutherland added.

"We really own our own plane? When did that happen?"

"McKnight Realty is really the owner. I bought it instead of that couch factory you yelled at me for not buying a few months ago."

"Okay. I may have lost it…a bit. Usually when I marry people, they disclose multi-generational portfolios of investments which made you…"

"Us. We are an 'us.'"

"Made us a tad better off than really comfortable, and now we have a plane. Why didn't we use it when we flew to Hawaii?"

"We didn't have the plane then, but we flew first class," Sutherland reminded her.

"First class was nice, but we still had to wait to board, wait for the plane to taxi, wait for our luggage—a lot of waiting."

"Agreed. Which is why I wanted this weekend to be no waiting for anyone but each other."

Agnes nodded her head. "Nice one, Mr. McKnight."

"Sometimes I don't mess up."

"Sometimes you don't. Should we nurse our ales or let the people standing by the door race for our table?" Agnes asked.

"On the count of two…"

"And we're up and out. Don't get run over." Agnes bounded up and out.

In the fall sunshine, Agnes grabbed Sutherland's hand. "I'm hanging on to you, so you don't get mysteriously lost again."

Sutherland held her hand until they reached another gallery. He opened the door and bowed.

Agnes smiled. "Nice."

§

Milo looked forward to a relaxing Sunday evening after a weekend spent hiking the North Shore with Mary Alice Bonner and her ever-growing pack of pups—Flash, Phoenix, Luna, and new pup Los. Unlike Luna, who only liked Milo when he had cream puffs, Los was all in all the time.

He wandered into his office to check his private investigator website set up for interesting cases only. People were looking for missing golf clubs, pets, or cars. Milo deleted those requests, complaining that nobody seemed to read or understand the word *interesting*. Next stop, the kitchen.

On his way, he debated what to do for dinner. No Sunday poker game, and it was Chef Martha's day off. He found himself staring at the drawer in the refrigerator marked *MILO*—Martha's solution to Milo's odd hour snacking.

He began constructing his favorite ham and cheese sandwich. As he added yellow mustard to one slice of bread, Milo debated whether to continue plodding through a mystery novel the critics erroneously described as suspenseful. Milo's phone vibrated with a news update: *Breaking News—Duluth Fire Department reports a plane down near Martin Road in East Duluth.*

Milo pocketed his phone, grabbed his completed sandwich, and began his trip through the Lakesong Gallery to his library. The news update rolled around in his mind. Sutherland and Agnes were due back this evening. Milo knew about Sutherland's purchase but had not yet seen the plane. He tried to dismiss the story. This plane crash was just an uncomfortable coincidence. As he bit into his sandwich, the uncomfortable coincidence continued to gnaw at him. He found it annoying, so he decided to bother Mary Alice.

"Milo?"

"Hey Blue, there was a plane crash near Martin Road."

"Do I or any of the dogs need to know this, Milo?"

"Probably not, but Agnes and Sutherland are due back in Duluth tonight on their new plane."

"Ahh, you are worried."

"I can't enjoy my ham sandwich without talking to someone about it."

"You need to talk to someone about your sandwich? I know what you prefer on your sandwich: bread, lettuce, lots of mayo, ham, and cheese…"

"Don't forget the mustard."

"Yellow, not spicy. I've been trained. Look, as charming as you are, and as much as I enjoy our banter, I am soaking in the tub with a glass of delightful Chateau Montrose Bordeaux."

"1852, just before the French truffle disaster?" Milo quipped.

"Cute. 2010. Besides, I have several life changing issues I'm working on right now, so go, take a late-night run to the crash. Or don't go. Don't care."

"I knew you'd have the right answer. What life-changing issues are you working on?"

"They need more sipping and soaking. Check with me tomorrow." The phone went dead.

Milo stood up, as did Jet the cat who was curled by the library fireplace. "I'm going out," Milo announced to the cat. "Care to come along?"

Jet yawned, stretched, and curled up in the opposite direction.

Checking GPS, Milo saw Martin Road was off Jean Duluth Road, but he lacked an address. "A plane crash has to be visible. Right Jet?" Jet, who cared little for the affairs of humans that didn't involve food, continued to sleep.

Considering this trip to be work, not pleasure, Milo drove his 2004 Honda Accord, reaching Martin Road in about ten minutes. The streetlights were blinking on, illuminating the dusk. "Nothing here but houses and trees," Milo muttered. As the road hair-pinned to the left, pulsing blue lights shone in the distance. Approaching the lights, he saw the cop car parked sideways across a wide dirt road, maneuvering to let an ambulance out onto Martin Road.

The activity in front of him gave Milo time to get the lay of the land. In an empty field on the left, he could see three fire trucks circling the smoldering hulk of what must be the plane.

Milo waited for the ambulance to clear, then began turning onto the road. The cop gunned his car back across the road, stopping Milo.

Milo didn't move. The lone policeman begrudgingly left his car. Milo lowered his window.

"This road is closed!" the cop barked, shining his flashlight in Milo's face.

Milo held up his consultant badge that he always left on the passenger seat.

The cop looked over the badge, becoming instantly more friendly. "I'm surprised anyone else would be here besides me and the firemen. I'm just here for crowd control."

Milo shrugged. "Was the plane landing or taking off?"

"Don't know. The fire guys have probably figured it out. The fire marshal is on the scene. I'm keeping people out."

"Where should I park?"

"Drive up the road past the crash, turn left, and leave your car off to the side. You're gonna have to walk into the field."

Milo thanked him, waited for him to back up his car, and drove on. The dusk had faded to pitch black, lit only by his headlights and the powerful work lights surrounding the plane. Milo parked as instructed. He slipped his consultant's card lanyard over his head and turned on his tac light.

The ground was rutted and uneven. Tall grass had to be kicked aside and flattened down as he walked. It was tough going. Sutherland had only spoken about buying a jet. A jet crash would have had more fire, more ambulances, and more than one lone policeman guarding the road. The fear that this crash involved Sutherland and Agnes had gone away.

So *why am I here?* Milo wondered as he tripped over an abandoned tire. *You're here because you're bored,* he answered himself. He held the tac light at his feet so he could better see where he was going and avoid stepping into a hole or tripping over abandoned farm machinery. Field mice scurried to get out of his way.

One of the firemen walked toward him, holding up his hand as a signal for Milo to stop. "Sorry sir, this is off limits. Someone should have stopped you from entering the field."

Milo again held up his lanyard, showing the fireman his police credential. "Milo Rathkey, Duluth Police Department."

The fireman nodded as he reached Milo. "Gary Knutson. Didn't think this was a police matter."

"What happened?" Milo asked.

"Young guy was taking off down that road there behind you. He achieved liftoff, apparently clipped that old silo off to the right while making a turn. His plane crashed in this field. A man from one of those houses down Martin Road heard it, called 9-1-1, and came running."

"Is he dead?"

"No, he was in the way. We sent him home."

"Not the witness, the pilot!"

"Oh yeah, okay," Knutson nodded his head. "No, he's actually in pretty good shape, all things considered. Nothing life threatening. Concussion, I think. Oh, his ankle was swelling."

Milo looked around in the darkness. "What was he doing here?"

Knutson shook his head. "We don't know."

"Is that road where I'm parked a runway?"

"Again, don't know. It's pretty rough, but it's wide."

Milo and Knutson continued onto the scene of the crash. Milo was introduced to the fire marshal, Paul Kutka.

"I think this is more a case for the FAA and NTSB than the Duluth Police Department," Kutka said.

Milo nodded, looking at the crumpled plane. "Single engine prop?" he asked.

The fire marshal nodded.

"Did the pilot say why he landed here?"

"He's sort of in and out. Got a hard knock to the head. Not making much sense."

"Mind if I look around the place? I'll stay out of your way."

"Suit yourself. Just be careful. The EMTs don't want to come back for you."

Milo trudged back through the field, disturbing the same field mice. They were not having a quiet evening.

"Now a plane landing in the middle of abandoned, rutted nowhere is interesting," Milo said to himself. "Was the pilot picking something up, dropping something off, or both? Was it legal or illegal?"

Once back in the Honda, Milo needed his brights to distinguish the road from the field as he slowly drove up to a dead-end circle. Creeping the Honda around the circle, his brights illuminated a barn with large sliding doors. Milo noticed a thick chain and sturdy padlock which screamed, *DO NOT ENTER.*

After sweeping a stand of pine trees, his lights shone on an old farmhouse. The house was not nearly as secure. The front door was ajar. *Why keep the barn padlocked but a house wide open?*

Getting out of the car, Milo fumbled for his tac light. He could see the broken wooden steps. Milo haltingly stepped, then grabbed a secure post and heaved himself up onto the porch. Shining his flashlight down, he looked for holes to avoid on the porch. *Pretty rickety.*

He kicked the door open. Milo smelled staleness immediately, but there was something else—a familiar sickening sweet odor. Scratching, scurrying feet told him that not all the field mice were in the field. A single stairway with a burgundy runner led up to the second floor. An oversized mirror hung on the wall to the right of the staircase, reflecting a table holding the remnants of what appeared to be a large dead plant. A dusty, oversized couch took up the rest of the hallway. The area to his left was clogged with living room furniture.

Milo stepped to his right, into what looked to be a dining room. Worrying about more critters, he swept his flashlight around the room before entering. Finding none, he carefully circled the table surrounded by chairs and stepped up to the half open yellow Dutch door. That sweet smell was getting stronger. *Let it be a dead raccoon.*

He shined his flashlight quickly from ceiling to floor several times, alerting any large critters so they could escape— away from him.

"Son of a bitch," he swore as the light came to rest on a still body lying beside a kitchen table. The body looked fresh. His heart skipped a beat. He might not be alone. Milo spotlighted the dining room again, corner to corner, floor to ceiling—no one. Milo stopped and listened—no sound.

I could be relaxing in the library with a ham and cheese sandwich and a cat right now.

He turned the knob on the bottom half of the Dutch door and approached the body. His light illuminated a pool of blood and bloody footprints. Being careful to avoid having his footprints join the others, he bent down, placing his fingers on the neck of the woman. There was no pulse, and the skin was cold to the touch.

Milo straightened up, stepped back, and called Police Lieutenant Ernie Gramm.

"Milo?" Gramm answered.

"Ernie, I'm at the scene of a plane crash off of Martin Road."

"Good for you, Milo. Call again sometime when you want to tell me about your odd hobbies."

"The pilot's going to be okay."

"What a relief! Now, if that's all, I'm going back to season twenty of *Midsomer Murders*. I'm only on the second murder. There will be another, and they will solve them all in ninety minutes."

"There's a dead woman in a farmhouse near the plane crash."

Gramm said nothing for several seconds before finally saying, "See Milo, that's something most people lead with."

"The body's stone-cold but hasn't been munched by critters...yet."

"Maybe the person was on the plane and walked to the farmhouse to die from their injuries."

"I kinda doubt it."

"Why, Milo? My Sunday night would be so much more restful."

"Restful is good. But…"

"But what, Milo? What?"

"The dead woman has scissors sticking out of her back."

"Again, Milo, you need to lead with that. Also, this is backwards. I call you out on a Sunday evening. You don't call me out."

"Okay, look, I'll go home, finish my sandwich, and you can call me."

"Is there blood?" Gramm asked.

"Yes."

"Don't step in it. I'm on my way."

2

Duluth Realtor Arial Jenkins padded down the hall to the bedroom she used as an office in her first-floor apartment. She bought the old three-story Victorian home for a steal and renovated it gradually into three cozy apartments.

She had come to love her home. Arial owned several old houses she had renovated into apartments, but this one on Fourth Street was her favorite. She felt safe and warm.

Arial clicked on her Tiffany desk lamp to review the Peterson file. Wally Schmidt Junior had finally passed away earlier this year after multiple brain aneurisms. Her client, Susan Peterson, claimed to be the sole heir to the old Schmidt Farm off Martin Road.

As Arial slammed the file shut, she heard the faint buzz of the microwave in the kitchen. Padding her way back down the hall, she removed her glass of warm milk, and added two packets of sweetener to the milk.

After taking the listing, she had proudly put up one of her large expensive signs at the farm's entrance. After all that trouble, Arial discovered that Susan Peterson's claim wasn't all that clean. A long-lost daughter of Walter Schmidt Junior first had to be declared legally dead. *It's only a matter of time. I already have a buyer. Legal delays happen all the time.*

Humming to herself, Arial brought her sweet milk and cookies to what she called her television corner, a cozy nook in the living room. Part of her evening ritual—watch the ten o'clock local news, and read two chapters in her latest historical fiction.

Curling up in a plush navy-brocade Queen Anne chair, her red curls resting against the favorite left wing, Arial clicked on the remote. The news had already started. The screen read LIVE ACTION CAM on the top and PLANE CRASH on the bottom. Biting into her cookie, Arial cocked her head upright in a bird-like fashion.

The plane appears to have been taking off from this dirt runway off of Martin Road when it clipped an old farm silo and crashed into the field you see behind me. The still unidentified pilot has been taken to the Essentia Trauma Center. His condition is not known at this time.

"Oh crap! Martin road? If that's my farm…ach, delay, delay, delay!"

§

Lieutenant Ernie Gramm picked up his partner, Sergeant Robin White, at her central entrance up-and-down duplex. When she first bought it, he questioned why she chose to live in the upstairs apartment. She explained rent from the larger first floor paid her mortgage, and the second floor had a much better view of the lake. Gramm understood. His Observation Hill house had a similar view.

Driving past the television trucks parked along Martin Road, Gramm grumbled about the media finding out about the dead body before he did.

"They're probably here for the plane crash, not the body," White said.

Gramm nodded. "You're right. I gotta have more coffee." He pulled up to the lone cop, who was now out of his car. "Evening, Lieutenant," the cop said, leaning in Gramm's window.

"Evening, Henderson. You've had a busy night."

He looked around to make sure no one was listening then whispered, "Sure have. You're here for the body, right?"

Gramm nodded.

"You will want to follow this road and turn left. Your consultant is already there, along with Doc Smith and the department generator truck."

As Gramm drove past the crash site and the blaring work lights, he wondered why the farmhouse was not lit up. "Henderson said the generator truck was there. Why no lights?"

"We could sit here in the dark or go and find out," White suggested.

Gramm clicked on his brights as he drove to the house, parking between Doc Smith's medical examiner's car and Milo's familiar Honda. He stepped over the cables running from the generator truck into the front door of the farmhouse.

Selina Sanchez, a police technician, walked up to the pair. "We're ready to go with the lights, but Doc Smith told us to wait."

"Why?" Gramm asked.

"He wants the media to leave so we don't attract their attention."

"Good plan," Gramm said, taking out his flashlight.

The two made their way around the roped-off section of broken steps and into the house. "Hey! Milo! Where are you?" Gramm yelled.

Milo yelled back. "Turn to the right, follow the light."

"At least you didn't say go into the light. I was hoping to get in a few more years before hearing that," Gramm muttered.

Milo was standing, holding his flashlight for Doc Smith, who was bent over the body. Without looking up, the doc said, "Nice of you two to join us."

"You know, Doc, we have a whole generator truck out there to replace Milo and his flashlight."

Smith checked his watch. "Fifteen more minutes and the TV boys will be gone."

"Boys and girls," White corrected.

Smith looked up. "Boys, a collective noun meaning everyone."

"Why not say girls, a collective noun meaning everyone?"

Smith shrugged. "Fifteen more minutes and the TV girls will be gone. Happy?"

"Can we get to the body?" Gramm questioned.

"Doc?" Henderson called over the radio.

Smith picked up his handheld. "Smith here."

"The last media truck just left."

Gramm keyed his radio. "Sanchez, turn 'em on."

The kitchen lit up like it was daylight.

"Whoa!" Smith said, squinting his eyes. "I never get used to that."

"Here's where you tell us she died of natural causes," White said, shielding her eyes until they adjusted.

"Certainly. I think this woman came upon a random pool of blood in her kitchen. She and her *many* friends danced in it. Then she laid down for a nap in the blood. She should be waking up any time now."

"And the scissors sticking out of her back?" White asked.

"Oh, that. It complicates the whole dance-nap scenario," Smith acknowledged.

"ID?" Gramm asked.

Smith shook his head. "Now that we have light, you two can begin your homicide investigation thing. No wallet or purse here."

Sanchez had put lights in all the ground-floor rooms, anticipating the search. Milo ventured back into the dining room.

"If you see blood, don't step in it," Smith called.

"Oh, I see," Gramm snapped, "don't walk in the blood. Good to know."

"It's late. He gets grumpy," White joked.

Gramm stayed to search the kitchen. White moved to the front hall. "Guys, I would drop my purse in the front hallway." There was no purse on the table. Looking at a too-large-for-the-space, dark green, velvet sofa, she spotted a soft, black leather backpack almost hidden between pillows. "I think I found something!"

Milo and Gramm joined her. "I would never have left my purse there," Milo teased.

"Noted," Gramm said. "Who's our victim?"

"Bring it in here!" Doc Smith demanded. "And don't smudge any fingerprints."

"Doc, we're not newbies!" White asserted as they all returned to the kitchen.

"It's late. She gets grumpy," Milo quipped.

Smith stood up, leaning against the table for support. "Lower back isn't what it used to be," he groaned, stretching out.

Handing Smith the backpack, White said, "This is not a purse. It's a chic and expensive backpack. Just for the record, the Gucci logo and this farmhouse do not match. That's my part of our homicide investigating thing."

Smith shined his flashlight into the backpack. "Lots of stuff in here." He finally found a clutch purse holding a driver's license and credit cards. There was no phone. Looking at the driver's license, he said the dead woman was Beth Hanson from Playa Del Ray, California.

Gramm shook his head. "Once again, a person comes all the way to Duluth just to die."

"On a Sunday night," White added to the complaint.

"Look on the bright side," Smith said while still looking in the backpack, "you're having a better Sunday than Beth Hanson."

Three forensics technicians arrived along with two of Smith's people and joined the group in the kitchen. Doc Smith handed them the backpack for bagging, then sat in the dining room, giving the technicians space to work in the kitchen. The cops and Milo trailed behind him.

"What do we know?" Gramm asked Milo.

"I know some guy flew a plane in here, don't know when or why. Then flew it out tonight, clipping that old silo at the end of the runway, interrupting my ham and cheese sandwich. Meanwhile, this woman…"

Gramm interrupted. "Milo. What the hell were you doing here to begin with?"

"Again, this woman's name is Beth Hanson," Smith scolded, always wanting to give a name to the dead.

"I was here and bored. I went investigating. I found Beth Hanson," Milo explained.

Gramm shook his head. "That doesn't answer my question as to why you are here to begin with."

"Read him his rights," Doc Smith demanded. "I wanna go home!"

Gramm recognized Doc Smith's impatience. "Before you go, when did Ms. Hanson die?"

"I would guess sometime today." Doc Smith said, getting up and walking away.

"Do we think Milo's pilot killed her and then tried to escape?" Gramm asked.

"Certainly, a possibility," White agreed.

"When did he become *my* pilot?" Milo questioned.

The group moved into the foyer and up the first three stairs, making room for Doc Smith's people to wheel out the body.

"We need to search the rest of this house," White said, looking up the stairs.

"No, let the forensics people finish tonight. We'll leave Henderson at the entrance and come back in the morning. We'll have more light and sleep," Gramm said.

No one objected. White led the way, bumping into a middle-aged man in a bright orange jacket, jeans, and a green-khaki fishing hat who was standing in the doorway. "Whoa, you can't be here. This is a crime scene."

"Sorry," the man said, stepping back, shoving his hands into the front pockets of his jeans. "I thought I should tell somebody what I saw as soon as possible."

"Where did you come from? How did you get in here?" Gramm asked. "This place is sealed off,"

"I live in the Shady Lane subdivision across the field that-a-way," he said, pointing behind the house. "I just walked over."

"In the dark?" White asked.

The man produced a tac flashlight similar to Milo's.

Gramm looked at White. "Have someone post a guard here at the house, too." Turning back to the stranger, Gramm asked him his name and what he saw.

"Bernie Waite. I'm a bird watcher…"

Gramm stared, trying to have that make any sense.

"I had my contractor put a special crow's nest at the top of my house. My neighbors think it's an eyesore, but I don't give a hoot." Waite said, chuckling.

Gramm's eyebrows drew together, and his lips pursed.

"Anyway, this afternoon I was in my nest looking east toward Hawk Ridge. I spotted three goldens in two hours today. It was tough. The sky was filthy with those red tail hawks. The Hawk Ridge web page said the count of golden eagles was eight, but I wasn't there all day. I figure I was lucky to count three."

To redirect the witness before Gramm slipped into nasty mode, White asked, "Mr. Waite, what did you see here at the farm?"

"The eagles don't usually head west. They like to fly near the lake to the east."

"No more about birds, please. Keep your comments about the plane." White commanded.

"Oh. Okay. Well, I was still counting eagles, like I said, when I heard this strange, loud sound behind me. I turned and saw a plane land on this road out here. I thought maybe he was in trouble and saw the road as his best chance to land, but I was wrong."

"Wrong?" White asked.

"Yeah, the guy turns the plane around in this circle. He gets out like I thought he would, but then strolls into the farmhouse like he lives there. He wasn't upset, like he was in trouble."

"How could you see that?" Milo asked.

Waite pulled long thin binoculars from inside his jacket. "Swarovskis. $163.28 a month. They'll be all mine in nine more months." He waited for the group to be impressed. They weren't.

"Then what?" Gramm asked.

"I went back to my birds. Then I heard the plane fire up again…"

"How much later?" Milo asked.

"It was getting dark because I was about to wrap it up for the day. I saw the plane take off as I was going down for dinner, so I stayed to watch. I don't know what happened, because, like I say, it was dusky dark. I saw the plane drop into the field—you know, kaboom. I called 911 and ran into the field to help the pilot. He was hurtin'. I tried to take his mind off the pain by talking about the goldens. He was quiet, so I think it helped."

§

Milo arrived back at Lakesong shortly after midnight. He headed immediately to the kitchen and the other half of his uneaten ham and cheese sandwich. Opening the refrigerator, he saw the plate he had so carefully placed between the butter and the lettuce was missing. "I've been robbed!" he yelled.

"Oh, was that your sandwich?" Sutherland asked, walking into the kitchen from the family room with an empty plate.

Milo whirled around. "You ate my sandwich?"

"Sorry, didn't know it was yours."

"Whose did you think it was? The cats'?"

"I would never take the cats' food. They have claws and teeth."

Milo began collecting lettuce, mayo, cheese, ham, yellow mustard, and another plate.

"I have to say, I never thought mustard belonged on a ham and cheese sandwich, but it was pretty good, tangy." Sutherland sat down at Martha's desk to watch Milo work.

"Do you want another one?" Milo asked.

"Agnes and I ate earlier at McSorley's. It wasn't enough. Your sandwich filled in the remaining holes for me. Where have you been?"

"I was checking out a plane crash on Martin Road," Milo said, adding the mayo to one slice of bread and mustard to the other. "I thought it might be you."

"Aww, you were worried about us."

"I was worried about Agnes. Good personal assistants are hard to find."

"What crashed?"

"A single engine prop job."

"When?"

"Late afternoon, four-thirty."

"And you've been there…" Sutherland stopped to count on his fingers. "six, seven, eight. Eight hours?"

"Well…" Milo placed two pieces of lettuce on the slice of heavily mayoed bread. "There was the dead body. Had to deal with it." Watching Milo's sandwich construction, Sutherland took mental notes.

Milo then put two slices of sharp cheddar cheese onto the mustard side and slapped a hunk of ham onto the lettuce. He slammed his sandwich together and took a bite. He smiled. "Delicious."

"Don't you want to cut that?" Sutherland asked.

"That lets the flavor out."

"You, Milo Rathkey, hater of green, put lettuce on your ham and cheese sandwich."

"The lettuce serves a purpose."

"Which is?"

"Keeps the ham and cheese from being attacked by mayo."

"I feel I should be writing this down, but I want to know more about this plane crash. I thought you said the pilot survived."

"I did."

"Then you said he died."

Milo took another bite. "Didn't say that."

"The dead body? You said you had to deal with it," Sutherland charged.

Milo shook his head. "Still jumping to conclusions. I thought I taught you better. The dead body did not belong to the pilot."

"Wait. Let me get this straight. You hear about a plane crash..."

"Got a breaking news thingy on my phone."

"You rushed out because you were sure it was Agnes and me in the plane."

"Just Agnes. We've been through this."

"Right, right. You get to the plane crash. The pilot is not dead, but there is a dead body."

"In the farmhouse. Beth Hanson from Playa Del Ray, California. Do you know her?"

"Should I?" Sutherland stood up, grabbed Milo's sandwich from his plate, and took a bite.

"I offered to make you one," Milo complained.

"It tastes better when it's yours, besides your murders make me confused and hungry. So, who is Beth Hanson from Playa Del Ray, California?"

"The dead woman."

"Does she have anything at all to do with the plane crash?"

"Possibly. We'll know more tomorrow. What did you bring me back from McSorely's?"

"A tankard of ale, but it spilled over Lake Michigan."

Annie the Cat walked into the kitchen and meowed loudly.

"What's her problem?" Sutherland asked.

"She was expecting a t-shirt."

3

Milo felt a weight on his chest as he roused. Without opening his eyes, he heard a duet of loud meows. *Both of them?* A cat's paw, claws in, stroked his face. Milo squinted one eye open to make out Jet, the resident black cat, perched on his chest, staring at him. Annie, Lakesong's calico cat, meowed sharply in Milo's left ear. Jet, the gentler of the two cats, pawed him one more time.

"Ugh! What do you want?" Milo demanded, turning to his side, forcing Jet to jump off. *How are you even here? Cats can't open closed doors!* Milo had tried to solve the mystery of the reappearing cats last spring, to no avail.

Another nasty meow from the normally aloof Annie told Milo something was amiss. Milo stood up and made his way to the bathroom for a shave and a shower. Jet followed him, urging him to move faster by weaving in and out of his legs. Annie nipped at Jet's behind if he stopped hurrying Milo along.

He reached his sink before saying, "You know guys, this would be quicker if you didn't try to trip me constantly."

If the cats understood, they didn't respond.

Milo continued his morning routine with his furry friends constantly underfoot. He returned to the bedroom, found the remote buried in his blankets and opened the drapes to a sunny Monday morning. Jet pawed at his leg. He looked down. "See, it's a beautiful day out. What is your problem?"

Jet squeaked.

The cats usually followed Milo through the gallery, the family room, and the hearth room before coming to a stop in the morning room. Today, they led the parade, looking back to make sure Milo was still moving.

Lakesong's chef, Martha Gibbson, greeted him before he could pour a cup of coffee. "I was looking for your friends, Mr. Rathkey. Darian forgot to feed them this morning. He yelled this bit of information as he ran to catch the bus."

"I knew something was wrong. Both cats mysteriously appeared on my bed this morning. Annie normally just sends in Jet."

"Their bowls are filled now," Martha said, looking down at the cats. "Go on now! Get your breakfast." Both cats sprinted to the hallway by the kitchen for their long overdue first meal of the day.

Milo looked at Martha. "I think they understood you."

Martha shrugged. "Of course. They're very smart cats."

He poured his coffee and sat down in the morning room, where Agnes and Sutherland were already sipping their morning smoothies. "The cats understand Martha," Milo informed them.

Sutherland folded his Wall Street Journal. "Of course."

Agnes added, "They're outstanding cats."

"So outstanding they open closed doors?"

"Don't look at me," Sutherland said. "The cats don't even acknowledge my existence—never have."

With that, Jet ran into the room, zoomed around the table, stopped by Sutherland, and squeaked.

"A shift in the universe, perhaps?" Milo wondered.

"I am speechless," Sutherland admitted. "What do I do now?"

"Squeak back," Agnes suggested. "Keep those lines of communication open." Agnes smiled at her business-proper, Monday-morning-meeting-ready husband. "So, Milo, Sutherland tells me you had a late-night adventure."

"Yes, and I blame you—both of you."

"How did we get dragged into this?" Sutherland questioned.

"You flew back from New York and a plane crashed. Naturally, I was forced to go check."

Looking at Agnes, Sutherland asked, "Did we add a plane crash to the end of our New York weekend?"

Agnes laughed and shook her head while Milo filled his fork with hash browns and ketchup.

"I think you were bored. You drove to that farm, saw the plane was not ours, and then figured as long as you were there, you might as well go looking for a mystery," Agnes charged.

"Pretty much."

§

Arial Jenkins had heard nothing new about the plane crash. How much of the farm was involved? What could she tell her client, Susan Peterson? Would this delay the deal? These questions were the cause of the gray cloud hovering over Arial's head this morning.

Her first stop had to be the Schmidt farm. Arial swerved onto the gravel road leading into the farm and was shocked to see a police car blocking the road. She slammed on her brakes and leaned on the horn. Her front bumper stopped inches away from the car.

Certain this blockade was in error, Arial continued honking until she heard a tapping on her driver's side window. A policewoman motioned for her to roll her window down.

Believing to be well within her rights, Arial flung her red curls back. "I represent the owners of this farm. I am required to inspect this property. You need to move!"

"Ma'am, this is a restricted area. Turn your vehicle around and leave."

"No! Not again! I refuse!" Arial shouted.

The policewoman unhooked the holster to her stun gun. "Ma'am, please leave the area."

Arial closed her eyes, slowly turning her head to the left, then the right, calming herself. "You people are trying to ruin me! You people paraded through that house for days like I murdered those two people."

The policewoman took out a notebook. "Your name, ma'am?"

Arial bobbed her head as if slapped. "Why?"

"Name please."

Arial put the car in reverse. "No! I'm leaving!"

"Step out of the car, ma'am," the policewoman ordered.

"No!"

"Step out of the car, ma'am," the officer repeated, her hand removing the Taser from its holster. "This is not a negotiation."

As she slipped out of her green Land Rover with her hands up, Arial's red curls flew in the direction of her name on the for-sale sign by the farm entrance. "That's me. Lt. Gramm knows me. I am always very helpful."

The policewoman keyed her radio. "Unit twelve to dispatch."

"Go ahead twelve."

"Sarge, I have a disruptive woman here at the Schmidt Farm who claims to have been involved in a murder."

"I wasn't involved!" Arial screamed. "I…"

The policewoman raised her hand for silence. Arial shut up. After a few moments, the radio came back to life. "Officer, this is Sgt. White, homicide. What's the woman's name?"

The policewoman read it off the sign, "Arial Jenkins."

"I know her. What is she doing there?"

"She says she represents the owners of the farm and wants access."

"Absolutely not. Tell her we will contact her later this morning."

"Ten-four. Did you hear that, ma'am?"

"Yes."

"Now, ma'am, turn your vehicle around and leave."

"I am distressed and dispirited. I really don't think you have any right to keep me from…"

The officer pulled out her handcuffs. "Leave now or I will arrest you."

Arial pursed her lips as she climbed back into her Land Rover and drove off in a subdued huff.

§

Gordy Peterson finished viciously deadheading the mums and daisies that bordered his sizable vegetable garden. After washing up, his nervous energy gave way to pacing in and out of the too small kitchen in his Moose Lake, Minnesota home. Passing the small mirror by the side door, he stopped to make sure the new gel was holding his conservative but edgy spikes in place. It was a new look for him, and he liked it. A smile sprouted across his narrow face, only to fade back into the scowl of concern. His pacing began again.

"Gordy, just stop! Stop pacing! Stop decapitating our flowers! Stop overthinking!" His wife, Susan, was a paralegal for a local law firm. It was a job that required calm deduction, which Susan delivered with the help of her daily dose of Xanax. Unlike Susan, Gordy was almost always wired, searching for solutions to things that weren't even problems.

"I'm going crazy here. This whole thing is crazy. We have to do something," he pleaded with his wife.

"No, we don't. We're going to do nothing." Susan Peterson didn't look up from her waffles as she ordered her husband to sit down.

"You said we should just leave the body there until we owned the farm. You said no one would find it. But they did, Sues! You were wrong!"

Susan cupped her hands around a hot cup of coffee.

"Maybe somebody saw us. It was broad daylight." Gordy's voice wavered.

"Gordy! Stop!" Susan snapped her head in his direction. Her tapered and highlighted, golden-blond bangs fell in her face. She whisked them back in exasperation.

"Maybe we should call that realtor lady—make up a story as to why we were there," Gordy suggested.

Susan's anger turned to disbelief. "Oh, yes, let's do that." She held a mock phone up to her ear. "Hello, Arial. We were at the Schmidt farm Sunday. We thought we'd tell you we were meeting my long-lost cousin. You know, the one I'm trying to declare dead, so I can inherit the farm. Oh, and now she is dead. Nobody saw us, but Gordy thought we should tell you so you can tell the police."

Gordy blanched. "Oh God, no. I didn't think it through."

"No, you didn't. Look at the upside. Now I inherit free and clear. No court deciding she's dead. We know she is dead."

"I don't want to go to prison," Gordy whimpered.

"Here, take one of my chill pills."

§

Gramm and White were eager to interview the still hospitalized pilot of the downed plane. Gramm walked up to Nurse Helen Thompson, the British nurse at the special services desk, and a colleague of Gramm's wife, Amy.

"Leftenant? You're here again."

"Morning, Helen," Gramm said with uncharacteristic cheeriness. "And, once again, it's *loo-tenant*."

White smiled. She liked Thompson and the British pronunciation that poked the bear.

"We are here to see a Kirkland Rafferty," Gramm said. "He was brought in last night after his plane crashed."

"A plane crash sounds serious. He's probably in ICU." Thompson hit a number of keys on her computer; screens changed. "I'm wrong. He's been admitted. Room 310 left tower. The elevators are on your right."

"Again with the left tower," Gramm said, remembering a suspect that recently spent a week in the left tower. "Does anyone stay in the right tower?"

"Right tower is for labor and delivery, Leftenant," Helen said without smiling.

Gramm nodded. "Good to know."

"Do you want to tour the right tower as long as we're here?" White teased Gramm on their way to the elevators.

Gramm gave her a look that said he was not amused.

A young man was having his vitals checked when Gramm and White entered his room. The nurse turned around. "You two cannot be here unless you are relatives."

Gramm flashed his badge. "Duluth Police. We need to speak to Mr. Rafferty."

The nurse seemed surprised but backed up to let Gramm show his badge to Rafferty.

"Are you Kirkland Rafferty?" Gramm asked.

"My father was. I'm Kirkland Junior. Call me KJ."

"This is Sergeant White," Gramm added.

"How badly are you hurt?" White asked.

"My pride mostly. My ankle won't need plates and screws—just a painful sprain. I have some scrapes and bruises and a pinched nerve in my shoulder that will need serious physical therapy. I've been better." He smiled and rubbed his hand over his cheeks. "However, all is not lost. This pretty face has been left untouched."

White enjoyed his humor, which was lost on Gramm.

"What were you doing at that farm?" Gramm asked.

"What was I doing at that farm?" KJ restated. "Not sightseeing. I was trying to not crash my plane. That was a giant fail."

"Why did you land at the farm to begin with?"

"I didn't land to walk my dog. Am I being charged with trespassing?"

"No, we just want to understand what you were doing there," Gramm repeated.

"You want the long, detailed version? I'm saving that for the NTSB."

White recognized that Rafferty was having fun, but thought Gramm was not enjoying it. "Yes, Mr. Rafferty, indulge us with the long version."

"I was on my way to Two Harbors and my fuel gauge suddenly dropped to empty. I didn't know if I had a serious leak or a bad gauge. That wide road was practically below me. I thought it was a safe place to set down."

"While you were there, did you go into the farmhouse?" Gramm asked.

"No. I only saw it when I landed. I jumped out on the wing and manually checked my fuel level. It was fine, more than enough to get to Two Harbors. So, I took off again, got lift, everything was great. Then I turned a little too soon and hit something with my wing."

"What's in Two Harbors?" White asked.

"Business."

"What business?"

"My business." KJ noticed that Gramm was about to erupt. "Sorry, long, detailed version, right? I am the owner and CEO of an eco-waste removal company. We're on the Minneapolis Tribune's list of the top twenty-five, black-owned businesses in the state, and you happen to be talking to possibly one of the top thirty under thirty."

"Impressive, Mr. Rafferty, but what does an eco-waste removal company remove?" White asked.

"Everything from ordinary construction materials to hazardous waste."

"Who were you meeting in Two Harbors?" Gramm asked.

KJ smiled a sly, secretive grin. "I would rather not say. It's a large contract. The negotiations are delicate. You get it, right, Lieutenant?"

Gramm was about to respond in the negative when the nurse reentered the room. "Mr. Rafferty is scheduled for an MRI. This will have to be continued later."

"When will Mr. Rafferty be discharged?" Gramm asked.

"You will have to ask the doctor in charge."

"Are you going to discharge him today?"

She looked at Rafferty, who gave her his best smile and then turned back to Gramm. "There are no orders for discharge."

Gramm stopped at the nearby nurse's station and handed his card to the woman seated there. "When Mr. Raffety is ready for discharge, call me."

The woman looked at the card, nodded, and clipped it to a chart with a note.

On the way to the elevator, White said, "He's a charmer."

"Charmer? Really? Bird man said this guy went into the farmhouse. Either Mister Charm is lying, or our bird man was mistaken. Have Kate do a background check on our pilot."

4

Arial's Monday morning began as a train wreck. She didn't go to the office after being threatened with a Taser, instead she went home to decompress—calm herself with a large cup of tea. She chose chamomile to de-stress and added a bit of tart cherry for easing anxiety, lemon for soothing anger, and honey to make it drinkable. Midway through her tea, her shoulders lowered. She was able to shake her bouncy red curls without discomfort.

The policewoman blocking access to the farm was rude and had told her nothing. She didn't see much damage, but wondered about the pilot. *Could it be KJ Rafferty? Why was he at the farm? Doublecross?* Now relaxed and back in control, she called Sergeant White to see if she could pump her for more information.

"Arial Jenkins," White said, reading the caller ID on her phone. "Funny you should call. We need to talk to you."

"Well, I need to talk to you too! Earlier this morning, some officer threatened to tase me for doing my job! I tried to explain I represent the owners of that Schmidt Farm on Martin Road, and your officer rudely stopped me from gaining access to the place."

"There was a plane crash there last night," White said.

"A plane crash?" Arial played dumb. "Who was killed?"

"What makes you think someone was killed?"

"You're a homicide detective, Sgt. White."

"Yes, Ms. Jenkins, thank you for noticing."

"I didn't finish. You're a homicide detective, which means someone was murdered on one of my properties—again."

"Lieutenant Gramm and I would like to meet with you. What time works for you?"

Arial gave herself an hour. "I'm free at eleven, but I have a question."

"Sure."

"What are you investigating?"

"See you at eleven." White hung up.

Arial's phone came back to life, this time with the caller ID of Mary Alice Bonner. She stared at the phone. "I'm stuck in a loop that will not end!" Arial said to herself as she took one last even breath and a sip of her tea before answering.

§

Milo arrived at the cop shop at the same time Gramm and White were returning from the hospital.

"Nice of you to join us, Milo," Gramm said.

"I was up late," Milo said by way of excuse.

Gramm looked at White, who was sitting on the other side of his desk. "I could have sworn we were all up late."

"But I need my beauty rest," Milo added.

"While you were doing whatever, White and I have already been to see the pilot who is resting his pretty face in the hospital."

"His pretty face?"

"His words. He's pretty puffed up about himself, but I think he's lying," Gramm said, recounting the discussion with KJ.

"Do we know any more about the dead woman?" Milo asked.

Gramm yelled for Officer Kate Preston, who rolled in her own chair. "Preston, what more do we know about our victim?"

Preston consulted her pad.

"Why do you even bother with that pad?" White asked. "We know you can recall everything,"

"To have a record in case I'm not here and you need details. Besides, my remembering everything tends to freak some people out."

Gramm stretched his neck. "What was the dead woman's name again?"

"Beth Hanson," Preston said. "She was an actress who waited tables."

"Was she in anything we would know?" White asked.

"I don't think she was ever in anything. Her employer at Señor J's Fresh and Healthy Mexican Food called her a wannabe actress."

"What else did Señor J say about her?" Gramm asked.

"There's no Señor J. Her boss is a guy named Larry. He said she worked there for about a year. She quit a week ago, saying she was going to be rich. He didn't know how. Apparently, employees come and go at the Fresh and Healthy Mexican Food restaurant all the time."

"Is it fresh and healthy?" Milo asked.

Gramm gave him a nasty look.

"Isn't everything in California?" Preston joked.

"More than we knew last night, but still not much," White said.

"There's more." Preston smiled. "I traced Beth Hanson back three years. Then she just disappears. I ran her ID through several databases, and I found a match for a woman named Tami Hannah. You know, five-four, 120, champagne-blond hair, blue eyes."

"There must be a million young women in California who match that general description," White said.

"But Tami Hannah had the same address as Beth Hanson?"

"Ahh, you didn't say that."

"Tami Hannah appears out of nowhere three years before Beth Hanson."

"Was our dead woman on the run?" White asked.

Preston shrugged.

Gramm picked up his phone and pressed the icon for Doc Smith.

"Smith here."

"Doc, we have reason to believe our Beth Hanson was using an alias."

"We're running her fingerprints—standard procedure," Smith advised.

"This is Officer Preston. How about dental records, Doc? Do you run those?"

Gramm leaned back, looked up at his office ceiling, and sighed. White mouthed the word 'nooo' waving Preston off.

Doc Smith cleared his throat. "I can tell, Officer Preston, that you and I have not yet had the dental record discussion. There is no dental database, but, if you want, I can send the dead woman's dental x-rays to every single dentist in the country to see if they recognize them."

Preston frowned. "But dental records are used all the time."

"To corroborate an ID, not to determine one. You tell me who she is, and I'll check with her dentist to make sure that's her."

"Oh, got it," Preston said. "Thanks Doc."

"How'd she die?" Gramm asked.

"I haven't finished yet, but the scissors in her back and a similar wound in her abdomen are hinting at probable cause of death."

"Stabbed twice? Was there enough blood for twice?" Milo asked, leaning into the phone on Gramm's desk.

"There's a splatter and pool in one of the bedrooms upstairs. Then a generous trail goes down the stairway, and the larger pool in the kitchen. It tells me she was attacked upstairs and tried to escape. Nasty couple of minutes. On a side note, a lot of people stepped in that kitchen pool. We have at least four sets of shoe marks."

"If you learn more, Doc, let us know," Gramm said.

"No, I get paid to keep it to myself." The phone went dead.

Gramm pushed his *end call* button. Before White could comment on phone etiquette, Gramm said, "See Robin, our conversation was over. No need for long goodbyes."

White folded her arms and huffed.

"Have we found the victim's phone?" Milo asked.

Preston shook her head. "I have IT searching for her carrier to see if we can get her records."

"Arial Jenkins," White said, "remember her?"

Preston piped in. "She was the realtor at the Hawthorn place."

"Right, well, she is also the realtor trying to sell the Schmidt Farm," White added. "She knows the seller and prospective buyers. On a side note, she showed up this morning at the farm and demanded access, and almost got arrested. I set up an appointment for eleven." White looked at her new smartwatch. "We should get going."

§

Kayla Maki had spent the summer in search of a new job and new direction. She saw no future in selling candles and soaps, after being kicked out of her kiosk in the Hermantown Mini Mall for threatening customers. She finished her court-ordered anger management classes and continued to work as an instructor at her father's archery range.

Every Monday morning, Kayla would go through the local newspaper's online help wanted section as well as other apps and write down three job prospects. Most of them involved being indoors, smiling and talking to stupid strangers for no reason. Kayla wrote those off immediately.

This week began with an ad for a salesperson at a sign shop. The position would require contacting clients, hanging signs, and setting up displays. That sounded livable. However, the sign shop was Sithens and Van Dyke. Kayla used to date Alex Sithens. When he dumped her, she got mad, barged into his sign shop, and threatened him with her knife—not her best moment.

Van Dyke would certainly remember her and not in a good way. Even though she decided to scratch that prospect and move on, Kayla shared the posting with her therapist.

"Apply. Of course, he won't hire you, Kayla," she said, "but rejection is one of your triggers. You have all the tools to calm your anger. Go there, be told no, smile, and leave. No threats and no knives. Remember, you control the situation. It does not control you."

Her therapist was right about one thing: Kayla hated rejection. With a clenched stomach, and her therapist watching, she emailed her resume to Van Dyke. Kayla concluded her session and drove to her dad's range. She would be busy with two clients this afternoon—lessons on the compound bow.

During a break between clients, she checked her email. Van Dyke was interested! In her! *He either doesn't remember me, or this is a setup.*

All the negative thoughts began flooding her brain. *Stop! I am in charge of me! I act. I do not react.*

§

Vincent Rembrandt Van Dyke could not believe his eyes. *Kayla Maki. I always thought she was pretty. She gets a little angry, but she is pretty. She can't stab me over the phone. This could be good.*

§

Mary Alice Bonner decided to work from home today in her lovely baby-blue and white sitting room—her room—the only comfortable room in this monstrosity of a house built by her late husband, James. She hoped the awaited call from her lawyer, Pat Wautkin, would end James' two-year hold on her even from the grave.

Her phone buzzed. She took a deep breath. "Pat, I hope you have good news."

"I have fabulous news!" Wautkin exclaimed. "We've identified what we think are all of James' offshore accounts. There's more than enough in them to satisfy all the claims from people James defrauded, plus a sizeable amount left over for you and Richard. My team should be emailing a complete breakdown to you before the end of the day. I'm seeing the probate judge tomorrow to get your funds freed up."

Mary Alice leaned back and smiled. "Pat, it's finally over, and I can breathe." After a brief moment, she sat up as if a client had come into her office—all business. "Good, I'll be going over the details tonight. Thank you and please thank your team for ending this nightmare."

"My pleasure. Recovering your money has been a satisfying journey."

"The evil ends today—this house will be razed," Mary Alice said without hesitation.

"Really? What will replace the hideous white whale?"

Mary Alice laughed. "A tasteful, comfortable home that will make me happy."

"Good for you. I'll call you tomorrow in case you have any questions about the report."

"My main question is, when will I have access to the money?"

"I'll have that information after I see the judge tomorrow."

Mary Alice thanked Wautkin again, hung up, and called Milo.

5

rial Jenkins appearance in the office Monday morning raised eyebrows because word had spread. Her fellow realtors all knew she had listed the Schmidt Farm, the sight of yesterday's mysterious plane crash. In no mood to chat, Arial scurried to her desk, sat down, and pressed the intercom.

"Gert, Gert, Gert."

Gert, the office manager, droned, "Yes, Arial."

"Gert, the conference room. I am in need!" Arial pleaded.

"Arial, we've been through this. Turn on your computer. Click on the conference room icon. Put your name on the schedule next to the time you want."

Arial's head jutted to the left in the fashion of a huffy peacock. The computer was not her friend. After several missteps, she managed to secure the conference room just as Gramm and company parked in front of the office. One realtor near the front window recognized the police from their visit last year during the Hawthorn murder investigation.

"Arial, what did you do now? Your police friends are here!" she yelled.

Arial darted to meet them at the door and hustled them into the conference room. She could almost hear other realtors whispering about her frequent visits from the cops.

Closing the door behind her before anyone was seated, Arial fumed, "When can I get back onto my property?"

"That's not our priority," Gramm said.

"It never is, and that's a problem," Arial declared. "I still haven't sold that Hawthorne estate."

"Are you blaming the police for that?" White wanted to know.

Arial swung her head to lecture White. "Yes! You kept me from showing that property for almost a month, the absolute critical time in a listing. The property's *newness* was wasted. Then dead body rumors spread. I am currently reduced to renting it," she fussed. "Luckily, I have found a reliable renter. No thanks to any of you people."

When did it become our job to sell her listings? Gramm thought as he and the others sat down.

White looked at Milo. "Looks like you will have a new neighbor."

"I'll have to stop over and borrow sugar," Milo quipped.

"No sugar borrowing! Don't bother her!" Arial muttered, "You have sugar. Who doesn't have sugar?"

Interrupting Arial's sugar rant, Gramm groused, "Let's get back to our current investigation. Tell us about the Schmidt Farm."

"I came prepared," Arial boasted, as she slid a slick informational pamphlet onto the table. "This will tell you everything you need to know."

Gramm stopped the sliding pamphlet with a slap of his hand and began to read. "Three hundred and eighty acres of prime development on the outskirts of Duluth, Minnesota, at the tip of beautiful Lake Superior," Gramm read. "The former Schmidt Farm is currently zoned agricultural but can easily be rezoned residential. That would match the surrounding land."

"Thanks for this, but I'm not in the market," Gramm said, handing the brochure to White, who handed it to Milo.

Milo thumbed through the brochure before asking, "This says 'former Schmidt farm.' Who owns it now?"

"Well." Arial took her time to ease into a chair at the other end of the oval table. "My clients will soon own it. They are going through probate."

"Probate?" White questioned. "Why? Who died?"

Arial cocked her head to the right. "Walter Schmidt Junior, of course. It was his farm."

"When did he die?"

"Eight months ago. Aneurysm. Brain exploded! It was apparently leaking for a long time, and nobody noticed. That happens when you live alone on a rundown farm, and no one knows you're there."

White was going to ask another question, but the picture of Walter Schmidt's leaking brain took over her thoughts.

"Who will own it after probate?" Gramm continued.

Arial's head bobbed up. "No, no, no, you can't bother any of my clients!"

White folded her hands on the table in front of her. "Ms. Jenkins, this is a homicide investigation. You've been through this before. You know if you don't cooperate, we can make this a formal interview at police headquarters."

"Aha!" Arial shouted, slapping her hands on the table. "I knew it! There's been a murder!" Arial settled down, quite pleased with herself—for a moment. "Wait, who was murdered? Am I in danger? Is that why you blocked me from..."

"Ms. Jenkins, please stop and let us ask the questions," White cautioned, afraid Arial's brain might start leaking.

Arial closed her mouth, folded her hands, and waited.

"Is the name Kirkland Rafferty Jr. familiar to you?" Gramm asked.

Arial's eyes widened. "Is he the victim?"

"You're asking questions again." Gramm closed his eyes and stretched his neck.

White took that as a sign that her boss' patience was waning.

"When was the last time you were in the farmhouse?" Gramm asked.

"What farmhouse?" Arial squeaked.

"The one on the property, Ms. Jenkins," Gramm said in an overly even tone. "I'm getting tired of these games."

Arial's eyes opened even wider. "I don't play games. I've never seen the property. I put out my sign by the road and paid a photographer to take drone photos of the land. That's what professionals do these days, take drone photos. Developers are standing in line to get this land. Any old farmhouse will be bulldozed." Her tight little smile turned up at the corners.

"So, you never entered the farmhouse?" Gramm persisted.

"No. Why would I? I'm selling the land, not a wretched farmhouse where an old guy's brain exploded."

Again, with the leaking brain, White thought.

"Maybe there's something valuable in there," Milo said.

Arial's chin tilted as she looked down at the group. "Not my concern. For me, it's all about that land."

"There are two barns on the property. One at either end of that wide road. Have you ever been in those?"

Arial shook her head. "Please—never!"

"One is padlocked. We will need to get inside. So, once again, who owns the property?" White asked. "If you don't tell us, we will serve you with the search warrant."

"Me? Why? What does that even mean?"

"It means you will be subjected to the whim of the court. The judge could order you to do any number of things, including being at the farm when we search both barns and that could take days."

"No! Just no!" Arial shook her head, sputtering about time being money and she didn't have time.

Gramm folded his hands, enjoying Robin's move. This was a bluff. The executor of the estate would be served, not the realtor, but from Arial's reaction, it was working.

Arial's frustration with the whole probate situation came tumbling out. "It's in probate. I've already told you that, Sgt. White."

"Ms. Jenkins, do not…"

"All of this…it's all become too much. My communication has been with Walter Schmidt's cousin, Susan Peterson. She expects to inherit any day."

"Address, phone numbers," White demanded.

Arial called up Susan Peterson's particulars on her phone and slid it over to White. "She lives in Moose Lake," she added.

Of course, Gramm thought. *A long drive to Moose Lake. There are houses near the police station. How come none of those people are ever involved in murders?*

White copied the information and handed the phone back to Arial.

"We found a body in the farmhouse Sunday night," Gramm said. "The death was not by natural causes."

Arial nodded. "Who?"

"A woman named Beth Hanson. Do you know that name?" White asked.

"No. Why was she there?"

"What were you doing Sunday night?" Gramm asked, ignoring more Arial questions.

"Me? Certainly, I'm not a suspect. Killing a stranger in a house I've never even entered—ridiculous!"

"Just procedure," Gramm said.

Arial looked up at the ceiling, trying to remember her Sunday activities. Suddenly, her bird-like eyes darted around the table. "Are you mocking me?"

White was taken aback. "Mocking you? How?"

"I was at yoga."

§

"In the future, if we find a body in any Arial Jenkins' listings, let's move it. Time for lunch," Gramm said as they stepped out of the realtor's office into the warm fall day.

"You know, if we could keep Arial Jenkins from yoga, Duluth might be murder free," White offered.

Milo's phone vibrated. He looked at the caller ID: Mary Alice. "Hello, Blue. I'm getting a new neighbor."

"What a coincidence," Mary Alice said. "I'm getting new neighbors, too. I'm told they have an odd living situation. There's a young, tall, good looking blond guy who owns his own business. His lovely new wife works for the third member of the household, a grumpy former cop and private investigator."

"So, it's you who's moving next door?"

"Temporarily. We have many life-changing events to catch up on. That's why you are inviting me to dinner tonight."

"I am?"

"The move has left Cook shaken, so I've given her the night off."

"If we're neighbors, we could just meet over the fence while I'm hanging out laundry," Milo said.

Mary Alice cringed. "That image is so disturbing."

"What time am I picking you up?"

"Seven, don't be late. You made reservations for seven thirty."

"Can I ask where I made reservations?"

"I'm in the mood for frescos and fine wine. So, you have chosen Bellisios in Canal Park."

"Just down from the lift bridge."

"I'm going now, Milo. Pick me up at seven."

"Wait, why are you moving into the Hawthorn place?"

"I'm having the White Whale pounded into little bits."

"Of course. I should have thought of that."

"Life-changing events, remember." She hung up.

Milo put his phone in his pocket and noticed that Gramm and White were staring at him. "Apparently, I have asked Mary Alice to dinner this evening."

"I like her style," White said. "I should have taken notes."

"Speaking of dining, where are we going for lunch?" Gramm asked.

"New Cambridge Café is just down the street," White said. "I used to eat there sometimes when I first started out on the force."

"Which way is it?" Milo asked, looking up and down the street.

"Here we go!" White said. "You're going to pretend you don't know it and then everyone in the place will know your name!"

Milo feigned hurt. "I could have sworn you picked the restaurant. How would I know where it is?"

White looked at Gramm, who only shrugged. She led the way to the blue-brick New Cambridge Café on the next block. Milo thought it was a good choice. Solid, clean wooden tables, no tablecloths, with old school, ladder-back, wooden chairs. Three high-boy chairs fronted a bar-like eating arrangement that overlooked a portion of the kitchen.

A young hostess who did not seem to recognize Milo led them to one of the four top tables.

"Do you know this man?" White asked the hostess while pointing at Milo.

The woman shook her head. "Sorry, no. Should I know you, sir?"

"No, please excuse my friend," Milo said. "She has hallucinations, but otherwise, she's quite harmless."

The woman dropped three menus on the table and quickly departed.

A waiter arrived with glasses of water. "My name is Quincy. I'll be your waiter."

"Quincy?" Milo questioned.

"Wait, wait, wait!" White almost shouted. "I've been down this road before. You and Milo were in the army together, right?"

"Army?" Milo asked. "I was in the Navy."

Gramm actually smiled. "Robin, Milo is at least thirty years older than this kid."

"Forgive our friend here," Milo said. "I was explaining to your colleague at the door that she suffers from malnutrition phobia, a serious condition that occurs when she hasn't received enough nourishment. It has taken over her life. So sad."

White took a deep breath and waited for Quincy and Milo to drop their act and admit they were long-lost friends or enemies, or Quincy was his son—something.

Nothing. Quincy simply went over the specials and said he would return to take their orders.

Sitting back in her chair, White began to check out the menu. "Okay, maybe we've lucked out and nobody here knows you. This may become my favorite lunch place."

Milo was about to say that may not be entirely true when Bruno Burton, the Cambridge Café's owner, burst through the swinging kitchen doors. He was a huge mountain of a man with an infectious smile. "Milo Rathkey, my friend! You have finally graced my humble restaurant with your presence!"

White put her elbow on the table, laid her forehead in the heel of her hand, and shook her head. "I knew it! I knew it!"

Milo jumped up. "Bruno! Long time no see!"

When the bear hug was over, Bruno stepped back. "You are thinner. That's not good."

"Bruno, I would like you to meet my friends, Ernie Gramm." Bruno shook Ernie's hand. "And this poor woman is Robin White. She has trust issues."

"Sure. Why not," White said, also shaking Bruno's hand.

"Milo, my life saver! He found Krakatoa."

"Krakatoa?" Gramm asked.

"My dog, years ago. He ran after a squirrel and couldn't find his way back. I was frantic. I hired Milo, who brought Krakatoa back to me." Bruno snapped his fingers at Quincy, who rushed over. "This meal is on the house."

Gramm was starting to object, but Bruno was insistent. After he left, White asked, "You found lost dogs?"

"It was during a down time. I was living on free food from Hank at the Chinese Dragon. Bruno's check kept the lights on. Beside I grew fond of old Krack."

"Pitbull, Rottweiler, German shepherd?" White asked.

"Yorkie," Milo said.

White laughed.

"Those small dogs are feisty and hard to find."

"Bruno doesn't look British," Gramm said.

"Armenian, I think," Milo said. "Why would you think he was British?"

"I don't know," Gramm said. "Maybe the name of this place, Cambridge Café, led me to believe that...never mind."

Quincy returned to take their orders. White ordered the Great Lakes Blueberry Salad. "Blueberries, apples, pecans, and blue cheese. This might be worth all the aggravation Milo puts me through."

"I didn't do anything," Milo defended himself. "I eat out a lot and I'm a friendly guy."

Gramm picked the Lester Park Burger with bacon. "Nobody tell Amy about the bacon," he admonished.

"Do you think if Amy doesn't know, that makes bacon heathier?" White chided.

"It's the theory I'm going with," Gramm countered.

Milo ordered the Superior Street Hot Beef Sandwich. "I see it comes on eight grain bread," Milo said.

"It does, sir, toasted," Quincy said.

"Lose seven of those grains—white bread, toasted. Does it come with mashed potatoes?"

"It does."

"Gravy?"

"Of course."

"And Diet Coke," Milo added.

"Of course!" White exclaimed. "Gramm not telling his wife about the bacon, and you ordering Diet Coke—turns unhealthy into healthy."

"Glad you approve," Milo quipped.

"Our case, let's review what we got," Gramm ordered.

"We have a dead woman in a farmhouse. We have a crashed plane with a pilot in the hospital. We don't know if those two things are connected. And we have a realtor who causes a murder to happen every time she goes to yoga," White summed up the case.

"Let's have Preston check on the name of Walter Schmidt's lawyer. He's probably the executor. That's a needed conversation," Gramm said. "And let's do that before we trek over to Moose Lake to talk with Susan Peterson."

"We could just call," White suggested.

Gramm shook his head. "I like to look people in the eye when they lie to me."

"Maybe they won't lie," White offered, accepting her salad, delighting in the pile of blueberries before digging in.

Gramm took a bite of his cheeseburger, then gestured to Milo, who was spooning gravy over his potatoes. "Time for your line, Milo."

Milo obliged with his oft-repeated phrase: "Everybody lies, but only one person is lying because they're the murderer."

6

Officer Kate Preston was on a roll. She had finished her homemade lunch—a chicken and veggie bowl—called probate court and had the lawyer's name for Gramm and White. With excitement, she confirmed the last slot on the Saturday jump with the Duluth Skydiving club. Placing it on her calendar, she spotted the trio coming back from lunch. Preston pushed her chair into Gramm's office.

White, Gramm, and Rathkey were settling into their usual chairs when Preston began her report. "Walter Schmidt's attorney is a man named Wilson David. I called him. He's local and willing to help us with the contents of Schmidt's will." Preston sat down in her chair.

Gramm, furrowing his bushy eyebrows, took a deep breath. "I know him."

"Problem?" White asked.

"He's a bit…scattered. He writes notes to himself and then sometimes forgets where he puts them."

"Charming," White mused.

Gramm asked Preston for the lawyer's number and then, with a sigh, punched the numbers into his phone and put it on speaker.

"The law offices of um…um…um…Wilson David," a man answered.

"Could I speak with Wilson David, please? This is Police Lieutenant Ernie Gramm."

"Speaking."

"Mr. David, I understand you handled the probate of the Schmidt Farm on Martin Road."

"I did? Let me check."

Gramm shook his head as rustling sounds could be heard from Mr. David.

"You are correct. I am…or did. Is there anything else?"

"Are you aware there was a murder committed on that farm yesterday?"

"A murder?" Mr. David questioned. "Do I need to note this?"

"It occurred just before the plane crash." Gramm couldn't resist having a little fun.

"Plane crash? My, that's a busy place. Do I need to note that? I have a red sticky pad for unusual occurrences."

Gramm looked at White, who gave the thumbs up. "Sure, give it the red. I just need to know the contents of the will."

"Will? I've drawn up many. Which one?"

Gramm looked up at the ceiling in a *Why Me* posture. "The will of Walter Schmidt Junior. He died recently."

They could hear fumbling and chair rolling in the background. "Here it is, with a black sticky note! Walter Schmidt Junior died. Did I send condolences?"

"I have no idea. We're requesting the contents of Walter Schmidt Junior's will. Who inherits?" Gramm asked.

"Yes, I have it here." David began reading his notes. "He was called Wally, but his legal name was Walter, like his father. The hospital social worker got in touch with me. Apparently, Walter listed me as his emergency contact. She just left a message that said he died—brain aneurysm. I think you're wrong, Lieutenant. That's not murder."

Gramm sighed. "Walter Schmidt was not the person murdered."

"Oh, good, I'm glad we got that straightened out. Anything else I can do for you?"

"Yes!" Gramm almost shouted. "Who inherits the farm?"

"Oh, yes, certainly. Hang on a second." There was more paper shuffling. "He left the farm to a woman who did not come to the will reading, his daughter, Anna Schmidt."

Gramm's bushy eyebrows drew together.

Preston began typing.

"We were told that a different person was inheriting. A woman named..." Gramm looked at White.

"Susan Peterson of Moose Lake," she whispered.

Gramm repeated the name.

"Give me a minute," the lawyer said. Several minutes went by. "Yes, here it is. A cousin, Susan Peterson, inherits if they cannot find Anna Schmidt."

"Anna Schmidt is missing?" White asked.

"That would be a blue note...wait...found it. Disappeared. Thought to be in California. No one's heard from her for at least seven years."

"Police Consultant Milo Rathkey here. How old was Anna Schmidt when she disappeared?"

More shuffling. "She was two gallons of...no, that's not right...wrong note." The group once again heard the sound of a chair rolling across the floor and more shuffling. "I've got it," he called from the other side of the room. Rolling closer, he added, "She was sixteen. I've completed everything the court requires to locate her—put advertisements in a number of Minnesota and California newspapers asking for Anna Schmidt to come forward. Those rarely work, though. No one reads legal notices anymore."

"What happens if she stays lost?" Gramm asked.

"Then she loses out, and the property goes to Ms. Peterson."

"How does that work?"

"Well, there is a hearing on Monday before Judge Hoffer to determine the inheritance."

"So, Anna Schmidt has until then."

"Well, she would if she hadn't called me two days ago."

Gramm shook his head and looked at White, who shrugged. "I thought you said no one reads legal notices anymore."

"Funny about that. Anna Schmidt did."

Gramm waited for more. Nothing. "Wilson?"

"Yes?"

"If Anna Schmidt called you, why are they going ahead with the hearing?"

"The petition to have her declared dead is ongoing. I urged the woman who called me to be in court with a valid ID. I'm afraid a phone call doesn't count for identification. We get a lot of that. Phony calls claiming to be dead people. I guess they think they will inherit. It's a lot more complicated than that."

"So, there's a good chance Anna Schmidt is still missing."

"Oh yes! A very good chance."

"Is that farm worth fighting over?" White asked.

"Definitely! Wally Junior bragged to me it was worth millions, not as a farm, but as real estate development."

"Did Walter tell you why that dirt road on the property is so wide?" Milo asked.

"I've never seen the farm. Walter Schmidt Sr. ran it as a dairy farm. My father was the Schmidt's lawyer originally.

"Why did Anna Schmidt leave?" White asked.

"I don't know that either. I didn't ask. Walter Schmidt Junior—Wally—and I met for maybe an hour a number of years ago—not a chatty guy. He told me what he wanted in his will. I drew it up. He came back and signed it. That was the full extent of our interaction."

Gramm thanked him and hung up.

"Wow!" White said. "That was amazing."

Gramm stretched his neck. "He's gotten much better—still scattered, but he did have…"

"Time out, shirts," Milo interrupted.

Gramm stopped stretching and looked at Milo. "What? Mind lint? Already?" he asked, referring to Milo's odd way of thinking.

"Not yet, but is the…"

Preston sat up, interrupting. "The dead woman is Anna Schmidt."

"Bingo!" Milo said. "She left town at sixteen. Our dead woman is early twenties. It fits."

Gramm looked at Preston. "Nail down exactly how long ago Anna Schmidt disappeared." He dialed Doc Smith. "We may have to dig up Walter Junior to get a DNA match."

§

Milo left Gramm's office to think about the missing Anna Schmidt and check his phone. He had a missed call from author Ron Bello. Earlier in the year, Bello had written a bestselling account of one of Milo's more famous cases. Ron made money and Milo fell into an uncomfortable celebrity. Interest in Milo peaked in the spring and, much to Milo's relief, had now somewhat abated. Milo did not look forward to a sequel.

Before calling Bello, he dialed Martha.

"Mr. Rathkey?"

"Heads up. I won't be home for dinner."

"Thank you, but your dinner companion already called."

"How thoughtful of her," Milo quipped. "Did you know she's also going to become our neighbor?"

"I know the whole story," Martha said.

"Can you tell me?"

"Not mine to tell, Mr. Rathkey."

"I missed Ron's call. Any idea what that's about?"

"I have no idea. I am your personal chef, Mr. Rathkey, not your personal assistant. I suggest Agnes is a better person for that."

"But you and Ron keep company."

"Keep company?"

"Ugh. I've been hanging with Gramm too long."

§

"Wilson David was right, Anna Schmidt disappeared a little over seven years ago," Preston said, re-entering Gramm's office. "At the time, her father filed a missing person's report. In the notes, it says he thought she left with a twenty-three-year-old man."

"Where's the mother?" Gramm asked.

"Kate, find out everything you can about Anna Schmidt," White said.

"Let's not get carried away," Milo said. "We don't know for sure our victim is Anna Schmidt."

"Milo giveth and Milo taketh away," White laughed.

Gramm glared at him. "No, you don't. You called this. You're sticking with it. If you're wrong, we'll blame you for wasting our time."

Preston, long used to this banter, waited to make sure it was over.

"Preston, don't just stand there. Go!" Gramm ordered.

"On it!"

§

Not wanting to talk directly to Bello about another Milo Rathkey book, Milo called Agnes on his way back to Lakesong, but only reached her voice mail. *She's probably checking on the construction or doing something with that artsy foundation of theirs.* Milo sighed. *I'll just have to put on my big boy pants and call Ron myself.*

Bello answered on the first ring. "Milo, thanks for calling back. I need to conversate with you," Bello said.

"The last time you *conversated* with me, I ended up in the New York Times and on several TV and radio shows," Milo complained.

"You're welcome. I'm sure you enjoyed it all. I know I did, and so did my bank account. Ca-ching. Now as to the new book…"

"Have you ever met Morrie Wolf?" Milo asked.

"I have not, but…"

"Morrie can make people disappear in the trunk of a car in the middle of Lake Superior. He owes me a favor."

"Milo, Milo, Milo. Last time you threatened to choke me like a chicken—didn't happen."

"I got busy."

"Despite the threats to my person, I would still like to sit down with you for a formal interview on the case involving you and an airplane explosion."

Wanting to divert Bello, Milo tried the personal touch. "How are you liking your rental in Lakeside?" Milo asked, referring to the bungalow Agnes owned before marrying Sutherland.

"Love it. In fact, Agnes and I have agreed on a really long-term lease."

I don't like the sound of a really long-term lease. "Look, Ron, I like you personally. You're a nice guy but go write about someone else. I do not want to be the star of your book. Just write about the murders—blood, gore, stuff that sells."

Bello sighed. "Milo, I never intended for you to be the star of anything. It just happened. You are a fascinator. People are interested in you. They want to know how you do what you do."

"Don't know. Never have. That makes me extremely uninteresting. The other day I was talking to myself and fell asleep," Milo kidded as he parked his Honda between the Rolls and Bentley in the Lakesong garage.

"Yeah, I have no idea why anyone would want to read about you. Let's see, you're a wealthy man who solves complex mysteries in a highly theatric manner because you enjoy it. That's not usual. The people want to know what you, Milo Rathkey, have done recently. I want to tell them."

"I got dressed this morning," Milo said as he walked through the gallery to his bedroom.

"That's fascinating, but don't tell me the particulars now. Wait until I can record all the tidbits."

"I'm going swimming now, Ron, and I've discovered my phone doesn't work well under water."

Bello was about to ask how he discovered that, but Milo had already hung up.

§

Full of endorphins from his swim and refreshed after a shower, Milo meandered to the fancy portion of his still mostly empty master walk-in closet and selected a blue dress shirt, slacks, and new blazer for his dinner with Mary Alice. He shaved and ruffled his always forgiving dark curly hair.

Not wanting to be late, Milo strode through the gallery on his way to the garage, debating which car to drive. Sutherland and Agnes surprised him. "Whoa, why so fancy?" asked Sutherland.

"Not for us, I hope," Agnes teased. "A burgundy blazer! So unexpected." The couple was enjoying their pre-dinner cocktails, watching the activity on Lake Superior. Random sailboats were maneuvering around a salty on its way to the harbor.

"My guy at N&J sold me this. He said it would set me off from the herd," Milo said.

"My guy at N&J sold you that?" Sutherland could not believe it.

"Not your guy. I changed guys. *My* guy at N&J sold me this. He's much more with it. Not as stodgy."

Sutherland feigned shock. Agnes elbowed him. "Get the name. Your guy is kind of stodgy."

"As wonderful as this fashion conversation is," Milo interrupted, "I have called you two here to advise me on cars."

"The Bentley," Sutherland said.

"The Bentley," Agnes echoed.

"I haven't given you the choices," Milo complained.

"Sorry," Sutherland said. "What are the choices?"

"My dream car," Milo said, referring to the '87 Mercedes 560SL he bought last year, "or the Rolls or the Bentley."

"You forget the Vespa in the back of the garage. Oh, and also Goliath in case of early snow," Sutherland added.

Agnes raised her hand. "I change my vote. I like the sound of Goliath, whatever that is."

Milo shook his head. "No Vespa, and no Goliath, which, by the way, Agnes, lives in the utility garage with the snow-mobiles and basketball scoreboard."

"That huge green thing with a snowplow?" Agnes asked.

"Yup," Milo said.

"I change my vote back again," Agnes laughed. "The Bentley."

"No Rolls or Mercedes?"

"The Mercedes is a sports car, and the Rolls is way over the top," Agnes advised.

"What's wrong with a sports car?" Sutherland pulled away. "You said you love my Porsche."

"Ah, poor baby. Your Porsche is giggly and fun but messes up my hair. Lakesong's Bentley is a loving hug that doesn't."

"Call me Bentley," Sutherland nodded, drawing Agnes's shoulder close to him.

Minutes later, Milo drove out of Lakesong in the always pristine, dark-blue Bentley. A mile down London Road, Mary Alice's front gates were open, a small welcoming sign that Milo always appreciated. He proceeded halfway down the long driveway before slamming on the brakes.

"What the hell?" he said to himself, as he gawked at heavy machinery parked on either side of the drive, making entry a slow process. Milo inched toward the front entrance, successfully avoiding cranes, dump trucks, and front loaders. He was particularly amazed at the machine with an ominous heavy ball dangling from a crane.

Mary Alice glided down the front steps as if the focal point of her front lawn was still the rose bushes. Milo jumped out and double timed around the car to open the passenger door. She smiled. "Nice blazer, but next time let me know that you've changed color palettes. My blue wrap dress and your burgundy blazer could have clashed."

"Oh, my god! Then what?"

"A cosmic catastrophe, I would suspect." Mary Alice slipped into the Bentley. As Milo situated himself, she added, "I knew the Bentley was the perfect car for this evening."

"Lucky I chose it."

"I called Agnes and told her, if asked, to push the Bentley. The fix was in."

"It's a conspiracy!"

"To the restaurant, Jeeves."

"It's Milo."

"To the restaurant, Milo?" Mary Alice shook her head, flicking her golden-blond hair behind her ear. "It lacks that certain joie de vivre."

As they drove the short distance to Canal Park, Milo inquired about the serious machinery in her front yard.

"Well, you know I've been remodeling."

Milo smirked. Mary Alice had been remodeling, changing her mind, re-remodeling, and then remodeling again for more than a year. "I noticed the wrecking ball. Is the crown molding in the library off by an eighth of an inch?"

"I don't get into the particulars, Milo. If my guy needs a wrecking ball to fix the crown molding, who am I to disagree?"

Two valet parking attendants rushed to the car when Milo pulled up to the restaurant, vying with each other for the experience of driving a Bentley even for a few feet. Once safely inside the restaurant, Milo and Mary Alice were escorted to their table. He couldn't help but notice the usual stares of the other patrons. He knew their stares were directed at Mary Alice, but he couldn't resist a little fun. "My guy at N&J was right. This blazer does attract attention. Sorry to upstage you like this."

Mary Alice smiled while batting the lashes surrounding her magnetic baby blues, and he was lost. She slipped into the booth where she was immersed in an Italian street-scene fresco on the wall behind her.

"You called in advance to get this table, didn't you?" Milo asked.

The waiter arrived to discuss their wine and appetizer choices, his eyes lingering on Mary Alice as they made their selections. Finished, she turned to touch Milo's hand, saying, "I might possibly have a favorite table, but I have much more interesting news."

That broke the waiter's gaze and sent him on his way with an order for the olive appetizer, a martini for Mary Alice, and a vodka gimlet for Milo.

"Does your news involve the crown molding, a ruler, and a wrecking ball?" Milo teased.

"I know you're just being facetious but let me set the scene. Remember long ago when we first met? Someone had just murdered that late husband of mine." Mary Alice smiled. "You remember him, the rude, red bearded man—angry all the time."

"Murdered you say? I vaguely recall."

"Vaguely? If I recall, you suspected moi." Mary Alice feigned outrage.

"Oh, not true. Not true. I thought it was Cook the entire time."

The drinks arrived with the olives. "I've been craving these imported olives all week," Mary Alice said. "Keep your intruding little fork away from the Halkidikis—my favorite."

Milo sipped his gimlet and speared one Greek olive stuffed with sun dried tomato because it looked the most normal. "So, Cook murdered your husband," he said matter-of-factly, getting the conversation back on track.

"She did not!" Mary Alice defended her employee. "And neither did I. You can't get them all right, Mr. Famous Detective. And speaking of famous detective," Mary Alice nodded at a woman, clutching Ron Bello's best seller, approaching the table.

"Mr. Rathkey, could you please sign my book?" the woman asked.

Milo took the book and the pen and flipped to the page with his picture.

"So sorry to interrupt your dinner," the woman said. "Is this your wife?"

Milo paused while signing his usual: *Book Clubs can be dangerous!* "She's my father's third wife."

Mary Alice laughed. "He kids. I'm his father's fourth wife."

The woman snatched back her book, mumbled thank you, and left quickly.

"I always wonder," Milo said, "do people carry those books with them everywhere in case they bump into me?"

"It's a small city. They're bound to find you somewhere,"

"Ron Bello wants to write another book about me. I'm trying to discourage him."

Mary Alice smiled. "Oh, come on, you love it. People ask for your autograph. The newspaper mentions you all the time. He's making you famous, or is that infamous?"

"He's taking my mind off of the fascinating woman that's moving into the Hawthorn Estate just to be near me," Milo said.

Mary Alice shook her head, speared a feta-stuffed olive, and savored it with great deliberation. "I was told the poor destitute is moving in because she will soon be homeless."

"Homeless? How homeless?"

"You're the detective. Put it together. Here's a hint: a wrecking ball is not a lawn ornament."

"Oh yeah? Here I thought it was a bold choice in outdoor decoration." Milo pointed to several olives with his fork until he got the okay from Blue to make it his. "Are you really going to knock down your house?"

"Oh, Milo, that monstrosity was never mine. It was the property of Mr. James Bonner. The new house will be mine. Guy, my contractor, is…"

"Wait. You have a guy named Guy?"

Waving one hand and spearing her deep-purple Kalamata with the other, she chided, "Don't interrupt. My guy, Guy, is teaching me how to operate the wrecking ball so I personally can take the first few whacks. My therapist and I think it will be cathartic."

"Wouldn't a sledgehammer to the bathroom wall do the same thing?"

"You're thinking too small."

"Sounds expensive."

Mary Alice's blue eyes sparkled even more. "Yes, it is, and that's the best part. That angry guy we spoke about previously is paying for all of it. My lawyer found all his hidden money. Some will go to repay the people he conned, but the rest comes to me. I checked. It's significant."

"How significant?"

"Puts me between you and Sutherland—pauper."

"If I'm a pauper, don't eat the expensive olives. We'll have to wash dishes."

"I don't think they charge you by the olive."

The waiter approached and attempted to take their dinner orders, but Mary Alice waved him away. Waving seemed to be a theme tonight. It amused Milo.

"You could have stayed in Lakesong. We have several empty guest rooms," Milo said.

"We'd get caught sneaking around, and what would Sutherland and Agnes think? So young and impressionable."

"I'd worry more about the cats. They're so Victorian," Milo said.

"That's the other thing. All my dogs are afraid of cats."

The waiter returned again. Mary Alice ordered the shrimp and asparagus risotto. Milo opted for the Italian sausage risotto.

"Maybe we can go Shakespearian," Mary Alice smiled. "You can throw pebbles at my window and recite poetry. Of course, you will have to climb that ten-foot fence."

"The fence has a gate."

Mary Alice laughed. "Of course it does. I still want the pebbles tossed and poetry memorized. Start practicing."

"The tossing or the memorizing?"

7

Milo had been slowly upping the lap count to his morning swim routine, but had failed to allot more time to complete them. It finally caught up to him and he was late arriving for his Lakesong breakfast of eggs, bacon, and hash browns. Sutherland and Agnes were already eating and chatting.

"Late night?" Agnes asked.

"Mary Alice is moving next door," he mumbled as he poured his coffee from the ever-present urn.

Sutherland looked at Agnes, who shrugged. "Mary Alice? Why?"

She's bulldozing the White Whale," Milo said, as if that was something everyone did from time to time.

Agnes grew silent, remembering that house and the demise of her old boss, James Bonner.

Milo continued, "She's renting the Hawthorn place in the meantime. We will see her when she hangs out the laundry."

Sutherland laughed. "That image! Wow!"

Milo was about to respond when Annie, the calico cat, clawed at him, impatiently demanding her bacon.

Martha arrived just in time with Milo's breakfast. He broke off pieces of bacon and handed them out to Lakesong's furry friends.

"Who knew a Tuesday could be so dynamic? Let's pile on. How's your plane crash, dead body discovery going?" Sutherland asked, finishing his patented green breakfast smoothie.

"We're pretty sure it's not you or Agnes. You're both too old. The victim is in her early twenties. I'm betting it's the runaway daughter of the farm's recently deceased owner, Walter Schmidt Junior."

"When did she run away?" Agnes asked.

"About seven years ago,"

"High school. Tough times. Lots of drama," Agnes mused.

A forkful of hash browns stopped in mid-flight. Milo stared at Agnes.

"Was it something I said?" Agnes laughed. "Did I solve the case?"

"High school drama!" Milo exclaimed. "The kids along Martin Road, what high school?"

Sutherland shrugged. "In my day, kids who lived up there went to East. Why?"

"In my day? Good grief," Agnes joked.

"We may not have to dig up Walter Schmidt Junior."

"Ew," grimaced Agnes, scrunching up her nose. "Why would you do that?"

"DNA proof that our victim is Anna Schmidt," Milo said.

Jet, who had lost his piece of bacon under a hutch, meowed for more.

"Sorry Jet. I'm afraid your papers have been lost," Milo said, petting the cat's silky black fur, "and no amount of DNA is going to tell us who you really are."

Jet rolled over, exposing his belly. Milo attempted to pet his silky black fur but received several love bites on his thumb. He shook his hand free, and promised, "We'll tussle later, Jet, I have research to do." Jet followed Milo to his office.

"I guess Jet has research to do, too," Agnes quipped.

Sutherland put his arm around his wife's shoulder. "Apparently, you did it again, my dear. You solved another case, and this time you didn't have to knock me off my bike."

"I didn't solve that case. Milo did."

"You saved my life with a fabulous flying tackle."

Agnes leaned back against Sutherland's chest. "I don't like to think about anything like that. I almost lost you."

"How about construction? Will that cheer you up?"

"Sure. Anything that's about us being safe and secure." Agnes got up and took her smoothie glass to the sink in the kitchen.

Sutherland called after her. "I ran our mini-glass-dome plan past the Historical Society one more time. They're still not budging."

"Historical society? So early in the day." Agnes returned to the morning room and snuggled up next to Sutherland. "Be still my heart. You really know how to charm a girl."

"Did I mess up?"

"No, just tell me."

"The Society feels that a second glass dome would not fit with the Jacobean style of the house."

Agnes shook her head. "Your mother's glass dome didn't fit either, but it's fabulous."

Sutherland sighed. "I know, but it doesn't seem to matter. Look, these people really have no authority, and if you love it, we'll do it. But I'm a member of that society and I've voted to deny other people's plans. I support historic integrity, but I love our dome idea."

"Milo could get Morrie Wolf to threaten a few people," Agnes suggested.

Sutherland winced. "My square corners of right and wrong are a bit more rounded, but I don't think they're that round yet."

Agnes laughed. "Luckily, we both love our alternative plan, which they have already approved. Are you going to take time off to supervise this construction, Mr. Sexy Real Estate Developer?"

"No, I'm far too important. I'm leaving it to the outstanding Lakesong house manager. I understand she is the best at this sort of thing."

Agnes closed her eyes. "You know that your Lakesong house manager has absolutely no experience in construction. She might be overreaching. Besides, this Lakesong house manager may not be available. She may be busy being Mr. Rathkey's personal assistant solving murders, or Mr. McKnight's wife doing—whatever."

Sutherland stood up, leaned over, and kissed Agnes one more time. "I'll leave that to you to figure out. All I know is Lakesong loves you and trusts you, as do I. Nothing bad will happen with you in charge, no matter your title."

"Does project supervisor come with a raise?"

Sutherland shook his head and looked down at the floor. "Sorry, things are a little tight these days, especially after our extravagant trip to New York. Check with me in the new year."

"Are you saying I shouldn't have ordered the liver sausage sandwich?"

"It was the onions that broke the budget."

§

Milo marched into the cop shop and headed straight to Ernie Gramm's office. He arrived at the same time as Officer Preston. "High School!" he announced to Gramm.

Preston sat down and echoed the same thing. "I agree, high school!"

White, having put her long, black hair into her work ponytail, got up from her desk to join them.

Gramm stretched his neck to the left for a thirty-second hold. "Well, Robin, both Preston and Milo have said 'high school' for no apparent reason. You want to get in on this and maybe tell me what's going on?"

White sat down, placing both hands around her coffee cup, settling into her chair. "I'm in the dark."

"Anna Schmidt disappeared in high school, probably at the end of her sophomore year," Milo announced.

"There are yearbooks in high school," Preston chimed in.

"Yes!" Milo agreed.

"I'm listening," Gramm said.

Preston continued. "Anna was a junior varsity cheerleader, and she belonged to the Spanish Club…"

"And the drama club," Milo added.

Taking what she perceived to be Milo's challenge, Preston countered, "I know she had the lead in that year's production of *The Little Mermaid*."

Gramm's eyebrows knitted together. "If either of you reads the review, I will stop listening."

"Patience," Milo advised. "There is a point. I found two other people who turn up in almost every picture of Anna Schmidt: Grace Hannah and…"

"And Bill Pendergast," Preston finished Milo's sentence.

Milo offered a fist bump, to which Preston responded in kind.

Gramm straightened up. "So, this was the long way of telling me we may have identified two people who knew Anna Schmidt well."

"Yes!" Preston said. "And can identify her body."

"I'm almost impressed. Why are we all sitting here fist bumping? Somebody find these people! I need more coffee!"

"Already done," Milo said. "Grace Hannah is now Grace Pendergast. They're married."

"Very tidy," White said.

Not to be outdone, Preston added, "The Pendergasts live in one of those subdivisions just off of Martin Road."

Gramm leaned over his desk. "Enough talking about them. Let's interview them."

All three got up and headed back into the bullpen area. White called the Pendergast home and arranged the first interview with Grace.

Gramm rose from his chair, left his office, and walked over to the coffee bar, only to find the pot empty. He turned to the group. "This is a lesson, children, for when you become old, irritable, and in charge. This coffee pot is empty!" he bellowed and calmly stood to the side. Two newbie patrol people scampered to the pot. Together, they made coffee and cleaned up the area.

Gramm smirked and stepped up to the newly made coffee to pour his cup. "One of the few perks of being in charge."

He settled back into his office, completing a series of morning neck and back stretches. Taking another sip of coffee, he pressed the blinking message button on his office phone.

Doc Smith here. A dental match for Anna Schmidt is not going to work. Call me.

"Of course not. That would be too easy!" Gramm grumbled just as White walked back into his office.

"Are you talking to yourself?"

"I'm talking to Anna Schmidt," Gramm complained.

"Tell me what chair she's sitting in so I can avoid her."

"Very funny. Sit down, we are going to hear bad news from Doc Smith. Join me."

Preston poked her head in the door and whispered to White, "I forgot to ask. What is today's coffee?"

"I'm holding off on the pumpkin spice latte until October. This is an apple crisp, oat milk macchiato," White said, raising her cup.

Gramm shook his head. "Oat milk?"

91

"Yeah, I saw a documentary on that," Milo added, poking his head in the door. "Tiny farmers up with the sun, milking those oats on tiny three-legged oat milk milking stools."

Gramm leaned back in his chair. "Robin, does Milo have any outstanding warrants?"

White smirked.

"Wait, maybe Walter Schmidt's farm was an oat milk farm. That's why there weren't any cows," Milo mused.

"Is anyone here armed?" Gramm insisted, his head resting on the back of his chair. "Please, just shoot him…or me."

The phone rang. Gramm sat up and pushed the speaker button. "Gramm."

"It's Doc Smith. Don't you return phone calls these days?"

"I was in the process but got held up by a discussion of tiny oat farmers," Gramm shared, knowing Smith had little or no humor.

"I…don't…need to know. My dental experts tell me that the stabbing victim has had extensive dental work, negating any pediatric work."

"Define extensive?" White asked.

"Caps, a couple of extractions, braces. I propose we continue our plan to exhume Walter Schmidt."

Wanting to avoid the expense of an exhumation, Gramm threw out another solution. "We have a woman that is a cousin to Walter Junior."

"No, a match to her would only show a relation. A match to Walter would positively tell us if the victim is the daughter. Of course, we could avoid the expense if you can find Anna Schmidt's mother," Doc Smith said.

Gramm looked at Preston, who was shaking her head.

"That would be Elsa, Walter Schmidt Junior's first wife who died when Anna was seven. Wally accidentally ran her over with a tractor."

"Accidentally ran her over with a tractor?" White was incredulous. "Was she sunning herself in the cornfield?"

"Oat field," Milo corrected. "It's an oat milk farm, remember?"

"Ernie, maybe the oat farm business is Milo's path to mind lint."

Doc Smith cleared his throat. "I'm sorry, but unless I just joined the comedy troupe, none of this applies to me. Plus, I'm not finished."

"Go," Gramm urged.

"We pulled several partial fingerprints from the scissors…"

"And?"

"They are a match for a Clara Schmidt."

"Clara? Who is Clara Schmidt?" Gramm asked.

Preston sat up. "Clara Lehto married Wally Schmidt Junior a short time after Elsa died in that tanning accident. She left Wally a year before Anna disappeared."

"Okay, Doc, are you saying Anna Schmidt was murdered by her long-lost stepmother, Clara?" Gramm asked.

"That's your department," Doc Smith said. "I'm just reporting that the partial fingerprints on the murder weapon belong to Clara Schmidt. We have her prints from immigration."

Gramm looked at White. "Put out a BOLO on Clara Schmidt."

"Do we have a description?" White asked.

Doc Smith interrupted. "Look, I've got a busy day. Do we dig up Walter Schmidt or not?"

"Remind me, do we need a relative's permission?" Gramm asked.

"We could ask Anna Schmidt, assuming that's her on the slab in the morgue. Or you could ask Clara Schmidt, assuming you can find her. However, I think a court order would be easier."

"What if we had an old friend to ID Anna Schmidt?" Gramm asked.

"Why didn't you say that earlier? If someone can ID her, we don't have to go through any digging." Doc Smith hung up.

Gramm took a sip of coffee while he gathered his thoughts. "Let's go with the ID but continue to get our ducks in a row on the exhumation, just in case." Gramm called Dutch Wilson, the county attorney.

"Gramm, got another puzzle you want the pieces to?" Wilson asked, referring to a recent case.

"Not this time. I'm not saying I want to do this, but if I wanted to dig up a dead guy, what's the process?"

"Look, I have some really exciting zoning variances I'm working on, but I can hold off on all that fun. Give me the particulars."

"Tell him it has to do with milking oats," Milo suggested.

Gramm turned to White. "Why can't you buy normal coffee?"

"Just don't ask me what I'm drinking."

8

Grace Pendergast agreed to meet the police at her home. She explained that both she and her husband Bill worked mostly from home for her real estate developer dad. Bill was at a job site, but she was available all day.

As they drove into the Martin's Landing subdivision, Milo remarked on how all the new homes were close together. "Better like your neighbors."

"We can't all live on estates," Gramm quipped. He found the narrow three-story house that belonged to Grace and Bill Pendergast and parked the police Interceptor on the short driveway.

Grace, a young woman who's worried look aged her, met them at the door. She guided them to a large-windowed front room that she called her office. Gramm, White, and Milo sat on three orange, swivel-barrel chairs arranged around a glass coffee table. Grace turned her desk chair around to face them. She offered coffee. They all declined.

Sitting very straight, hands folded in her lap, Grace began, "Your call took me by surprise. I don't know what I can tell you about Anna. She left so long ago. We were tight in high school, but I haven't talked to her or thought about her in forever. How did you even find me?"

"We looked for Anna in old yearbooks and found you two shared several clubs. You look different than you did in high school."

Grace laughed. "Don't we all. You mean the hair?"

White nodded.

"I was in love with Anna's long, straight, blond hair. I had to have it. It was a lot of work, Champagne-blond, plus keratin treatments every six months. Kids! Hers was natural. Mine was expensive. Besides, Bill prefers my natural brown, short, curly hair. I do, too." She fluffed up the curls."

"You are the only person who referred to her as leaving," Milo asked.

"Well, she did! What do other people say?"

"Disappeared."

Grace scoffed. "Please! Anna was no magic fairy. She left. Ran to California with some theater guy."

"Did you know him?" White asked.

"No. He was with the Duluth Playhouse. I didn't do plays there—just high school. I knew his first name was Ted. She called him her Teddy Bear. That's all I know."

"Were you and Anna close?" White asked.

"Like I said, we were. Why are you digging up old history about Anna?"

"We have reason to believe that she recently returned to Duluth," Gramm said.

"So what? Is returning to your hometown a crime now?" Grace joked. She grabbed a handful of orange chewy candies and offered the bowl to the group. "If she had come back, she would have called me."

"Did she?" White asked. "Call you?"

"No." Grace offered the bowl of candy a second time, taking another handful herself.

Gramm leaned forward. "A woman was found murdered Sunday evening on the Schmidt farm. That woman might be Anna Schmidt." Gramm stopped for a reaction. He was disappointed.

Grace stared ahead and absently reached for another orange slice. As she chewed it, she murmured, "That's terrible. Life can be terrible."

"Are you okay?" White asked, thinking Grace might go into a sugar coma.

Grace attempted a deep breath. "Yes, I'm…it's a…Anna?"

"We don't know yet. One more question," White said. "Did you know Anna's stepmom, Clara Schmidt?"

Grace blinked. "Clara? Yes, I knew her. She left too—before Anna."

"What can you tell us about her?" White prompted.

"I didn't know her well. She was younger than Anna's dad. She had an accent like Swedish or something. Nice to me when I was over."

"Do you have a picture of Clara?"

Grace shook her head. "Anna spent most of her time at my house or the theater. Her father was mean."

"Because you knew Anna, and she no longer has any family here, we were wondering if you could identify her," White said.

Grace grabbed yet another orange slice. "You want me to look at a dead body? A friend I haven't seen in years?" She bit her lower lip and turned away. "Don't you have other ways to identify bodies? Like with science?"

"Sometimes in our line of work, we forget how upsetting it might be to see a dead person outside of a funeral," Milo said. "Maybe your husband could do it."

"Why would you ask Bill?"

"We've seen yearbook pictures—Anna and your husband, Bill. He seemed to be a close friend, too. Maybe he could…"

"No! He's too busy. I'll do it!" Grace chirped.

White wrote the address to the morgue on her notepad, tore off the page, and handed it to Grace. As they left, White called Doc Smith to alert him that Grace would be there to ID the body today. Gramm added that maybe forensics could grab Grace's fingerprints while she was there.

§

Tamara Busker sat across the desk from Agnes Larson McKnight, who was flipping through a construction schedule.

"Nifty office," Tamara remarked. "Convenient for work people. Separate entrance, very nice."

Agnes smiled. "This is my house manager's office, and my personal assistant's office."

"Oh, I thought Mr. Durant said you were married to…"

"That too. It gets confusing."

"I bet."

"Ms. Busker, in checking over the construction schedule, it looks like you are going to do the skylights in the main house and build the room over the garage first," Agnes stated.

"It's going to get cold next month. We feel it's best to get both areas enclosed. Then the crews have the winter months to work inside. Your architect has signed off. Oh, and call me Tee. Everybody does."

Agnes smiled. "We are looking forward to working with you, Tee. You come highly recommended by Creedence Durant."

"He has been our best marketing person. Ever since we renovated his house, he's kept us in work. Two other remodels, that soup kitchen on Lake Avenue, and now a mansion expansion. Our crews are busy and happy."

"I'm happy to get a bathtub that isn't down the hall." Agnes explained the current arrangement in Sutherland's old suite of rooms.

Tee laughed. "No one would believe that story driving through those fancy gates."

"I know. It makes me giggle too." Agnes moved the schedule into a folder. "When do we begin?"

"We've already started. If you look at the back of the house, we are assembling some of the equipment we need and the supplies."

Agnes jumped up. "Oh, I have to see!"

She led Tee through the gallery to the terrace, where they saw scaffolding being laid out on the lawn and workmen directing a crane onto plywood supports. In the middle of Tee's explanation, Martha's younger brother, ten-year-old

Darian, appeared. Martha had directed him to take their drink orders.

"Coffee would be great," Tee said.

"Same for me, Darian, but why aren't you in school today?" Agnes asked.

"Teacher workday," Darian said.

"Come see," Agnes invited. "The construction people are getting ready to begin."

"Oh, I know! I've been watching them all morning!" Darian smiled.

Agnes introduced Darian to Tee.

He was about to leave when he turned around and said, "The house is excited. It hasn't been fixed in years."

"Fixed?" Agnes asked.

"Yes, the house likes to look new." Darian left to tell Martha about the coffee orders.

"The house is excited?" Tee asked.

"Darian says the house talks to him or lets him know how she's feeling. I don't know exactly how it works, but if Darian says Lakesong is happy, we're happy," Agnes said.

Tee nodded. "If we encounter ghosts, that's extra."

Agnes laughed.

§

Grace Pendergast unwrapped a caramel, placed it in her mouth, and began nervously folding the wrapper along its creases. Wanting to run home, she kept redirecting her thoughts to a pleasant, beautiful place—the North Shore of Lake Superior, where she and Bill had hiked a week ago.

Closing her eyes, she visualized the red and gold leaves and felt the warm sunshine on her skin. When she slowly opened her eyes, her reality was still the county morgue with white-tiled walls and a strong smell of chemicals, especially bleach.

An older woman wearing a white coat emerged from one of two swinging doors and beckoned her forward. "Grace Pendergast?"

Grace nodded.

"Can I see some ID?"

"Really? Why? Do people randomly come here to look at dead bodies?" Grace asked, digging around in her purse.

"You'd be surprised," the woman said. "We need to make sure who is making the identification in case someone wants to question it."

Grace fished out her wallet, opened it, and showed the woman her driver's license. The woman copied it and asked Grace to follow her.

The smell of bleach had grown stronger as they walked down a short hallway to an autopsy room. Stepping just inside the swinging doors, Grace tried to avoid looking at the single gurney and sheet covered body.

"If you feel upset or queasy, just say so. The chairs are right beside you. We don't want you fainting," the woman said.

Grace nodded, keeping her focus on the tile floor.

The woman gently folded the sheet down to reveal the face of Anna Schmidt—actually only the white-blond, hair. She had been positioned so her head was turned, hiding most of her face.

"She's turned away," Grace mumbled.

"When a person dies, and the face lies on one side for some time, blood pools on that side. It is disfiguring and often interferes with identification."

"I don't know."

The attendant gloved up and turned the dead woman's head, so she was facing Grace. The large, dark patch around the cadaver's eye covered her cheek from her nose to her ear.

"Oh," Grace whispered, "she was always so pretty."

"For the record, can you say this is Anna Schmidt?"

"Yes, that's Anna, but I can't do this anymore. It's horrible."

"That's all," the woman said. "You can follow me out."

§

Gramm drove the police Interceptor up over Thompson Hill on his way to Moose Lake. "I remember in the old days, the old highway ran through Moose Lake. Then they built I-35 and bypassed it," Gramm said to White and Rathkey.

"Good story. Milo, do you have Tylenol?" White asked.

"Excedrin or nothing," Milo said.

"Fine. Six or seven will do…for now."

Gramm frowned. "I know you consider my reminiscing boring, but I consider it historical background for you."

"More historical background. I remember driving to the cities with Sutherland's father," Milo said. "We'd stop off at Tobie's in Hinkley. I'd have the hot meatloaf sandwich."

"Fascinating." White emptied the pockets of her parka, finding nothing. "Maybe there's strychnine in the glove compartment."

After a long period of silence, Milo questioned, "Where are we meeting Moose Lake's finest?"

White checked her phone. "The Lazy Moose Grill."

"Lazy Moose?" Milo asked. "They're all lazy unless it's rutting season and then they try to kill you—at least the males do. Oh, and it currently is rutting season."

White grimaced. "We go from reminiscences of old highways to Milo's twisted nature stories. Love road trips with you two."

Gramm drove in silence. White watched for rutting, killer moose as she programmed the GPS for the Lazy Moose parking lot. Along with a friendly five-foot cardboard cartoon of a smiling moose welcoming visitors to the café, there was also a sign advertising an Agate Festival.

The Lazy Moose was a hopping lunch destination. A perky hostess showed the three to a six top table in the back. Before the hostess could scamper away, Milo asked about the Agate Festival.

"Oh, too bad. You just missed it," she informed him. "But don't worry, they hold it every year," she added, as if these visitors might think about staying in Moose Lake for a year to catch the next festival.

Amused, Milo pressed. "What happens at an Agate Festival?"

The hostess glanced back at her station in case other visitors were waiting. They weren't. "It's all so much fun, but you should fer sure not miss the Agate Stampede."

White told herself to ignore it, but she couldn't. "An agate is a rock, right?"

The hostess nodded.

"Ahh, how do rocks stampede?"

The hostess laughed at the absurdity. "Rocks don't stampede, silly, people do. We got two dump trucks, one blue, one orange. My Uncle Rob drives the orange one. Anyways, we all start lining up at dawn on both sides of the street. Everybody's excited—talking, laughing—you know, catching up. They drive the dump trucks two blocks with their backs up, dumping rocks, coins, and dust everywhere. At the blast of the horns, we all rush for the rocks. I've done it since I was a baby. It's great."

"Fun," White said, trying to keep the sarcasm out of her voice. *Babies and flying rocks—sounds idyllic.*

"Check out the specials on the menu. They're great. I'll send Becky over," the hostess said as she left.

Becky was an older woman with a pad, pencil, an over-abundance of chewing gum, and no humor. "What can I getcha?" she asked.

"Do you have strychnine?" White asked.

"My cousin got some weed laced with that stuff once. It almost killed her. I'd stay away from it if I were you," Becky advised, as serious as Doc Smith.

White buried her head in the menu, stunned that the server would take her seriously.

"I'll have the Bigfoot Bacon Cheeseburger," Gramm said, "with fries."

Milo ordered the Bacon Barnyard Burger. White opted for the Minnesota Wild Rice Meatloaf Burger, proclaiming it was in memory of Milo's boyhood trip to Hinkley.

They were halfway through their meal when a fortyish woman walked in and scanned the crowd. Her rose-gold, long hair brushed the shoulders of her navy suit as she spoke to the agate loving hostess. A man with brown, tousled hair, wearing a pink polo shirt with a Moose Lake logo, and plaid pants was waving to people at various tables. He joined her.

The hostess pointed to the six top table in the back. The waving man's tousled hair gave him a younger look than the woman's professional suit.

"We are the Petersons," the woman announced as they reached the table. "I'm Susan, and this is my husband, Gordy."

Gramm motioned for them to sit down and waved at the server.

"There are three of you?" Susan questioned.

Gramm did the introductions. There were nods and handshakes. "Thank you for meeting with us today," Gramm said.

The couple nodded. "Is this about my farm?" Susan asked.

"Your farm? It's our understanding it's not your farm—yet," Gramm said. "Is that correct?"

"Yes, but it will be ours in a few days. We have some minor procedural hurdles."

They ignored the menus. "I don't see how this is a police matter," Gordy said.

Milo noticed Gordy began polishing his silverware.

"We're not here to talk about your wife's inheritance. The police matter concerns the body of a woman found in the farmhouse on that land. We are investigating her death as a homicide."

"A homicide? In my farmhouse?" Susan asked.

"In the Schmidt farmhouse, yes," Gramm said.

"How was it discovered?" Gordy asked.

The server arrived with her notepad and greeted the Petersons like old friends. She asked if they wanted their usual. They nodded, and she left.

"As awful as that is, I don't see why we were called," Susan asserted once the server had left.

"When was the last time you were in that farmhouse?" White asked.

"Never!" Susan blurted. "I have never seen the place. I probably never will. Once I own it, I'm going to sell it. I already have a realtor in place."

Gordy went from silverware polishing to stabbing at the lemon in the bottom of his water glass with his straw.

"Ms. Peterson, how are you related to Walter Schmidt Junior?" White asked.

"Wally and I were second cousins," Susan said.

"Did you know Wally's second wife, Clara?" White asked. "Maybe you have a picture of her?"

"I knew of her, maybe met her once or twice. Why?"

"Routine," Gramm said.

"Were you and your cousin close?" White asked.

"Oh no, he was...I don't know, a distant relative. It was a family dance we did. I would invite him to a family reunion. He would say no because he hated everyone in the family. One year I asked after Clara, and he ranted on that she left him, and he divorced her. That's how I knew."

"The man was foul," Gordy added, having pulverized his lemon.

"Today, I talked to my boss. She's a lawyer. She said that if Wally's will only mentions me and Anna, Clara has absolutely no claim."

Gramm's and White's phones buzzed at the same time. White looked at the incoming message and showed the message to Milo.

Neither Gordy nor Susan spoke.

Gramm nodded at White, who announced, "We have positively identified the murdered woman found on the farm as Anna Schmidt."

Susan opened her mouth, but nothing came out.

Milo excused himself to call his lawyer friend, Saul Feinberg. Probate and dead inheritors were beyond Milo. He needed some information on how finding dead Anna Schmidt complicated things. The answer he got caused him to whistle.

Milo returned as the server was delivering the Peterson's food and the next ten minutes were taken up with eating and small talk about Moose Lake and agates, again.

"Let me ask you a question, gentlemen," Gordy said to Gramm and Rathkey. "Have either of you ever considered a BlowVee?"

From their blank stares, it was obvious that neither knew what he was talking about.

"The BlowVee is my vacuum haircut system. It's a hot product and you could say I'm riding the wave." Gordy chuckled as he ran his hand through his bouffant seventies style blow combed hair. "I'm the regional distributor. I can get both of you a deal."

"Is that what you do for a living?" Gramm asked.

"Well, it's one of my business endeavors. I'm an entrepreneur."

Milo leaned back, pushing the few remnants of his Bacon Barnyard Burger away from the edge of the table.

"This discovery of Anna Schmidt throws your inheritance into question."

"No, it doesn't!" Susan insisted. "Walter may have left his farm to Anna, but if she is deceased, it all comes to me. She's deceased." Pointing at White, she added, "You just said she's dead. That makes me the sole heir."

Milo took a deep breath and blew it out slowly. "Our medical examiner says she died sometime last Sunday. She was still alive when Wally Schmidt Junior died last month. Even if she wasn't at the reading, she inherited the farm, and it now goes to her heirs, not you."

Gramm's eyebrows shot up.

"No!" Susan shook her head. "That land is mine! We will fight that. Who says that dead woman is Anna?"

"A friend from high school," White said.

"High school? That was years ago!" Susan shouted. Other people in the restaurant turned and stared. Gordy grabbed her arm to quiet her down. Regaining her composure, Susan took a different approach. "Who was the trespasser who illegally entered my farmhouse to find the body?"

Milo raised his hand. "That would be me, but it was part of another police investigation."

"Investigation into what?"

"A plane crashed while taking off from the farm. The pilot had been on the ground, possibly in that farmhouse. Searching the farmhouse was within police jurisdiction."

"A plane? A pilot? A dead body? Was someone holding an open house on my land?" Susan demanded. "All of this is trespass!"

The conversation was getting loud and contentious. Gramm decided it was time to bring it back to the point. "Your inheritance is not our problem. Our problem is finding the person who murdered Anna Schmidt. Where were both of you on Sunday?"

"Us?" Gordy exclaimed. "We were here in Moose Lake. We didn't even know Anna Schmidt was alive. We wouldn't need to kill her. We were having her legally declared dead.."

Susan stood up. "I think in the future you need to talk with my attorney." She slapped a card with the name of her employer on the table. She and Gordy walked out.

The server arrived with the check.

"Who pays for them?" Milo asked.

Gramm took the check. "The City of Duluth."

"I take it from what you told the Petersons that Grace Pendergast positively identified the body," Milo said.

"She did. The missing daughter returned only to be murdered."

§

"Not the low-key Lazy Moose lunch I expected," Gramm said climbing back into the car. "What do we think about Susan Peterson?"

"Ms. *my land* Peterson really wants that farm," Milo said.

"They could have traveled to Duluth, killed Anna Schmidt, and drove back to Moose Lake Sunday afternoon," Gramm said.

"If they killed her, why leave the body in the kitchen of the farmhouse?" White asked. "There's a lot of land there. Just bury her."

Milo shook his head. "I don't think grave digging is one of Gordy's side hustles. I will bet they thought they had lots of time to dispose of the body at their leisure."

White laughed. "At their leisure? Most people do not want to be disposing of a days-old dead body."

"Maybe they're dumb enough to think the demolition would bury it."

"That land is motive. We need to check alibis," Gramm ordered.

"I wonder how IT is doing on finding Anna's phone records?" White asked. "She could have called the Petersons."

"Why?" Gramm asked.

"Maybe she discovered they were trying to have her declared dead," White said.

"Continue," Gramm urged.

"If somebody tried to declare me dead, I'd want to have a little chat!" White said.

"The cats are constantly trying to declare Sutherland dead," Milo said.

"Off topic, Milo, and irrelevant," White said.

"Sutherland doesn't think so."

"Let's pull Susan Peterson's phone records, too. Meanwhile, Clara's fingerprints on the murder weapon still make her suspect number one," Gramm said.

§

Sutherland was in the midst of making his pre-dinner martini when he spied what he thought was a construction crane faintly lit by the back lawn lights. "We have a crane!" he exclaimed.

"Kinda late in the season," Milo said.

"Maybe it was a seagull masquerading as a crane?" Agnes joked.

"I'm not talking about birds!" Sutherland insisted, walking over to the windows for a better look. "What's a *construction* crane, not the bird crane, doing in our backyard?" Sutherland asked.

"Oh, that crane is going to put in our lovely skylights," Agnes said.

Sutherland raced for the stairway. Taking two at a time with his long legs, he hurried up to the second floor and turned around, expecting to find Agnes still at the bottom. She was at his side. "I can do that too."

Sutherland smiled. "So you can."

Together, they walked the next flight of stairs to the empty third floor. Looking up, they saw a hole in the roof covered by a blue tarp.

"That's a big hole," Sutherland said.

"It's going to be a big skylight."

"What about the one for the bedroom?"

"I think they will cut that hole tomorrow," Agnes said. "You know we're floating in our living room."

"Floating?"

"Yes, floating. This floor we're standing on will not be here in a couple of days. It will be gone to give us a vaulted ceiling in the living room."

9

Sunshine all week and today it pours. "Interviews here today," Gramm groused as he made his way back to his office from the coffee station. "Preston, whaddaya got?"

"They released the pilot from the hospital," Preston reported. "He is now at the Canal Park Inn."

Gramm sat back, sipped his coffee, and raised an eyebrow at White's store-bought cup. "That's not office coffee!"

"Of course not."

"You and everyone else around here told me you drink office brew on Wednesday. Today is Wednesday."

"Everybody lies," White said, mocking Milo. "Besides this is Chukku Kappi."

White was met with a blank stare.

"Ginger coffee," she continued. "It's good for coughs and colds. I feel one coming on. It's medicinal."

"You and the pilot are kindred spirits. You lie about coffee, and, according to our birdman, the pilot lies about being in a farmhouse,"

"What did he say when you confronted him?" Preston asked.

"First interviews are informal, friendly. Let him think the lie worked," Gramm said.

White added, "Second interviews are much more uncomfortable."

"Since he's been released, shouldn't that second interview happen today in case he leaves town?" Preston asked. "I'd like to listen."

"First, we have another task for you."

Preston took her iPad out of her backpack. "I know you're going to say something about my memory, but I feel better writing things down," Preston persisted, "so, there's a record."

White shrugged. "Suit yourself."

"So, what's the task?"

"Yesterday morning, Grace Pendergast told us our victim left for California with a man named Ted. Find him."

"Ted who?"

Gramm shrugged. "Well, Anna apparently called him Teddy Bear."

"Description?"

White laughed. "He was in his twenties seven years ago. Check out the Duluth Playhouse."

"We don't have a picture, really aren't sure of his name, or his age—piece of cake." Preston said, thinking she had been around long enough to step into the fun banter of the group.

§

Agnes stood at the window, mesmerized by rain splattering against the construction vehicles on the back lawn. Milo shuffled in and began pouring a needed cup of coffee. Sutherland was buried in his *Wall Street Journal*. Only Jet was active, zooming from one room to the next.

The intercom broke the silence to announce that Ron Bello was at the gate. "How does Debby know Ron Bello?" Milo demanded.

"Who's Debby?" Agnes asked, not really caring.

"The intercom is Debby. I gave her that name," Milo said, "in honor of a pretty weather girl from my past."

Sutherland folded his paper and hit the *gate open* button on his app.

"You opened the gate! Maybe I don't want to talk with Ron," Milo complained.

"Maybe I do," Sutherland countered. "I'm thinking I should be the subject of his next book." Sutherland opened his arms in a grand gesture. "Sutherland Freskin McKnight, commercial real estate developer by day, crime fighter by night."

Agnes turned and did a double take at Sutherland's false bravado.

"I never realized when you snuck downstairs at night in your jams, you were off fighting crime. I thought you were raiding the refrigerator."

"Ron Bello is at the door," Debbie announced.

"Again, how does Debbie know it's Ron?" Milo asked.

Sutherland jumped up and headed for the door.

"I think your answer just left the room," Agnes said.

Martha arrived from the kitchen with Milo's breakfast, expecting a normal uneventful morning. Instead, she was greeted by Milo's pronouncement, "Debbie knows Ron," Martha paused. "Who's Debbie?"

"The intercom," Milo explained.

"I see. Perhaps a second cup of coffee?"

"Also, Sutherland fights crime at night in his jammies."

"Sounds like low blood sugar, Mr. Rathkey. Maybe pancakes and syrup along with your eggs and hash browns?"

"Or we could go the other way. Maybe a green smoothie," Agnes suggested.

"Never give Milo a green smoothie!" Ron Bello bellowed as he entered the room. "It could destroy the space-time continuum."

Martha smiled. "Morning, Ron. I'm going back to my kitchen. None of you are invited."

Bello, being familiar with Lakesong's rhythms, poured himself a cup of coffee and sat down at the end of the table opposite Sutherland. Annie the cat came by to scope out the situation in case the visitor was also getting bacon. Assuring herself that Bello was baconless, she moved to Milo and received her share. Jet followed his calico mentor.

"Sutherland insists you write a book on his crime fighting exploits," Milo said.

"In his jams, holding a ham and cheese sandwich," Agnes added.

Sutherland put down his empty smoothie to proclaim, "One and all, there was a time, after my father passed, that I sat alone at this table. The quiet was soothing. Then I received a call from Dad's attorney with the time and place of the will reading. He asked me a life-changing question—did I know a Milo Rathkey? I should have said no and taken passage to Madagascar."

"Taken passage?" Milo questioned.

"It's an old-fashioned term," Agnes said. "If you did take passage, I would have been sad and have had the vapors."

Bello shook his head. "I need to start taking notes the second I come through Lakesong's gates."

§

In advance of a second interview with pilot Kirkland Rafferty Junior, Sgt. White decided to re-interview bird watcher Bernie Waite. If she could avoid the *golden* chatter, he may have more to add to his story. He was the only eye-witness they had.

He answered on the first ring.

"Mr. Waite, this is Sgt. White of the Duluth Police Department. I want to briefly go over your recollection of the events last Sunday night."

"Sunday. Lots of eagles."

"The events at the Schmidt farm concerning people."

"Oh, right."

"You said you saw the pilot of the plane run out of the farmhouse. Is that correct?"

"Yes, he came running out of the house. I can't be sure, but he seemed to be carrying something under his arm, like a briefcase. I think he fell or tripped on something. When he got up, he was limping."

"Anything else to add about what you saw?"

"Oh yes. You want to know all of it? The whole day?"

"Yes, Mr. Waite, the whole day—human parts only."

"Yeah, I get that a lot. Okay, no birds. The whole day was odd. No one had been near that field of birds in months and then Sunday it was Grand Central. I spotted three people coming out of that house. Not together, mind you. About two there were two." Waite chuckled at his joke. "They rode off in a white car. Then a while later, about three, that plane landed and the pilot…"

"Two people came out first?"

"Yes."

"Before the plane?"

"Yeah, an hour or so before the plane. So annoying, upset my birds."

"How did you happen to see them?"

"I was following a tail who flew over my patch. I saw those people leave."

"Tail? Patch?" White asked.

"Sorry, a redtail hawk, and my patch is the farm. I know it doesn't belong to me, but the tails fly over it all the time. I certainly am not going to see birds in my neighborhood—too many people."

"Were these two people running like the pilot?"

"They seemed to be taking their time. No one tripped or fell."

"Could you recognize them if we showed you pictures?"

"My binoculars are good but not that good. Besides, I only saw them from the back."

"Two men?"

"No, a man and a buffy."

"Again, what does that mean?"

"A buffy, pale—yellow plumage."

"So, a blond woman."

"Blondish. Buffy. Not dark like the man."

"One more question. Did you see anyone enter the farmhouse earlier in the week? Say a very blond woman, a different buffy?"

"Not on Sunday?"

"Any other day?"

"On Saturday. I saw her getting dropped off by a taxi or I guess they call them an Uber and walk in. I don't know if she left. Two of the tails were hunting, and I stopped watching the farm to watch them."

"Thank you, Mr. Waite. Would you mind coming in to make a formal statement, and we'll need to take your fingerprints? It's just procedure."

"You want my fingerprints? Wow! Am I a suspect?"

"Not at this time. The prints are just for elimination."

"Are you sure I can't be a suspect? I've never been a suspect before."

"Okay, Mr. Waite, you're a suspect."

"Great! Thank you."

White went into the Gramm's office. "It seems Bernie Waite was watching as many humans as birds this weekend."

Gramm looked up. "Bernie, our bird watcher?"

"Yup. Not only did he see Rafferty leave the farmhouse, earlier in the day he saw two people leave. A man and a woman."

"Are we thinking the Petersons?"

"I am. The woman was blondish; the man had dark hair. And he also saw another blond woman enter on Saturday but didn't see her on Sunday."

119

"Was Bernie staking out the place? Does he want a job? We could use him."

"I'm thinking the blond woman could be Anna Schmidt," White said.

Preston leaned in the office door. "I got something big for you."

"Great!" Gramm said, leaning back in his chair. "Go for it,"

Preston was all smiles. "Anna's *Teddy Bear* is really a guy named Teddy Bear. Theodore Bear is an actor who used to work at the Duluth Playhouse."

"So, Teddy Bear is Teddy Bear. Great work!" White exclaimed.

"How did you find him so quickly?" Gramm was equally impressed.

"I could lie and tell you all about my clever detective work, but the truth is, he found us. He's sitting in the lobby." Preston turned to leave but then turned back. "Oh, and he says he's Anna Schmidt's husband."

White looked at Gramm. "Bear was not one of her aliases."

Before Gramm could get up and go to the lobby, Milo and Teddy Bear walked in together.

"Ernie, this guy was in the lobby waiting for you," Milo said. "Meet Ted Bear, husband of Anna Schmidt."

Bear was tall and buff with a fashionable beard stubble. His face was asymmetrical, almost as if two divergent faces had been glued together—oddly handsome. He wore a gray bomber jacket, jeans, and a black baseball hat—LA casual.

Gramm stood up and shook Bear's hand across his desk. Gramm introduced White. White noticed Bear's hazy, gray eyes, which contrasted with his black clothes and hat. They were striking.

Bear sat down on the edge of Milo's usual chair. Milo rolled in another.

"So, Mr. Bear, are you Anna Schmidt's husband?" Gramm asked.

"Yes, but I'm not the important one here. My Anna is. She is my muse, my love. Where's my wife!" he demanded.

"I can tell you're concerned, but first tell me who you are, other than Anna Schmidt's husband."

"I, sir, am an actor! Anna and I are both actors."

"Can I see an ID? You say you're her husband," Gramm continued. "Do you have any proof of that?"

Bear unzipped a side pocket on the arm of his jacket and produced a wedding certificate, handing it to Gramm, who looked at it, and offered it to White.

"Why do you have your wedding certificate with you? I don't even know where mine is," Gramm said.

"Anna told me to bring it in case we ran into any legal problems with the sale."

Gramm nodded. "We still need to see your ID."

Bear reached into the same jacket pocket and brought out a bright orange Ridge wallet and popped up his driver's license. "The wallet blocks RFID signals," he said.

Gramm looked at the license, handed it to White, who wrote down the license number and other information.

"What is an RF…" Milo was about to pursue the blocked signals, but Gramm was not in the mood.

"What brings you here to the Duluth police station?" Gramm interrupted.

"To find Anna. I have been playing a riveting Sherlock Holmes at the Majestic Regional Theater in Long Beach for the past twenty-two weeks. They wanted to extend me, but I had a luxury car commercial to shoot…steamy and sensual. I nailed that!"

"Let me rephrase," Gramm said, having had his fill of the *actor*. "What brings you here to the Duluth police station—today?"

"I followed the clues to my muse," Teddy gazed off, pleased with his rhyme.

White also had enough. "Mr. Bear, answer Lt. Gramm's question now!"

"Shall I begin at the beginning of my odyssey?"

Gramm sat back, folding his arms.

"In LA, in our line of work, you've got to be flexible— use all of your creativity. Be prepared to do it all. Anna is currently turning her talents to writing treatments. She gets her inspiration from the newspaper, especially personals and legal notices. She takes dull, legalese slices of life and expands them into wild, creative scenes with real people and authentic situations. It's so amusing and entertaining. She is wonderful."

Reading the personals. Is this how she found out about the will? White wondered.

Gramm was still silent, staring and waiting.

"Should I continue?"

The 'yes' came from White.

"She disturbed my meditation one morning about a week ago shrieking, 'Teddy! They're looking for me. The old man died. That wretched farm is mine. Acres of nothing but money.'"

"We laughed and laughed at the irony. She ran away from that farm, and all the joy it sucked from her soul. Let me tell you, LA is an expensive place to live. Money from that farm will keep us going. Anna insisted I finish my Sherlock and my sexy commercials while she came back here to sort it. I haven't heard from her since. so, like I said, I followed the clues to my muse." Once again, he stared off, enjoying his rhyme.

"What took you so long?" White asked.

"Well, one commercial turned into three. I was a hit. It was a good payday."

"How long was she here?" Gramm resumed.

"Two weeks exactly. She left the day she read that ad. Anna said she was going to stay at the farm. When I landed, I rented a car. I wanted a flashy convertible, but the best I could do was a dull gray SUV…"

"How did you know the location of the farm?" White asked.

"I'm from here. I picked up Anna many times from that tomb of gloom until she couldn't stand it anymore."

Gramm absently rubbed his thumb with his forefinger. "Go on!"

"When I got there this morning, your police tape was blocking the road. I couldn't go in. I couldn't stay there. I didn't know what happened. I was about to succumb to panic when I saw the for sale sign and the realtor's number. She led me to the lawyer, which led me to you. Clues to my muse. Now, I'm here. Where's my Anna?"

"I'm afraid we have some bad news," White said.

"We have reason to believe that Anna Schmidt was murdered on Sunday evening," Gramm said.

The hazy eyes became watery. Were these actual tears or an actor's ability to display emotion?

Bear collapsed into the back of the chair. The watery eyes closed. "I am devastated. I cannot deal with this. What do I do?" Two tears ran down his face. Once again, drama or grief?

"You could help us by identifying the victim," Gramm said.

Bear's eyes shot open. "You've got to be kidding. How could you ask that of me? I am bereft! Wait, you people do that on detective shows, don't you?" Bear closed his eyes once again, hands balled into fists, clasped to his chest. He took a quick, deep breath and let it out slowly. "You're right, of course. I must do this. It will be healing. I can deposit my devastation into my bag of actor's aids. Anna would insist."

Gramm clenched his teeth, leaned forward, and called Doc Smith.

"Smith here."

"Doc, our victim has another visitor."

Ignoring Gramm's phone call to Doc Smith, White asked Bear if Anna had any pictures of her family, especially of her stepmom Clara Schmidt.

Bear smiled. "To paraphrase a favorite movie line, Anna's family was not big on good times and noodle salad. Jack Nicholson. Such delivery."

"Which means?"

"No pictures of pretty picnics in that family. Anna said Clara was her role model—skipping out on her father. Why the interest in her stepmom?"

"We think she might have returned to Duluth too," White said. "We need to talk to her."

"Is she a suspect? Is she dangerous? Should I be worried?" Bear asked.

"At this point, Clara Schmidt is definitely a person of interest."

"Is your name really Teddy Bear?" Milo asked.

"Only to my beloved."

10

After a short break in the early morning downpour, the gray skies over Duluth were again darkening when Gramm and White drove off in the police Interceptor to interview their pilot. Canal Park can be dicey with high winds and rain. Milo came prepared with the Lakesong SUV.

The Canal Park Lodge was the first in a row of hotels along the narrow strip of land that led to the famous Aerial Lift Bridge. The lodge was modern with an expansive view of Lake Superior.

The dark clouds opened up just as the three were parking their vehicles. Milo, remembering he had the SUV, searched the back seat for an umbrella, something he never carried in either of his cars. However, always-prepared-Sutherland made sure there were umbrellas in all the official Lakesong vehicles.

"Good old Sutherland," Milo said to himself as he grabbed the green and white striped umbrella and kicked open the door against the wind. As quickly as possible, he popped up the umbrella against the incessant side-driving rain.

Gramm and White, not having a Sutherland to equip the police Interceptor, flipped up their collars and ran for the door. Milo followed, fighting the wind that was grabbing the umbrella.

"How do you have an umbrella?" White demanded.

"I plan ahead," Milo answered.

"Doubtful," Gramm grumbled as he wiped his shoes on the mat, shook off the water from his coat, and walked to the reception desk. Showing his badge to the greeter, Gramm said, "We are here to see Kirkland Rafferty Junior."

"Is he a guest here?"

"That's what we are told."

The woman clicked a number of keys on her computer, picked up her phone, and dialed Rafferty.

"Mr. Rafferty, there are police officers here to see you," she said. She listened, nodded for no reason, and hung up. "Please make yourself comfortable in our lounge area. Mr. Rafferty said he will be right down," she said to Gramm. "We have hot coffee on the buffet."

White and Gramm sat down in the yellow lobby with dark wood trey ceilings. Someone had tried to brighten the area up with some orange flowers in tall skinny vases. Milo stood, not knowing what to do with his umbrella, almost never having one with him.

"There's an umbrella stand by the front door," White said.

"Pretty public. How do I make sure no one steals it? It's Sutherland's."

"It's an honor system. No one steals someone else's umbrella," White insisted.

"Where's your umbrella?" Milo demanded. "I bet someone stole yours. Probably stole hundreds of your umbrellas over the years."

Gramm looked up. "I'm out in the rain on a day when I said suspects will come to me. Milo, put your damn umbrella in the damn umbrella stand or I will shoot you in both knees and you'll have to crawl out to your car!"

"I need a chart. Which offenses get me shot in which places?"

"Right now, I'm working on knees. If that changes, I will let you know."

A limping KJ emerged from the elevator balancing two packages of honey buns on a cup of coffee. His left foot was in a boot.

Gramm stood.

KJ spotted him and limped over.

Milo also stood and announced to all, "I have to put my umbrella in the umbrella stand or apparently I too will walk with a limp."

KJ, having never met Milo, said absolutely nothing.

"Ignore him," Gramm ordered. "He has a metal plate in his head and thunderstorms confuse him—something about the lightning."

While waiting for Milo to return sans umbrella, the other three sat down. KJ put down his coffee and honey buns and winced slightly as he fell lopsidedly into an overstuffed, brown-leather chair.

The pilot, using his good arm, straightened himself out and began opening one of the packages of honey buns with his teeth. "I hope you don't mind. I have a fast metabolism and have to eat constantly."

"Little Debbie's," White said, "always a good choice."

"We have a few follow-up questions," Gramm said.

Milo returned from the umbrella rack and sat down with a steaming cup of coffee.

Gramm introduced Milo, who had not attended the first round of questioning.

White inhaled the aroma of Milo's coffee. Milo pointed to a coffee urn on the buffet.

"We're here to conduct an interview!" Gramm said in exasperation. "But as long as you're going, get me a cup, too."

"We're glad you decided to stay in town," Gramm said to Rafferty.

"No choice. The NTSB folks are up here going through my plane. I have to be here for that. This hotel has room service and strong Wi-Fi, so I can heal and conduct business. I'm not complaining."

Milo grimaced, remembering the hours of tedious NTSB interviews after he caused a plane to crash last winter.

"Have they interviewed you yet?" White asked.

"Not yet, but I'm sure they're planning to blame me," KJ scowled. "I landed because of a faulty gas gauge and then clipped an unlit silo on takeoff. It was dark. I didn't see it. No matter, they will chalk it all up to pilot error because that's what they always do."

Or so says the pilot, Gramm thought. "The last time we talked, we asked if you had been in the farmhouse and you said you hadn't,"

KJ took a large bite of his honey bun and began chewing with gusto.

"We have a witness that says he saw you running out of the farmhouse carrying a briefcase or suitcase."

"A witness? That's crazy. There was no one there. It was almost dark when I landed, and besides, there's nothing there but acres of farmland. What's your witness? A woodchuck?" KJ laughed at his joke and took another bite of his honey bun.

"Funny, you couldn't see the silo in the dark, but you could see the size of the farm," Milo said.

"I saw the acres of nothing on the way in when it was lighter. I needed a wide-open space to land."

"But not the silo on the way out?" Gramm asked.

"Not the silo," KJ answered, finishing honey bun number one, and tearing the wrapper on number two with his teeth.

Gramm shook his head. "Now that your blood sugar is nice and high, it's time to tell us what you were really doing on the farm."

"Man, I told you, my gas gauge suddenly dropped to empty, so I landed on that road to check my fuel level. Your witness is dead wrong."

"A woman was murdered in that farmhouse on Sunday, and so far, you're the only person we can put there," White said.

KJ jerked back and winced. "That's crazy too. I didn't kill anyone. I don't even know anybody in this place! I was on my way to Two Harbors."

"Do you know a woman named Anna Schmidt?" Gramm asked.

"No."

"Clara Schmidt?"

131

"No."

"Susan Peterson?"

"Another no!"

Milo jumped in. "Arial Jenkins?"

KJ paused, laughed, and bit into honey bun number two. "You guys are something else. I'm going to need more honey buns if you are going to name every person in Duluth."

"Still need an answer to Arial Jenkins!" Milo insisted.

Chewing robustly, KJ mumbled, "Never heard of her."

"So that's your story?" Gramm asked.

"Yeah, that's my story."

"How long are you planning to stay in town?" Gramm asked.

"It will be several days to complete the NTSB grilling, plus get my plane sorted out with the insurance company."

"Call us if your plans change."

Rafferty nodded.

"We need your fingerprints," White said.

"Already got 'em. I'm a pilot. My fingerprints are on file with the FAA."

As the trio left the hotel, Milo grabbed his umbrella. His growling stomach announced that lunch might be in order. Gramm suggested Everybody's House for a tasty burger and to watch Milo eat green onions and sour cream. Milo declined. "I'm in the mood for Chinese."

White sighed. "The Chinese Dragon it is." She texted Preston.

§

Susan Peterson had called in sick to work. She sat at her kitchen table, head in hand, untouched coffee cooling in a cup by her elbow. Gordy slammed the door, returning from the Moose Lake Police Station. "They took my fingerprints, Susan. They're gonna prove we lied!"

"Oh, shut up," Susan erupted.

Gordy tried to avoid an argument by remaining silent. He poured a cup of coffee and took several sips.

"I'm sorry, Gordy. Look. We didn't expect her. We had to improvise. It didn't work."

"That's the understatement of the year," Gordy mumbled.

"What?" Susan demanded. "What did you say?"

"I said goddamn right it didn't work. Let's just go, you said. Leave the body here, you said. No one will find it. When we demolish the house, everything will disappear, you said."

"Shut up and let me finish. We improvised. We'll improvise again."

Gordy shook his head. "I don't know anymore. I burned our clothes and shoes from Sunday."

"That's good. See, you're already improvising."

"But we didn't wear gloves. They're gonna know we were there."

"The house could burn down—struck by lightning," Susan suggested.

Gordy sighed. "I bet they already have our fingerprints. The time to burn the house was Sunday—like I suggested. But you said no one will ever find the body."

"Shut up Gordy."

§

When they arrived at the Chinese Dragon, the group was escorted to Gramm's favorite table in the back. Gramm let Milo know he was exceedingly hungry after watching KJ savor those honey buns and not in the mood for the usual Milo insanity. Henry Hun, owner of the Chinese Dragon and Milo's high school friend, handed out the menus. He included Milo, which was unusual given Milo's predilection for ordering the same thing—Chicken Egg Foo Yung, no scrimping on the gravy.

"Milo gets a menu?" White asked.

Gramm groaned. "Just let it go."

"I have to give a menu to my new client," Henry said.

Milo cocked his head to look at his friend. "New client?"

"I'm now your agent. Didn't the famous author Ron Bello tell you?"

"I want to hear the specials!" Gramm demanded.

Ignoring Gramm and the *famous author* comment, Milo drilled down. "Agent? Why would I need an agent?"

"Because you're a terrible businessman," Hank answered. "I am much better."

"Specials?" Gramm mentioned once again.

"Ron Bello writes a best seller about you. He makes big bucks. What did you get? Writer's cramp from signing autographs. Don't worry, I will look out for your interests and charge you only twenty percent."

"Twenty percent of nothing is..." Preston joined the fray.

"Ah, but it won't be nothing," Hank said. "I'll negotiate a good deal with Bello's publisher, including movie rights."

"Movie rights? Who plays me?" Milo asked.

"Right now we're thinking Danny DeVito—short, curly hair, and not too pretty."

"He's bald!" Milo exploded, attracting stares from nearby tables.

"Specials?" Gramm demanded, gesturing to those other tables. "Anyone?"

Hank sighed, but acquiesced. "Chinese barbeque or char sieu with steamed white rice and blanched choy sum."

"That's a special you can get behind Milo. You like barbeque," White said.

"What gives you that idea?" Milo challenged.

"You own half of that barbeque food truck in Canal Park."

"Ours doesn't come with chard stew. Sounds gross."

"Char sieu, not stew, you heathen!" Hank shouted, attracting even more attention.

"An agent shouldn't scream at his client," Milo insisted.

Hank yanked his menu away from Milo. "I resign. You're too difficult."

"It's for the best. I think Chris Helmsworth should get the first shot at playing me."

"Hemsworth!" both White and Preston shouted.

Gramm cleared his throat. "I am an officer of the law. I carry a weapon. I'm going to discharge that weapon unless someone brings me food!"

Unfazed, Hank turned to him. "What would you like?"

"I'll take the special."

Preston and White asked for the same.

All eyes turned to Milo. "So, you burn the stew…"

Hank talked as he wrote, "Chicken Egg Foo Yung, don't scrimp on the gravy." He walked away.

"He knows me so well," Milo said.

§

After lunch, the four stood protected from the rain under the Chinese Dragon awning, waiting for a group decision on their next step. "Let's go talk to Bill Pendergast, Grace Pendergast's husband," Gramm suggested.

"Why?" Preston asked. "We already talked to his wife, and she identified the body."

White took this question. "Grace was her friend. Bill was her boyfriend. I guarantee his view of Anna Schmidt differs from his wife's."

"For the record," Gramm said, "I hate this part of a new case, first interviews with everyone and their brother."

"I want to know what's in that barn, the one with the padlock," Milo said.

"We just got the search warrant for the barn," Preston said after checking her phone.

"Good, Robin and I will go talk to Bill Pendergast and the Preston-Milo team can see what's in that barn. Check out a bolt cutter," Gramm suggested.

"Big thrill for you. I have Lakesong's SUV. Not many people get to ride in it," Milo said as he and Preston walked toward the nearest parking garage.

"Bigger thrill for you. I have a police car," Preston retorted. "Lights and sirens, baby."

§

White called Bill Pendergast. He agreed to meet them on the site of a new subdivision that was being built several miles from the Schmidt farm, also along Martin Road.

"All this building, yet Duluth still has a housing shortage?" White said to Gramm as they parked the police Interceptor and emerged into what should have been a cacophony of hammering, sawing, and nailing. Ten homes were being worked on all at once in one corner of the construction site. It was silent except for the rain.

White spotted two trailers off to the left. One had three movable metal steps leading to a dented door with no window. Gramm pushed open the door without knocking. The office was comprised of two desks, some bad fluorescent lighting, and walls covered in plot maps. "We're looking for Bill Pendergast," Gramm said to the only occupant of the office.

"You found him," the tall, blond man mumbled. Pendergast looked up from a set of blueprints on his desk and stood to shake hands. "I've got all the permits for this project on file and up to date. What's the problem?"

Gramm introduced White and himself. "We want to talk to you about Anna Schmidt."

"On yeah, that. I forgot," Pendergast mumbled. "This rain is the last thing I needed." Leaning back in his chair, staring at the officers, he motioned for them to sit on two metal folding chairs.

"We understand that you were a close friend of Anna Schmidt when you were in high school," White said.

Pendergast smiled. "Well, yeah, Anna and I were an item, and Grace idolized Anna, so all three of us hung out a lot.

137

Grace told me you had her identify Anna's body. That was pretty upsetting for her."

"Have you had any recent contact with her?" Gramm asked.

"Anna? No, I haven't seen her since she left town eons ago. She broke up with me and broke my heart. I healed and married Grace. Good move on my part."

"She didn't try to contact you recently?"

Pendergast shook his head.

"Where were you this weekend?"

"Here! Working! Like always!" Pendergast shouted. "Sorry, we're behind—have to get these houses enclosed before winter. This rain…"

"Did you know Clara Schmidt, Anna's stepmom?" White asked.

His brow furrowed. "A little. I know she did a runner a year before Anna dumped me. I became the strong shoulder to cry on. Then Anna did a runner too."

"Do you have any pictures of Clara?"

Pendergast shrugged. "No."

"Can you describe her?" White asked.

"Short, thin, long brown hair, pulled back mostly—that's all I remember."

§

"This is a waste of time. I can check out a bolt cutter from the equipment room," Preston said as she pulled up to Bingham Hardware, per Rathkey's instruction.

"This is personal. I like this place. Besides, I may need a bolt cutter someday," Milo responded.

Preston shrugged. "Okay. Your dime."

They walked into the massive warehouse like store, the same one Milo shopped at last spring where he saw a man buy seven identical winter hats. He waved to the kid behind the counter, who didn't wave back. Preston stopped and stepped back outside, remembering she had to call Wilson David. She felt the lawyer needed to be reminded to meet them at the farm.

"I want to make sure he didn't misplace the sticky note to meet us at the Schmidt farm," she told Milo as she left to make the call.

Milo found the bolt cutters, selecting one that claimed to be a thirty-six inch, super heavy-duty cutter, good for cutting padlocks, fences, and steel wire. "This will do it," he said to himself as he maneuvered the long, awkward handles, opening and closing the cutters.

The kid behind the counter, who had ignored Milo's wave, was the same one that waited on Milo this past spring. "Remember me?" Milo asked, trying again just to be friendly.

"Nope," the kid said, running a price scanner over the bolt cutter.

"I was here last spring buying batteries and some guy in front of me bought seven winter hats."

The kid briefly glanced at Milo, then went back to the transaction. "I remember the hats. I hope he enjoyed them."

"I doubt it. He was murdered."

The clerk stopped and stared. "How do you know?"

"I work with the cops. They fished the guy out of the St. Louis River. By the way, will these bolt cutters cut through a thick chain?"

"If it says so. Why was that guy murdered?"

"He bought too many hats."

The clerk almost smiled. "Those were ugly hats. FYI, chains are expensive. Cut the lock."

"Good to know," Milo said, feeling more confident in this growing relationship.

Looking more closely at the bolt cutter, the clerk said, "The Ziamatic Heavy Duty may be overkill."

"It's a really big lock," Milo said.

Preston re-entered the hardware store, found Milo at the checkout counter, and laughed when she saw the bolt cutter. "We're cutting a half inch chain, not an I-beam."

"FYI, we're cutting the lock, not the chain. Locks are less expensive," Milo said.

Preston shrugged. "Sure, why not? Buy a million-dollar bolt cutter but worry about the cost of the chain."

§

Peggy Brune, Mary Alice's party planner, joined her boss on the back patio of the Hawthorn estate. "I have finished addressing the invitations, Mrs. Bonner, and Venmoed the deposit to the caterers."

"Wonderful, Peggy. My *Wrecking Ball Brunch* is progressing nicely. I hope today's rain doesn't reappear."

Peggy smiled. "It wouldn't dare."

§

Wilson David was checking the sky for more rain while he waited for Preston and Rathkey to arrive. Milo exited the police vehicle, bolt cutter in hand, tag still attached, while Preston handed the search warrant to the lawyer.

David looked at the paper. "What do I do with this?"

"I think you read it, approve it, and get out of the way," Milo instructed.

"Give me a minute." He read it over, double checked the signatures, and nodded for them to proceed.

"A Ziamatic heavy duty bolt cutter," Milo said as he heaved the cutter up and fumbled getting the lock into the teeth of the cutter. Squeezing the bolt cutter's handles, the lock came apart with barely a snap. Preston undid the chain and began sliding one of the large barn doors open, setting off a screaming air horn.

Wilson David, startled, turned and ran down the road away from the barn. Milo, who still had ear damage from an explosion nine months ago, dropped the cutter, turned his back, and clapped his hands over his ears. Preston reached for her air buds in her jacket pocket and quickly shoved them into her ears to block the sound.

Looking down, she spotted a braided fishing line that ran parallel to the barn door. She followed the line to a stick lying by a large, flat rock. Lifting the rock, the ear-splitting scream stopped. A now silent air horn was half buried in the ground. "Booby trap, but why?" she said, taking her ear buds out.

Milo turned back, shaking a finger in his left ear. "Quite a doorbell. I think we need this at Lakesong."

Mr. David crept up to the pair and yelled, "Is it safe?"

"Well, it's quiet," Milo yelled back.

"Given the locked chain and the ear piercing screech, someone really doesn't want this barn opened," Preston said. She looked behind the other still closed barn door. "I think I spot a twin. Cover your ears, in case I'm unsuccessful," she warned, taking the bolt cutter away from Milo.

"Hey, that's my bolt cutter!" Milo complained.

Preston ignored him, walked over to the second barn door, and found another strand of fishline. The set up was the same, a stick holding up another large flat rock. "Unimaginative, but effective," Preston said as she cut the second wire and removed the rock before it could fall and assault their ears a second time. Triumphantly, Preston returned and handed Milo his bolt cutter. "Thanks."

Milo looked at the large device. "You defiled my Ziamatic Heavy Duty Bolt Cutter, cutting fishing line."

"I saved your hearing."

David waved his arms in protest. "This is all beyond my job description. I have your warrant. The barn is yours. I'm out of here!" He scurried to his car. Seconds later, he was just a dot disappearing down the wide farm road.

Preston opened the second barn door, letting late day sunlight stream into the dark interior. "What is this?" Preston asked, looking at a barn filled with old tires piled haphazardly four and five tires high. "You said this was a dairy farm. Where are the cows?"

"Hiding under the tires?" Milo suggested.

"No cows. Lots of tires. It's getting late. What's our next move?" Preston asked.

Milo looked around. Pointing to the south side of the barn, he said, "Over there where this mountain of tires end, I see cardboard boxes piled against the wall. I wonder if the locks, air horns, and tires are here to guard those boxes."

Preston pointed to the other side of the barn. "Over there, way in the back, the tires are different. They're not just thrown in. They're piled up straight. That could hide something, too."

"I don't like this," Milo said. "I'm going to tell Gramm." *Maybe a bomb squad. There may be lethal booby traps under these tires.* Milo turned and walked away.

While Milo updated Gramm, Preston began inching up the heap of tires, keeping her right hand on the wall. She climbed her way up to the area at the back of the barn where she had seen the tires piled straight rather than just thrown.

Milo turned back to see Preston leaning on the neatly stacked tires. "Stop!" He yelled.

The stack gave way. Preston fell forward as a flame-driven blast exploded past where she had been standing.

Milo hit the ground.

"Milo!" Gramm yelled.

"Can't talk." Milo hung up. "Preston! Preston! Are you okay?"

Milo heard muffled noises but couldn't make out words. He moved to a crouching position and massaged his ears, hoping they would come alive. "Crap, I can't hear shit. Preston don't move. Shotgun blast."

The massaging helped. Words were floating through. Nothing made sense. Relieved Preston was still alive, Milo shouted, "Don't move!"

"Hole…wrist…belly…garbage…gross."

Worried about the shotgun, Milo again shouted, "Look up! Don't move!"

There was a silence that worried Milo. "Preston!"

"…triggers…

"Triggers, like two?" Milo shouted.

"Yeah."

"Stay down. Don't move."

"…Doc…"

"Doc? Why? Oh, shit."

11

"Kate," Milo continued shouting, "Do not move. There may be more booby traps" If she was responding, Milo wasn't hearing. Fighting panic, Milo shifted into professional mode. Professional mode for Milo meant talking to himself. "I gotta get help now!" Calling the desk sergeant, he hurriedly explained the situation and asked for a bomb squad, six radios, EMTs, and a tech with a drone.

"The nearest bomb squad is in Crow Wing County. I need authorization to get them," the sergeant advised.

"Get them anyway! I need them moving! Now!" Milo screamed.

"Do you know you're yelling?"

"I know. I can't hear."

"I'll call Sanders…"

Milo hung up. He was not a pacer but trying to keep tabs on both the road and Preston, he became a pacer. A simple barn opening had developed into a sensory assault, a near fatal shotgun blast, and Preston disappearing in a pile of tires. "Preston, I can't hear you if you're talking, but I'm going to keep talking to you. I've got people coming. Don't move!" he yelled.

The desk sergeant called back, also yelling. "Good news. Deputy Chief Sanders okayed the bomb squad. They are in McGregor, on a false alarm—on the way now."

"Great! Much closer." Milo hung up just as the tech with the drone skidded to a stop next to Milo's SUV.

Milo recognized Sergeant Skip Aikin. They had talked drones when Milo bought his own. Milo continued to pace back to Preston. Aikin popped the back of the SUV, and seemed to take forever easing out of his car. Milo met him at the rear of his vehicle.

"Skip! We gotta get moving."

"I'm moving as fast as I can. Why are you yelling?"

"I can't hear. I'll try to tone it down. We have tires, shotgun booby traps, and Officer Preston in the middle of it. I can't hear her. I don't know if she's okay. We have to get her a radio ASAP."

"Well, this Matrice 600 can deliver that and more," Skip said as he flipped the drone's arms up and attached two spotlights. A wire held a small basket filled with a radio and a blanket.

"Maybe some water?" Milo suggested.

Skip shook his head. "Not until she's cleared by the EMTs."

"Why?"

"Shock. Trust me. Just show me where she's at," Attempting to lift the drone out of the SUV, Skip said, "Here, take the other side. Help me set it on the ground."

This drone was much larger and heavier than Milo's personal drone. After setting the machine on the ground, Milo stepped away to give Skip room to work. "Here we go!" Skip said as the drone's six blades sped up to a blur, lifting the apparatus.

Skip kept the drone hovering overhead as he and Milo walked to the edge of the barn. "Stop here," Milo ordered. "We can't go any further. The place is filled with booby traps. Preston is at the back of the barn on the right side." Milo pointed to a hole in the tire wall made by Preston when she fell. "A loaded shotgun is pointing over her head."

Watching the video on his phone screen, Skip guided the drone over the tires, hugging the right side of the barn. Milo craned his neck to see the screen over the technician's shoulder, careful not to get in the man's way.

Skip stopped the drone's forward progress at the back of the barn. He then guided it along the back wall until he found the deep hole in the tires.

"There she is!" Skip announced.

Preston was huddled, knees up, head down, her back against the barn wall. There was no blood, only tires.

Skip pointed to the screen. Two wires came out of a straight wall of tires, ending at a shotgun attached to a support on the back wall. "I've gotta disarm that shotgun. I'm going to drop the basket to the right and then set it off. The weapon is not pointing at Preston."

Milo nodded.

Preston looked up at the drone. A good sign.

"Can you go any faster?" Milo demanded.

"No. Calm down. I'm working."

As the basket dangled in the hole, Preston haltingly stretched out her legs, one at a time, and maneuvered over several tires to reach it. She grabbed at the blanket and radio.

Milo immediately keyed his radio. "Preston are you okay?" he yelled.

"I...I think so," she whispered.

Still not hearing her, Milo looked at Skip.

"She says she thinks so," Skip repeated.

"Preston, talk bigger if you can. I can't hear much."

"It's hard...fell...lost breath for a bit."

"We see the wire on the second trigger of that shotgun. We're gonna pull it. It's gonna be loud...again. Put in your ear buds and don't move."

Milo and Skip watched her reach across her body with her right arm to get the earbuds from her left jacket pocket.

"What's wrong with your arm?" Milo asked over the radio.

"Hurts."

"Lay down. Knees up. Put the blanket over your body, head too." Skip ordered.

Preston threw the blanket down over her legs, laid on her right side, drew her knees up, and finished pulling the blanket over her head as best she could.

Skip maneuvered the drone to the back wall, releasing the basket cord. It and the basket fell harmlessly away.

"What if we need to get more stuff to her?"

Skip nodded. "I have spare baskets, but only one drone. If you're looking for something to do, keep track of the baskets. I don't want to leave one behind." He put on his earmuffs and offered a set to Milo. "They'll keep what little hearing you have left."

"My ears appreciate it," Milo said, putting on the protective muffs.

Skip keyed his radio. "Here we go, Preston. Hunker down."

The drone moved left. Skip inched it sideways until a leg almost touched the wires. Taking a deep breath, he jammed the drone to the left and snapped it down. Flame shot out of the shotgun barrel with a screaming blast lighting up the back of the barn. Skip and Milo took off their ear protection.

Skip returned the unharmed drone to hover over Preston, who was peeking out from under the blanket. "Is it safe?" she asked over her radio.

"Yup," Milo said. "but there may be more of Junior's gadgets, so stay where you are. The bomb squad and EMT's are on the way."

"Call Doc Smith, too."

"Doc Smith? The Doc is a coroner. You need EMTs."

"Do you see what's under the tire I fell on?"

"A pile of old clothes," Milo said.

"It's a dress, Milo."

Skip zoomed in on the blue flowered fabric just as Preston added, "And the dress has bones."

Tires screeched to a stop in front of the now open barn. Skip and Milo turned to see White running towards them.

"How is she?" White demanded.

"She's okay," Milo yelled. "She's in the back of the barn. Skip got her a blanket and a radio and discharged a booby trap shotgun over her head. Gotta call Doc Smith," Milo said as Gramm moved toward them.

Gramm's eyebrows slammed together. "Who's dead?"

"I don't know. A pile of old clothes," Milo said.

White grabbed a radio from Skip. "Preston, this is White. What's the situation?"

"The pile of old clothes has bones. I wanna get out of here."

"No!" Milo commanded. "Lay down! Relax. Breathe."

"How about water? And something for my wrist. It hurts."

Milo looked at Skip, who shook his head. "It's the EMTs' call."

"I hear a siren," White said.

As if commanded, a lone ambulance, full lights and sirens, raced up the dirt road to the barn, and skidded to a stop in front of the assembled group. The driver jumped out. "Where do we go?"

Skip showed him the video. "She's there."

"We're waiting on the bomb squad," Milo advised. "Booby traps."

The EMT took a radio from Skip and asked Preston a series of questions. When the medical interrogation was over, Preston once again asked for water and something for pain.

"We didn't want to give her anything in case she was going into shock," Skip explained.

"You did the right thing. Do you have a basket for that drone? I think water and ibuprofen will be okay."

Skip brought the drone back to the front of the barn and set it down while he sent Milo to get a second basket from his vehicle.

"This is basket number two," Milo informed everyone. "Skip put me in charge of the baskets."

"A red-letter day for you, Milo." Gramm understood Milo. He could sense his friend's stress. Humor usually helped.

Doc Smith arrived. "Why am I here?" he asked.

"Preston is in the back of the barn, in some old tires."

"I see the tires, Milo, but again, why am I here?"

"Preston!" Milo yelled over the radio. "Talk to Doc Smith."

"I see clothes and bones, and I don't like it."

Skip pointed his monitor toward the Doc and played a recording.

"Okay, that's a human skull. Now I know why I'm here."

"I'm getting creeped out here. It's hard to breathe again." Preston said, her stress showing in her voice.

Doc Smith grabbed the radio away from Milo. "Doc Smith here. A little trick I learned years ago. Give the body a name. Talk to it. It will seem less creepy."

"Body?" Preston asked. "Are you sure it's a body, Doc? Not a dog or a cow?"

"Give it a name. Talk to it," Smith repeated.

Skip had delivered the water and ibuprofen, and the drone was hovering, keeping eyes on Preston. She was sitting up, had her blanket up to her chin and had her eyes closed. Her lips were moving. The radio button was off.

More officers arrived. Plans were being made in advance of the bomb squad. The day was fading. Lights were being set up around the barn.

White broke away to radio Preston about how she was doing.

"Better. My new friend, Hermione, and I have been chatting. She's a good listener."

White looked at Doc Smith. "Is she okay?"

"She's fine. I have full on conversations with many of my clients. Only worry if they talk back."

"Clients?" White questioned.

"Can't call them patients."

"Who the hell tries to kill people for opening a damn barn!" Gramm barked. Milo realized Gramm was anxious about Preston and let the comment go without a response.

"How did you get the bomb squad?" Gramm asked.

"I called the desk. They checked with my good buddy, Deputy Chief Sanders, who okayed it. I know I kinda went over your head, but I didn't want to take the time to explain the situation to you and then have you explain to him."

"You're not hurting my feelings, Milo. This entire expense is now on him." Gramm almost smiled.

§

"I'm home, Grace," Bill Pendergast shouted. "It started to pour this morning, so the crews had to knock off early. We've got to get these houses enclosed. Any more delays and your dad will chew me out again, maybe even fire me."

Grace was at her desk in the kitchen. "Daddy will never do that."

"Never say never, Grace. He only hired me because I married you. I do a good job, but he just…"

The dog in the pantry began to whine, scratch, and whip his tail against his crate. "Better take your dog out."

"You kept him in the crate all day, again?"

"Honey, he scares me out in the yard alone. You love him. I don't want to take the chance of losing him. Please, just take him to work with you," Grace said.

"Grace, we have a fenced-in backyard. Nothing bad will happen." Pendergast let the excited dog out into the backyard, threw the ball for a while, then returned to the kitchen. "The cops came to work today to ask about Anna," he said.

Grace began seasoning the steaks for dinner. "What did you say to them?"

"Not much. They wanted to know if I heard from her recently. They asked about us—me and Anna before she dumped me." He walked over to Grace and put his arms around her waist. "Getting dumped was the best thing ever. I won the lottery with you."

Grace leaned back against him. "I won too. Salad and corn with your steak?"

"Sure." He planted a kiss on her head and broke away to get a beer from the fridge.

"Did they ask you anything else?"

"Just where I was Sunday morning."

Grace put the salad in the fridge. "Weren't you here? You usually sleep until I get back from my run."

"Usually, but I had work at the job site."

§

Agnes needed her late afternoon French press coffee. Heading into the kitchen, she found Martha cutting fresh veggies for Sutherland to steal before dinner.

"Coffee time for me," Agnes said.

"I can get it," Martha offered.

"Don't be silly, you're busy," Agnes said.

"I'm ahead of schedule. I'll make the coffee and we can drink it together in the gallery," Martha offered. "We haven't been able to do this for an age."

Agnes picked her favorite spot in a small seating arrangement by one of the floor-to-ceiling windows. Martha joined her with the coffee tray. "Is this a Mrs. McKnight moment or an Agnes moment?" Martha kidded.

"Definitely an Agnes moment, Martha. We are going to sit here, watch the gray cloud covered sky, and talk about how great it would be to own Lakesong."

Martha laughed. "You do."

"Shh," Agnes admonished. "Mrs. McKnight owns Lakesong. Agnes does not."

Martha sat down in one of the cushioned wicker chairs and took a sip of coffee. "Where have you been lately? This is your first afternoon coffee break all week."

"Lakesong hasn't had any issues, and Milo hasn't needed an assistant lately, so I have morphed myself once again. Creedence Durant and I have been changing the Laura and John McKnight Foundation into the McKnight Family Foundation."

"Is it just a name change?"

"No, we are expanding the focus from exclusively funding the arts to include helping people. We're starting with local foster kids—scholarships and clothes." Agnes reached for one of Martha's cookies. "I never realized how complicated this all is. There are so many rules we have to follow to give money away. For a break, I sneak upstairs from time to time to see how my bathtub is coming along."

"Your bathtub? Aren't you remodeling the entire north end of the upstairs?"

"Sure, but it's all about finally getting a bathtub in the bathroom, attached to the bedroom where I sleep."

Martha laughed. "I have that kind of bathtub."

"Oh, rub it in."

They both laughed.

"So, that's my catch up. What have you been doing?" Agnes asked.

"I have been tending to a lovesick young man."

"Jamal?" Agnes guessed.

"Of course. Kelly, the cheerleader, has moved away. Her father got a promotion and the whole family moved to Atlanta."

"Oh, no!" Agnes exclaimed. "Young love thwarted by geography. In my romance novels, that's cured by a handsome stranger, or, in Jamal's case, a beautiful young girl."

"If only it was that easy. He really liked Kelly. She was good for him—studious. I worry about his grades. Last night we were playing a little one-on-one and Jamal let slip the Coach said his play was off, not bad, just off." Martha sighed. "I was never a teen boy. I'm just taking it day by day —not sure what's going to come walking down the driveway every day."

"Maybe Sutherland could help. He was a teenage boy once, I think," Agnes offered.

Martha smiled. "I'm sure he was, but I don't want to bother him. Remember, he's my boss."

Agnes smiled and shook her head. "He's also your friend."

"I asked Ron, and he says not to worry, it will work itself out."

§

What had started as a routine blustery day had become a long, extraordinary ordeal. Selena Sanchez powered up her lights an hour ago, illuminating interior of the barn and the road out front. Other techs had set up several tent canopies in case the morning rain returned.

Milo and Gramm stood under one of canopies watching the headlights of the three bomb squad vehicles turn onto the wide, rutted farm road. At Gramm's insistence, space had been left for the vehicles near the front of the barn. A policewoman directed them to the spot.

A man dressed in a dark blue jacket and pants exited the lead car. Gramm began to speak, but the man walked to Milo. "Rathkey! What are you doing here?"

"Graveson! How the hell are you?"

"Good, good." Graveson looked into the barn. "What are we doing here?"

Milo turned to Gramm. "This is police Lieutenant Ernie Gramm. Ernie, Greg Graveson."

The two shook hands and Milo explained the situation.

Graveson's squad assembled for instruction. Along with his people, two dogs stood at attention. "People, we have three devices tripped so far, two non-lethal air horns, one lethal shotgun. There may be more devices. Our priority is to clear a path up these tires and extract Officer Kate Preston from a pit in the back of the barn. We then scan the tires in the rest of the barn for other devices and let the medical examiner remove human remains from the bottom of the pit."

The bomb personnel donned protective coats and helmets. They began slogging over the mound of tires, checking for trip wires and booby traps. The dogs were head down, sniffing the tires. After about an hour, the squad cleared a narrow area to the pit.

EMT's, also wearing protective clothing, were motioned to approach. After struggling up the tires, one jumped into the pit and checked Preston for injuries. Satisfied that she had not been shot and had no broken bones, they lifted her up to the stretcher.

Gramm could see she was arguing about getting on the stretcher. His radio lit up. "Dammit, Preston, get on the stretcher!" he yelled. She complied.

While she was being carried down the tires, Doc Smith was climbing up. "Did you disturb the body?" he asked Preston as they met halfway.

"I fell on it!"

"So, you disturbed it," Smith grumbled.

"Yeah, I guess."

Once the stretcher-bearers reached the ground, Preston handed her radio to the police tech, taking her time to stand.

"How are you feeling?" Gramm asked.

"My wrist hurt, but it's better now."

"Go to the ambulance."

"I'm really okay," she protested.

Gramm turned to White. "Did I stutter?"

"No, you did not," White said sternly.

"I didn't think so." He turned back to Preston, who raised her hands in mock surrender.

"I'll go with her," White said. "She needs another lecture from the department safety officer."

Gramm scowled. "Last spring, she plows a motorcycle into a suspect, and today, without orders, she almost gets shot and falls into a pit with a dead body. Yeah, I would say she needs …something."

White stepped into the ambulance as the doors were closing. Gramm watched the red taillights disappear. He turned abruptly and looked into the barn. "Tires?" he asked Milo.

"I have no idea," Milo said. "I'm wondering why no cows?"

Graveson returned to the front of the barn. "Once the medical examiner removes the body, we will start clearing the rest of the barn. Do you suspect there are more bodies in here?"

"We didn't know there was even one," Gramm said.

"Booby traps?"

"Don't know. Could be," Gramm said.

"We'll work on the assumption that there are more, so we'll work all night to clear the barn. We have no other option."

Gramm nodded.

12

Milo knew he was awake but kept his eyes shut, hoping to fall back for second sleeps. Yesterday's adventure in the booby-trapped barn had taken more out of him than he realized. Unfortunately, his brain had powered up and second sleeps were not on its agenda. *I have money in the bank. I don't have to work. Sleep.*

Jet dashed Milo's last hope for more sleep when the black cat jumped up on the bed. He tiptoed onto Milo's chest, and gently pawed his face. Milo opened one eye. Annie, the other cat, sat on the unused pillow. As a Calico, she refused to get personally involved.

Opening both eyes and scratching Jet's nape, he mumbled, "Okay, okay, I'll move." Ever since arriving at Lakesong almost two years ago, Milo had adopted a morning swim routine. It kept the girth around his middle from expanding. He rarely missed it, but this morning was going to be a pass.

While chatting with the cats, he mentioned he would swim twice as far tomorrow. Even they doubted it.

Showering and dressing were again fraught with peril as the cats crisscrossed in front of him, a move that puzzled Milo as it slowed him down. Eventually, Milo and the cats paraded into the morning room just as Agnes and Sutherland were finishing their breakfast smoothies.

"Good of you to join us," Sutherland said.

Milo stopped. "That's Gramm's line. Have you been spending time with him?"

"Only on poker nights," Sutherland said. "Unlike you, I do not declare homicide as my vocation or avocation. Clearly, in the future, I will stay in town on poker nights, so you don't go unearthing more dead bodies."

"We found another one yesterday."

"You're kidding," Agnes gasped.

Milo explained the barn, the tires, the trip wires, and Preston's pit mate.

Agnes grimaced. "Ugh! Poor Preston."

"Two bodies in less than a week, and you were complaining about how unexciting your life had become," Sutherland said.

"Was I?"

Martha interrupted with Milo's half lumberjack breakfast. The cats gathered by Milo's chair for their tithe of a piece of bacon—Annie for eating, and Jet for playing.

"Both killed by the same person? Is this a serial murderer situation?" Sutherland asked.

"No, yesterday's body was not fresh," Milo said.

Agnes turned away, "Ugh!"

Milo went through the shareable particulars and possible suspects coming last to KJ Rafferty, the pilot. "He claims he landed there because of a faulty fuel gauge."

Sutherland, who had been quietly taking it all in, suddenly responded, "There are two problems with that idea."

Milo, not expecting a Sutherland critique, stopped talking.

"In my flying experience and…"

"…as a passenger?" Agnes asked.

"Well…no…I can fly a plane. I soloed in college. You didn't know me then."

By the look on Agnes' face, he knew this was going to be a conversation later but continued to talk. "I keep it current but haven't used it in a few years. I would have to upgrade to fly a jet like the one we took to New York. Besides, I enjoy being a passenger with my lovely wife."

"Yeah, lovely. Back to my suspect!" Milo demanded. "What is the problem with the pilot's landing because of a faulty gas gauge?"

Agnes waved Milo away. "You can wait, Milo. I just learned Sutherland's a pilot."

"Don't you two ever talk?" Milo countered.

"We take part in…other activities," Sutherland stated.

Milo spread his hands out wide. "I don't want to know. What's the problem with the landing?"

"If a pilot has an emergency, they alert the nearest tower, in this case Duluth International Airport. There are also several small airstrips between Duluth and Two Harbors to land on. We're not in rural Alaska. There's no reason to land on an old farm road unless you're out of gas and the engine in sputtering."

"He didn't mention sputtering."

"Also, if your pilot is that concerned about fuel, he or she could manually check once he landed. With most planes, it only requires getting out on the wing."

"Our witness says the pilot ran out of the farmhouse and back into the plane."

"The fact that he took off again, without checking, tells me there was nothing wrong with the gauge."

"He did crash into an old silo," Milo added.

"That's not about fuel, but I'm sure the safety folks will address it. Also, I haven't been to that farm, but picking out a road from the air is not safe. No, I think your pilot knew about the runway and meant to land there," Sutherland said.

"Good to know."

"Who is the second victim?" Agnes asked. "Officer Preston's barn buddy?"

"We don't know yet. All I know is that farm is overflowing with dead bodies. One per building. We haven't even checked out the old barn or silo."

"I think we're finalizing the sale of a duplex on 16th Avenue East today," Sutherland said.

Both Agnes and Rathkey looked at him.

"What? Not as exciting as Milo's work?" Sutherland feigned disappointment.

§

Arial Jenkins startled when her ringing phone displayed the Duluth Police Department. Hesitantly, she answered. "Arial Jenkins here. How can I help you?"

"Arial, this is Sergeant White. I'm calling to give you a heads up on what we found at the Schmidt Farm."

Arial held her breath and braced for more bad news. "What now?"

"Two things. First, the barn was filled with old tires. We cleared them last night. Now it's up to the state pollution people to dispose of them. Most of the expense will fall on the property owner."

"No! Stop it!"

"There's more. The dead woman found Sunday night in the farmhouse has been identified as Anna Schmidt, daughter of Walter Schmidt Junior."

"What have you people got against me?"

"Arial, I assure you that none of this is personal," White said.

"Have you informed Susan Peterson or does that fall to me?"

"She knows about Anna Schmidt, but I think you may be missing the point."

"Which is?"

"Anna Schmidt died this past weekend, meaning she was alive when her father died—at that point she inherited the farm, not your client. I think Anna Schmidt's heir now inherits and I guess that would be her husband, Ted Bear."

Arial was quick to pick up on the business end of that statement. "I think he called me a couple of days ago. He will need someone to sell that farm for him."

Goodbye Susan. Hello Teddy, White thought.

"One more question. Did you know Clara Schmidt?"

163

"Clara Schmidt? Of course. Short, brown hair. Strong Finnish Accent."

White was taken aback. She didn't expect Arial to know Clara Schmidt. "Umm, tell me about her."

"I don't remember much. She was quiet, shy even, a good knitter though, perfect bobbles."

"Bobbles?"

"It's a knitting stitch."

"I guess I didn't take you for the knitting circle type."

"I'm a realtor, Sgt. White. Clients don't just materialize. I have to get out there and schmooze. I belong to a lot of clubs and organizations."

"Is yoga one of them?"

"It is."

"We may ask you to stop that," White joked.

"Trust me. I'm thinking about it."

§

His circumstances were dire. Van Dyke needed someone fast. His late partner, Alex Sithens, had been the lifeblood of their business. Vincent was going down, never to recover. He had put off calling Kayla as long as he could. Vincent hated talking to people but froze when talking to pretty people. *Kayla was pretty. She probably still is.*

Sitting on his tall stool in the back room, Vincent stared at his phone. He uncoiled one of his red curls that reached his chin. *I should get a haircut. That would help. Would that help? I don't know anymore.*

Looking over the painfully honest resume Kayla had sent, Vincent crossed one gangly leg over the other. He began to read the resume out loud.

Sold soap and candles. Threatened customers.

Maybe the soap and candle buyers were mean and nasty? Vincent thought. He read on.

Went to anger management class. Passed.

Worked with archery clients and have not stabbed them or shot them with an arrow.

Unusual, but definitely shows an upward trajectory. He flipped the page to read the recommendations. There was only one. *Her dad likes her.*

I'm desperate. She's pretty, and she can't stab me over the phone. Vincent sighed. *I'm ready. Tomorrow morning, 9 AM.* He typed the email, closed his eyes, and hit send.

§

White hung up with Arial as Preston walked into the bullpen. Her fellow officers kiddingly warned her about trip wires and corpses lying under the coffee station.

"Thanks guys." Preston waved as she walked to her desk.

"They kid you because they're relieved you weren't seriously hurt," White said.

"I know. They love me," Preston called out and adjusted the wrap on her wrist.

"Sit down. Why are you even here?"

"I work here," Preston said, taking off her uniform jacket with one hand and sitting down at her desk.

"I told you to take the rest of the week off."

"All my vitals are fine. I'm wearing my wrist support, like the doctor told me. I woke up a bit stiff. Took some ibuprofen, and now I'm okay. I did keep falling in my dreams last night. A little disturbing."

"The department has people you can talk to, and you should be home resting," White advised.

"I know. I canceled my skydiving lesson for this weekend." Not letting White say what her face showed, Preston rushed on, "I made a promise to my pit buddy, Hermione, I would find out how she ended up there."

"Hermione? How do you know to call her a she?" White asked.

"I took a leap. What was left of the fabric looked springtime girly."

Milo walked in and noticed that Gramm's office was still dark. "Where's the boss?" he asked White.

"He's running late. Apparently, he had a busy day and night yesterday." White smiled.

Milo turned to Preston. "Why are you here?"

"I need to help Hermione," Preston said with a straight face.

Milo blinked. "Did you land on your head? Have the concussion people cleared you?"

"Is that a job title? Concussion person?" Preston asked.

Milo's response was cut off by Gramm striding into the bullpen area. He looked around, then proclaimed, "When we have a day like yesterday and I come in late, two of you must come in later. You're making me look bad."

Milo saluted, turned around, and said, "I'll be back in five."

"Milo! Thank you for the support. My office, now!"

White joined Gramm. Milo grabbed a chair and wheeled it in for Preston.

"How are you doing?" Gramm asked her.

"Healing. Eager to find out what happened to Hermione."

"Preston, why are you even here?" Gramm asked.

"Why does everyone ask me that? I work here!"

"I don't think she's been cleared by the concussion people," Milo said.

Gramm's eyebrows raised to about half mast. "Milo, I don't know any *concussion people* at that hospital."

"There should be," Milo added.

Gramm continued to grouse as he opened his window blinds. "Why do the cleaning people close these blinds every night?"

"On a case related note, my good buddy, Sutherland, says Rafferty's gas gauge story is bogus."

"You talked to Sutherland about our case?" Gramm asked.

"Well, more to his wife, Agnes. She's the sharper of the two."

"Agnes Larson," White said. "Our murder investigation mascot."

"Stop!" Gramm ordered. "How does Sutherland know anything about planes?"

"He's a pilot. I found that out this morning," Milo said. "Shocked me."

"If the gas gauge excuse is bogus, what was Rafferty really doing there?" White asked.

"Preston, as long as you're here, what did you find out about him?"

"He inherited a trash hauling business from his father and has changed it into an eco-friendly hazardous-waste removal business."

"You mean like tires?" Milo asked.

"Is that why he was there?" White asked.

Gramm's phone lit up. He looked at the caller ID. "It's the good Doc." He answered. "Whatcha got Doc?"

"Fingerprints. The following people were in that farmhouse."

Preston began one finger typing with her good hand.

"Anna Schmidt, Theodore Bear, Kirkland Rafferty Jr., Susan Peterson, Gordy Peterson, Bill Pendergast, Arial Jenkins, Walter Schmidt Jr., Milo Rathkey, and Clara Schmidt."

"Are you kidding me?" White mumbled.

"It's a fricking convention of lying suspects," Gramm groused.

"Everyone lies," Milo began, "but only…"

"Yeah, yeah, yeah," Gramm cut him off.

"Most of the fingerprints were on that table in the kitchen. Maybe they all had dinner together before they killed her," Doc Smith added.

"Was that a joke, Doc?" White asked.

"Morgue humor. Can't beat it."

"Doctor Smith, have you identified the barn body from yesterday?" Preston asked.

"Not yet. I should have something by the end of the day. By the way, did you name her?"

"Hermione," Preston piped up.

"You're right. Your Hermione is female." The phone went dead.

Gramm sat back in his chair. "Well, according to the good Doc, everybody was in that farmhouse, which means…"

"Not…" Milo interrupted.

"Not now, Milo!" Gramm admonished. "Let's jump on the Petersons first. They told us they were never in that farmhouse and the price of lying is they come to us. I don't want to trek all the way to Moose Lake. Schedule it for tomorrow—no excuses."

"I always wondered," Milo said, "is it called Moose Lake because the lake is in the shape of a moose, or is it because there are a lot of moose who live there?"

"Historically, it was a settlement of hunters called Big Moose there," White said.

"Big Moose?" Milo questioned. "Who would name a settlement Big Moose?"

White shrugged. "Your people, not mine."

"Can we get back to the case?" Gramm shouted.

"Arial Jenkins next!" White shouted. "She tops my list and money from the sale is her motive."

"I agree," Gramm said.

White dialed Arial's number.

"Sergeant, what now? I'm very busy," Arial answered.

"I'm furious," White countered. "You lied to us about being in that farmhouse. Your options are to come into the police station now, or we can send a patrol car for you. That comes with handcuffs."

"I'm on my way," Arial said meekly.

White looked at Gramm. "The Petersons? You want to call them, or should I?"

"You are on a roll," Gramm almost smiled.

White called Susan Peterson and was just as forceful as she had been with Arial. "Tomorrow at ten," she told Gramm after hanging up.

White set up the rest of the interviews and waited for Arial.

§

Mary Alice needed a caretaker. She was becoming much too busy to deal with any hiccups in the day-to-day running of her house. Last week, Peggy Brune suggested Fred Britain, the man who organized the parking at last summer's Lakesong wedding. Agnes seconded that recommendation.

Mary Alice had her doubts. How could a parking attendant do all the things she needed doing? But on their recommendations, she decided to give him a try. "I need to know if he and I are compatible," she told Agnes.

Agnes laughed. "Compatible? You're not going to marry him."

"I know, but I need him to do a lot of other things, such as walking the dogs, making minor repairs, and dealing with snow. I need someone to do all that without bothering me every five minutes."

Peggy had called Britain, told him to come to the Hawthorn Estate nine o'clock, Thursday morning, for a job interview.

Mary Alice looked at the twenty-five-year-old man sitting opposite her. He was woodsy in his plaid flannel shirt, dark trousers, and hiking boots. They were sitting on red tapestry chairs in the dark, wood-paneled great room of the Hawthorn

Estate, Mary Alice's temporary home. "Mr. Britain, your employment history does not show longevity. I see you have some university, but no degree as of yet. Is there a problem?"

"I'm doing what I like, a wide variety of jobs," Fred said.

"Mrs. McKnight recommended you. She said you successfully guarded the side gate at Lakesong, while directing deliveries for an important event she had planned."

The young man didn't respond.

"It was a wedding a year ago at Lakesong, next door."

"I remember. I don't know the name."

"You may know her as Agnes Larson?"

"Oh, Agie, yes. We've known each other for a long time." Fred smiled.

With two days to go before her Wrecking Ball Brunch, Mary Alice was in firm business mode. "I want to hire someone to help me with a project this Saturday. Are you free?"

He nodded.

"You would be in charge of parking. It would be similar to the wedding last summer. The people next door at Lakesong have graciously opened their property to us. I would need you to take charge of parking cars and getting guests on party buses that will shuttle between Lakesong and my soon-to-be-demolished house.

This is short notice, but do you have people that could park cars and guide people to the shuttle buses? Uniforms have been ordered."

"I do. It won't be a problem."

"Peggy Brune is my party planner. Do you remember her?"

"Yes."

"If you need anything, talk to her. You will find her in the front office. She will need your social security number."

Fred left the great room and went in search of Peggy. "Hi," he said.

"Hi yourself." Peggy smiled. "So, how did it go?"

Fred shrugged. "Mrs. Bonner has hired me to set up the valet parking."

"Good. You realize this is a tryout. She has a permanent job in mind, caretaker. I think you'd like it."

Fred nodded. "I understand. Thanks Peggy. How many cars are we expecting?"

"Still counting. Sit down; we can figure it out."

13

The morning was half gone when Agnes took a break to make her daily trip up to the second floor. Tee and her crew were busy. So far, no new bathtub, but Tee assured her it was ordered and on its way.

Agnes walked through the framing of what would become their bedroom, living room, and bathroom. A wide hallway was also being constructed, leading to the new room over the garage. For now, that room was to be their exercise area. The plans called for floor-to-ceiling windows and a double door leading out to a balcony. However, plywood currently blocked the view of the trees and the lake.

Tee walked over to her. "What do you think?" she asked.

"Every day there is progress."

"While you're here, let me show you what we discovered," Tee said. "We thought we would have to put in expensive exhaust fans in the garage to keep any fumes from coming up here. It turns out there already are exhaust fans that come on when the system senses fumes or smoke. Probably put in when horses went out of style and the garage was converted for cars. Of course, the equipment will all have to be replaced, but the holes and conduits are already in place."

Agnes smiled weakly in confusion.

Tee held up her hand. "I get it. Too much information, but I was curious about that ventilation."

"Curious? Why?" Agnes asked.

"This old ventilation mirrors our plans exactly. Someone put it in to protect a second floor from exhaust fumes."

"Really? So there was a second floor. Why was it removed?"

Tee shrugged. "I'm just the builder. I tell you about holes, conduits, and when bathtubs arrive."

Agnes smiled. "Thanks Tee. Another Lakesong mystery. See you tomorrow."

§

Arial Jenkins sat in Interview Room A with her hands folded on the table in front of her—no outrage, no huffing, no bouncing her red curls.

White and Gramm walked in and sat down. Gramm opened his fake folder as White clicked on the recorder and stated the date and people in the room. "Ms. Jenkins, you told us you were never in the Schmidt farmhouse…"

"I may have forgotten."

"Forgotten you murdered Anna Schmidt?" White asked.

"No! Are you crazy? I peeked in for a few minutes last week just to see if there were any valuable antiques. I wanted to make sure that Ms. Peterson knew to remove them. I do that for clients. I will do the same for Ted Bear, who you say now owns the property."

"Have you already called him?" White questioned.

Arial cocked her head, causing her curls to spill to the left. "Yes, I've talked with Mr. Bear, and I think we've worked out an arrangement should he inherit the farm."

"I gotta admire her," Milo said to Preston as they watched through the one-way glass, "life throws her a lemon, and she just chucks it back."

Preston nodded.

"Why did you lie to us?" White asked.

"I didn't lie, I simply for…"

White held up her hand. "You are wasting our time! Why did you lie?"

Arial pursed her lips and bobbed her head like an irritated peacock. "I knew it looked bad. But I have one more thing I may have forgotten to tell you."

Gramm's eyebrows rose.

"You never asked, so I forgot about it. I received a call, a horrible call, last Saturday from a woman claiming to be Anna Schmidt. I thought it was a prank. It caught me by surprise. I should have hung up. She began yelling at me, demanding I take my sign down in front of *her* farm. I was stunned. She was rude and abusive. I finally got my wits about me. I shouted she was a fake, and I already had a buyer. Then I slammed down the phone."

"Such a rude, abusive call slipped your mind?" White challenged.

Arial was silent.

"Who's your buyer?" Gramm asked.

"A nice young man from White Bear Lake…"

"Kirkland Rafferty Jr." Both Gramm and White blurted together.

"How did you know?"

"Did you happen to mention that name to your caller?" Gramm asked.

"What difference does that make?"

"We asked you a question?" White shouted.

"It may have slipped out," Arial mumbled and started examining her manicure.

White had enough. "Arial Jenkins, you have the right to remain silent…"

"All right," Arial yelled and slammed her hands on the table. "It was a mistake! But that woman was so nasty and threatening. I don't like to be ordered about. She needed to be put in her place!"

If the caller really was Anna Schmidt, she got Rafferty's name from Arial. Did she contact him? Did they meet? Milo wondered.

White stood up, shoved her chair back, and stood behind Gramm. "Ms. Jenkins, we are two seconds from hauling you into one of our cells for obstruction of justice!"

Arial's head snapped backward as if avoiding a blow. "That seems harsh."

"We asked you if you knew Rafferty. You lied and said no," Gramm said.

"I call him KJ. His real name must have confused me. All this, the plane crash, the body, it's been a lot."

"Why did Rafferty want to buy the property?"

"He didn't divulge his personal motives to me, but he is eager. I guess, like anyone, he wants to develop it."

"Ms. Jenkins," White said in a softer voice, "Is there anything else you want to tell us—something else you forgot?"

Arial shook her head.

"Did you find antiques in the house?" White asked.

"Great question!" Milo said.

Preston shot him a perplexed look. "Why? Who cares?"

"It's not about the furniture. It's about the age of the fingerprints," Milo said.

Arial flipped her curls. "No. Most of it was not old enough. It was modern cheap. I was hoping for old, sturdy, turn of the century farm pieces, but it was all something I could buy from any discount furniture place."

§

"So, Robin, does Ms. Jenkins just anger you, or are you replacing me as the bad cop?" Gramm wanted to know.

"She does rub me the wrong way, but I wanted to push her. We rarely see an angry Arial Jenkins. I wondered what that looked like," White said.

"Before you beat up Kirkland Rafferty, I need lunch," Gramm said.

"Me too. Beating up suspects saps my energy," White said. "Preston and I were thinking of trying that new take out, A Bale of Kale. Here's their menu," she said, holding up her phone. "They deliver."

Milo rolled his eyes at the idea that kale provided energy.

Gramm took White's phone and flipped through the menu. "I remember my old sergeant, Jablonski, had a pile of menus in his desk. It was easier."

"Didn't he go bald?" White asked.

For some reason, Milo found that funny and couldn't control his laughter.

Gramm handed back White's phone. "You and Preston have fun at A Fire Sale of Kale…"

"A Healthy Bale of Kale," White corrected.

"Laughing Man and I will be at the vending machines," Gramm said as he left his office. Milo followed close behind.

When they arrived at the vending machine, both stopped dead. A man in a green jumpsuit had the burrito machine open, and he was filling it with various sandwiches. One row, the important one, remained empty.

"We've come for the burritos," Milo said.

The man turned and smiled. "Sorry, not today."

Milo read the name on his jumpsuit. "Joe—can I call you Joe?"

The man shrugged.

"I don't think you realize the seriousness of the situation. The lieutenant and I are on a complicated murder case, and we need at least two vending machine burritos apiece to fuel our brains."

"Sorry."

"Joe, can you simply go back to wherever it is you get the burritos and get them?"

"No can do. The delivery to us was delayed. Next time."

Milo walked closer to the man. "Joe, you have the right to remain silent. Anything you say…"

"Milo."

"will be taken down and could be used against you.;."

"Milo!"

"What?"

"We can't arrest the man for not having burritos!"

"Yeah, but he doesn't know that."

"Yeah, I kinda do," Joe said, going back to loading the machine. "I tell you what." Joe turned around. "I'll give you guys a sandwich of your choice, free of charge."

"Egg salad," Gramm said.

"Tuna," Milo added, dejectedly.

Joe produced both sandwiches from his cart and handed them to Gramm and Milo.

"Chips?" Milo asked.

"You're gonna have to pay for those—different company."

With hunched shoulders, Milo shuffled to the chip machine. "This is a dark day."

"That guy takes burritos seriously," Joe said.

"He leads a sad life. The burritos are all he has going for him," Gramm said.

Back in the office, White and Preston opened Kale Caesar Salads and eagerly poured the small container of salad dressing over the yellow leaves.

White bit into her first forkful and grimaced. She reached into her mouth and pulled out a small white stick. "What is this?"

Preston found a similar stick in her salad. "I think these are stems."

"Shouldn't they have taken these out?" White asked.

"You would think so."

"And why are these leaves yellow? Shouldn't they be green?"

Gramm and Rathkey arrived back at the office and sat down.

"No burritos?" White asked.

"Not available," Milo said, with no joy in his voice.

Gramm looked at his sandwich. "This expires tomorrow. He gave us old sandwiches."

"We got a salad of sticks," Preston said. "I spent hours with a dead body yesterday and now I'm eating sticks."

"Dig in everybody. We've got another long day," Gramm advised.

§

Kirkland Rafferty Jr. had just hung up with Sgt. White when his phone vibrated again. It was that realtor, Arial Jenkins. Not his favorite person. He put her on speaker. "Yeah?"

"KJ, I wanted to alert you to a possible change of ownership of the farm."

"You said it was mine. I had right of first refusal!"

"You're not understanding. I didn't sell it to someone else. It's quite involved. According to police, the woman who was murdered in that farmhouse was the actual owner of the property."

KJ remained silent.

Arial continued. "It's all a legal mess right now, but she may have lived long enough to inherit."

"What's the bottom line, Arial?"

"Not to worry, I've got this. You're still first in line. Susan Peterson is out as the seller. A man named Theodore Bear is in. I've talked to him and now he's working with me as I work for you." Arial paused. "Umm, there may be a slight problem…for you. The police know you are my interested buyer."

"Damn it! You promised me confidentiality! I didn't want my interest to be public!"

"I had to tell them. That Officer White threatened to put me in jail."

The line went dead. KJ sat in his hotel room, gazing out at the lake, thinking about how to play this. *That's why the cops want to talk to me again. Ms. Jenkins just put me in the frame.*

Arial paused at her desk, thinking. *Why was KJ landing at the farm? Was he double crossing me and talking to Anna Schmidt directly? Find another buyer, Arial. Cover your bases.*

§

The tone of this KJ interview differed from the earlier one. The location was the gray-walled Interview Room B, not the bright yellow and dark-wooded lobby of a comfortable hotel with coffee and Debbie's Honey Buns. Gramm clicked on the recorder. White led the charge.

"You lied to us," White challenged.

Rafferty jerked, causing him more than a little pain.

"How are you doing?" Gramm played the good cop.

"Not much different. It's only been a day or two since I talked to you last."

"Was your engine sputtering, indicating a lack of fuel?"

"No, but I'm an instrument guy. If my gauge tells me something, I believe it. I don't fly flapping my arms."

"Since you're such a stickler for instruments, according to our experts, you didn't follow any of the protocol for having fuel problems. No mayday call to nearby airports. And choosing to land on an obscure dirt road is certainly not protocol, especially when there were better alternatives."

Our experts? Milo mouthed behind the one-way glass.

"I panicked."

"No, you didn't. We know why you landed at that farm. You wanted to buy it. Did Anna Schmidt not want to sell, or did she raise the price? Is that why you killed her?"

"No, and no, you've got it all wrong!"

"Now he's in a panic," Milo said to Preston.

"We found your fingerprints in the farmhouse," White continued to press. "You were there. The lies are piling up."

KJ took a deep breath. "Okay, last Saturday, a woman claiming to be Anna Schmidt called my company phone and left a message saying she was the rightful owner of the farm. She wanted to sell it fast. Dealing with her directly would cut out that annoying realtor. She wanted to meet on Sunday. That's why I flew to the farm."

"Then what?" Gramm asked.

"I went to the farmhouse, knocked, and called for her, but there was no answer. I pushed open the front door, calling for her again, and identifying myself. I did that in every room.

I was not in the mood to get shot for breaking and entering. I found her in the kitchen. Not breathing. I panicked and ran out, tripped on those rotted stairs, and hurt my ankle. It rattled me. That's why I lost control of the plane. Not a great day."

White decided to do a Milo and ask a question out of left field. "What do you know about all those tires in the barn?"

KJ leaned forward. "Tires? In the barn? How many tires?"

"You're concerned about the tires? Please explain."

"Another expansion of my story? Okay. My father's business was on the up and up until about ten years ago. He was going through a tough time. Bigger haulers were squeezing him out and the offers to buy his company were insulting. He got a lucrative contract to take tons of old tires and dispose of them. Normally, he would have done that through legal channels, but he told me he saw a way to make a killing and get back in the black."

"Bury them?" Gramm guessed.

"He told me he and this Schmidt guy cooked up a plan to bury them on Schmidt's farm. The only trouble was the nearby land was being developed. It wasn't an isolated farm anymore. I went off to college, and dad hung in until I graduated. He retired, and I took over. He told me Schmidt still had the tires, so I kept tabs on this property. When I saw Schmidt's Obit, I knew I had to act…buy the place."

"Did you dad agree?" White questioned.

"He's passed."

"Again, why do you care about tires?" Gramm asked.

"They're hazardous waste. We are an eco-friendly disposal company. I have a reputation for doing things by the book.

If it came out dad was responsible for polluting the land, it could ruin me and my plans for the company."

"But it wasn't you, it was your father," White said.

"Doesn't matter. Our competitors would have a field day. I need to buy this land and deal with the tires responsibly, but quietly."

"You fly in here to make that deal, but Anna wants a lot more money. You're enraged. You stab her," White said.

"Okay, I admit the gas gauge was phony. Anna Schmidt called me, wanted to meet, and do business."

White cleared her throat. "So, no bad gas gauge—you meant to land on that farm. And you did know Anna Schmidt…"

"I didn't know her. I talked to her once, if it even was her."

"When you found Anna Schmidt's body, why didn't you call the police or an ambulance?"

"She was long past needing an ambulance. Even I could see that. I knew I didn't kill her, but I wasn't the only one in that house that day."

"How do you know," White urged.

"I stepped in that mess of blood in the kitchen. There were other bloody footprints all over. I just hauled up and ran out of there."

"Once again, don't leave town," Gramm said.

"I think it's time I called my lawyer," KJ said.

Gramm shrugged. "Your call."

14

C offee breaks and neck stretches—Ernie Gramm was remembering a time when midmorning coffee breaks came with a strawberry danish. After a flair-up of arthritis last winter, Gramm's wife Amy, tired of his grousing, insisted he consult a physical therapist. He learned effective stretching techniques, and they helped. At first, he tried to hide them from the staff, thinking they would see them as a sign of weakness. Over time, he lost that sensibility and stretched when he felt his neck or back stiffening up.

"Back acting up today?" White asked as she walked into his office carrying her coffee shop cup.

"Just doing what I'm told to do. What's today's flavor?" Gramm asked.

"I caved—pumpkin spice latte. It helps my immune system."

Gramm was about to ask how pumpkin spice could possibly keep her healthy, but he was afraid she knew and would tell him. "Any progress on finding our prime suspect, Clara Schmidt?"

"That is becoming a problem. We found Clara and Wally's marriage certificate that lists her maiden name as Lehto and her place of birth as Oulu."

"Oulu, that's great. Not too far away."

"Not Wisconsin. That would be too convenient. It's Oulu, Finland."

Gramm groaned, "International, we don't need. What about family here in Duluth?"

"None. She has a brother in Helsinki, Leo Lehto. He filed a missing person report back when Clara first disappeared. The file indicates he checks in every couple of years," White said.

"Did the department follow up on the original report?" Gramm asked.

"Yes, two officers were dispatched to search the farm."

"Names?"

"Prepinski and Crandell."

"Well, forget that."

"I also checked with the Finlandia Foundation and Oulu Cultural Heritage Center. She was not a member of either organization. No one remembered the name."

Today, Preston, tired of being lectured on the benefits of rest, stopped off at her favorite café for a leisurely breakfast of steak and eggs. While waiting for her food, she made a few productive calls. Eventually, Preston joined the group and rolled her chair into Gramm's office. "What's new?" she asked, nonchalantly.

"Want to go to Finland?" Gramm asked.

"Sure!" Preston said, eagerly.

White shook her head. "He's putting you on. Clara Schmidt was originally from Oulu, Finland. I don't think our travel budget will extend to Finland."

"It won't. Find someone on the staff who speaks Finnish and have them make some phone calls. Let's see if we can talk to her brother," Gramm ordered Preston.

"Got it." Preston nodded as Rathkey joined the three.

"Clara Lehto comes from Oulu, Finland," White told Milo.

"Really? Gosh that's great! Who is Clara Lehto?" Milo asked.

"Our prime suspect, other than all the liars. Glad you're keeping up to date, Milo."

"Oh yeah, that Clara Lehto Schmidt." Milo nodded. "So, field trip to Finland?"

"No!" Gramm said emphatically. Gramm's phone buzzed. It was Doc Smith again.

"Have you found Clara Schmidt?" the medical examiner asked.

"Not yet. We have her maidan name as Lehto, born in Finland."

"Well, she died in Duluth. Preston's new friend, Hermione, is Clara Schmidt."

"Are you sure?"

"No, I'm guessing. I have a dart board with names. This time the dart fell on Clara."

"How did you ID her?" White asked.

"I'm pleased you want a course in victim identification. We checked her dental records."

"No," Preston corrected. "You told me that…"

"I know what I told you. I told you we couldn't use dental records if we have no idea who the dead person is, but in this case, we have a missing wife and a dead body. I took a guess. We checked with area dentists and one of them treated Clara Schmidt. The records matched."

"Doc," Gramm interrupted, "you told us Clara's fingerprints are on Anna's murder weapon."

"Yes, I did."

"That woman in the pit died years before Anna Schmidt."

"Once again, look at you, a junior medical examiner. We think the weapon that killed Clara Schmidt was a shotgun. There were pellets in the bones."

"So, you think she was murdered, then hidden in the barn?" Milo asked.

"That's your department," Doc Smith said.

"Only one conclusion," Milo said, "Anna Schmidt was stabbed by the ghost of Clara Schmidt."

"I'll share that tidbit. We always enjoy a good laugh here at the morgue." The phone went dead.

Gramm looked from Preston to White. "First, kill that BOLO on Clara Schmidt. Second, cancel all flights to Finland. What do we think?"

"I'm baffled," White said.

"Pumpkin spice not doing it for you?" Gramm mocked.

White looked at her coffee cup with disdain. "I suspect it's artificial pumpkin."

Preston asked, "How can long-dead Clara's prints end up on a murder weapon used last weekend? Do ghosts have fingerprints?"

"Interesting paranormal question to ponder, but from what I saw, that house is a musty, dusty museum. I doubt Wally did any cleaning. Maybe her prints were there from when she last used them years ago. Anna's murderer just happened to pick up those scissors," White guessed. "They were convenient."

"Or the murderer intentionally used scissors that Clara had handled to throw us off the track," Preston added.

They bandied about several other theories before Gramm noticed Milo wasn't saying anything. "Milo?"

"Let's go with Preston's theory. If the killer used Clara's scissors with intention, he or she didn't know Clara was in that barn any more than we did. Clara being blown away was a Wally Schmidt secret he took to the grave. I think we tell the media we found Clara Schmidt's body."

"To what end?" White asked.

"To stir the pot. If the murderer used the scissors intentionally, Clara Schmidt's resurfacing as a ten-year-old corpse is going to ruin somebody's plan. Let's see what happens." Milo sat back in his chair.

They debated broadcasting the discovery of the body or keeping that info in-house for now. After much discussion, they compromised, deciding to reveal it first only to potential suspects and then watch reactions.

With Clara Schmidt out as prime suspect, the people who made contact with Anna Schmidt moved up the list.

"One of them is our killer, but which one?" Gramm said.

"We can start with Susan Peterson," White said, looking at her phone. "She and her husband will be here within the hour."

§

Kayla Maki sat on the edge of a metal lawn chair behind her dad's archery building. She played with the fringe of one of the chair's faded plastic straps waiting for the call. Her throat was dry. She took a sip of water from her dad's old dented red thermos. Kayla took her phone from her pocket for the third time that morning. She checked to make sure her ring tone was on, and double checked she had read the email correctly.

Her phone lit up. Van Dyke was on time. That was a plus—not a time waster. She held her breath and reminded herself that this was just an exercise her therapist said would be healthy. After all, there was no way in hell she was going to get the job with the pointedly personal resume she sent. She began breathing and swiped the green button.

Van Dyke coughed and cleared his throat before whispering an unexpected question. "If I hire you, will you come to work?"

"Ah, I kinda think that would be a requirement. Right?" Kayla said.

"Well, not everyone I hired has…never mind. Come in. Let's talk."

"Really?" None of this was what Kayla expected. "In case you forgot, your partner and I were…close. I was the girlfriend who went a little nuts when he dumped me and…"

"I remember. You came in here and threatened him with a knife," Van Dyke said.

"So, you still want to talk to me about a job?"

"Can you be here in the next hour?"

"Absolutely, but full disclosure, I stabbed another guy last summer. He was mugging me at the time."

"Do you plan to stab me or my customers?"

"I don't threaten people anymore. Anger management and yoga." Kayla waited for the rejection.

"Again, can you be here in an hour?" Van Dyke asked.

"I can't today. I have clients. How about Monday morning?"

There was an uncomfortable pause. Kayla was sure she had blown it.

His voice became stronger. "Did he die?"

"Who?"

"The mugger."

"No, but he was messed up. I wasn't the only one to attack him. The llama did too."

"Monday morning then."

§

Preston left the office to escort the Petersons and their lawyer into the bullpen area.

"Divide and conquer time," Gramm said. "White and I will take Susan. Milo and Preston can interview Gordy."

Explaining that plan to the Peterson's brought the first objection from the lawyer.

"You cannot interview them separately," the lawyer, a woman named Michelle Zielinska, said. "I can't be in two places at once."

Gramm shrugged. "Okay with us. We were hoping to do simultaneous interviews and get you people back on the road to Moose Lake before dark. But we can interview Mrs. Peterson first, and then Mr. Peterson. Your choice."

"I want to get back," Gordy complained. "It's oyster night at The Lazy Moose. They run out early."

The lawyer took her clients to a less populated portion of the bullpen to discuss the matter. "I think I should be in both interviews, but the decision is yours.

"Why can't they talk to us together like they did in Moose Lake?" Susan demanded.

"I suspect because you lied. Lying to the police is serious, Susan. You should have known better."

"Fine, we've got time," Susan said. "I want us represented equally. I'll go first. Then Gordy. I've told him what to say."

"I can do an interview without a lawyer," Gordy objected. "I want to get home for dinner."

"Be quiet, Gordy. Having Michelle with each of us is the best decision."

"Like your decision to lie to the cops has been the best so far," Gordy mumbled.

Susan said nothing but glared at her spouse.

Being told the couple's decision, Gramm nodded and invited Susan Peterson and her lawyer back to Interview Room A. Milo watched through the two-way glass. Preston sat with a bored, fidgeting Gordy Peterson in the bullpen area.

White started the recording. Gramm began the interview, "You lied to us, Mrs. Peterson, your fingerprints…"

"I did. I admit it. I'm sorry," Susan blurted.

Putting her hand on Susan Peterson's arm, Zielinska said, "My client wishes to correct her earlier statement about being in the farmhouse."

"Let's hear it from your client," Gramm insisted.

"Gordy and I got a call from somebody calling themselves Anna Schmidt last Saturday. It was a shock. She said she was alive and well. She threatened to take my farm away from me. It had to be a hoax, so I called her bluff and demanded a meeting on Sunday morning."

"And did you meet with her?"

"Gordy and I debated the idea. I thought we were crazy to even consider it, but Gordy said it would be a nice drive—changing leaves and all. We drove up Sunday morning."

"What happened when you arrived at the farm?"

"The door was open."

"Open or just unlocked?" Gramm asked.

"Unlocked. We knocked, but there was no answer. I wanted to leave. Gordy pushed gently on the door with his foot, and the door opened! We called her name and identified ourselves. No answer. We looked into the downstairs rooms, calling out. We eventually made our way to the kitchen. It was awful. There was blood everywhere and a dead person with my scissors in her back."

Gramm was stunned. "Your scissors?!"

"Are you admitting killing Anna Schmidt?" White pressed.

"NO!" Zielinska shouted. "That was not a confession! What Susan means is they are a popular brand of scissors. That iconic orange handle has been around for years. My client has a pair; so do I; so do thousands of other people."

"Go on," Gramm urged.

"Gordy and I were shocked, stunned. We've never seen any death like that. We panicked. Maybe the killer was still in the house. We ran out of the kitchen and sped off! We couldn't get out of there fast enough. But now I feel so bad. We left that poor person lying there," Susan said, wiping away a tear.

"That poor person was your cousin, Anna Schmidt," White said.

"How would I know? The person was lying face down. The last time I saw Anna, she was six. I saw a grown woman."

"Why did you lie about being in that farmhouse?" Gramm asked.

"It would look awful. If it were Anna, it would look like we killed her to hang onto the farm."

Gramm nodded. "It does, especially since you lied."

"I didn't want to go. I told Gordy, I didn't want to go and leave her like that." Susan began to cry again.

White sat back in her chair. "That's a sad story, but let me give you our scenario, Ms. Peterson. Either you or your husband killed Anna Schmidt and left the body to rot inside the farmhouse. You figured you had plenty of time. Maybe you'd retrieve it after dark, or maybe you'd just leave it there until you inherited the land. How am I doing?"

"Totally wrong!" Susan shouted. "We didn't kill anybody! This is why we lied! We knew you would pin this murder on us."

"But you did leave a dead body lying there without reporting it," Gramm said.

Susan Peterson began to sputter about being frightened.

Zielinska again put her arm on her client and asked for a moment to confer. Gramm and White stopped the recording, turned off the mics, and stepped out of the room. They joined Milo in the anteroom.

"Robin, you accused her of leaving the body to rot? You have a dark view of human nature," Gramm joked.

"Dark perhaps, but it makes sense. Innocent people would have called the cops, but these two calmly walked to their car and said nothing. No urgency."

"Calmly? Remind me, how do we know that?" Gramm asked.

"The birdman. KJ came running out of the house. The couple before him walked out calmly," Milo said.

The lawyer motioned for Gramm to come back in. He and White returned, restarted the recording for a second time, and waited.

Zielinska began. "I must point out that my clients were under extreme stress, having just seen a dead body. Most people never come across such a sight," Zielinska said.

"We panicked and ran!"

White shook her head. "We have a witness that describes you two as calmly walking to your car."

"Witness? There was nobody there," Susan protested.

"There was, and our witness puts you in yet another lie."

"Look, Lieutenant," the lawyer said, "you can nitpick Ms. Peterson all day, but in her mind, they were running to the car."

Gramm decided to follow Milo's recipe and stir the pot. "We found the body of Clara Schmidt in the barn earlier this week. She had been dead for years."

"We didn't kill her either."

§

Gordy Peterson had been pushing his hand through his semi-spiked hair, leaving it a bit ragged. He hunched over the table, crinkling his plastic water bottle.

"How did the trip to Duluth come about?" Gramm asked. "Sues got a call from someone claiming to be Anna, who was yelling and screaming, calling her a thief, saying she would never get the farm. Sues challenged the woman to a meeting..."

"Challenged?" White questioned the verbiage.

"Yeah, pretty much. Sues didn't think it was Anna. meah, no one has heard from this woman in years and then she suddenly pops up. I doubted all of it. It was a con."

"A con?"

"Yeah. You know, shaking us down for money."

"Why did you come to Duluth?"

"Well, I thought it would be nuts to have anything to do with this hoaxer, but Sues said we had to come. She said it would be a nice drive."

"Was it?" White asked. "Your wife told us you thought it would be a nice drive."

"She did? No, she wanted the nice drive."

Gramm looked at the attorney who said, "Really, Lieutenant? Is this the most important question you could ask?"

"It goes to credibility."

"Maybe Susan suggested the drive, maybe I did. I don't remember," Gordy said, running his hand through his spikes again.

"Tell us about entering the farmhouse," Gramm ordered.

"We knocked. The door was unlocked, so after getting no answer, we walked in and saw her."

"Who?"

"This dead person in a lot of blood."

"Where was the dead person? What room?"

"The kitchen."

"What did you do next?"

"We left. I thought we should call the cops...you guys, but Susan said no."

Zielinska asked for time to confer with her client.

Gramm stood but stopped before leaving the room. "We know Ms. Zielinska represents your wife, but are you sure she represents you?"

Gordy nodded. "Sure! We're a team."

Gramm and White left the room, joining Milo in the observation room.

"I think his attorney is telling him he just set his wife up for an obstruction charge," Gramm said.

"Are we believing Gordy or Susan?" White asked.

"Would a man who sells a BlowVee lie?" Milo asked.

The attorney waved them back in. Gramm groaned and stretched his back.

Once Gramm and White sat down, Zielinska charged ahead. "My client didn't realize the weight of his words. He would like to amend his last statement to..."

Gramm raised his hand to stop the verbiage. "We get it, counselor, but we would like to hear from your client."

Gordy cleared his throat. "Susan and I both thought we'd wait before calling the police."

"Or never calling the police," White added.

Gordy shrugged.

"We need a verbal response, Mr. Peterson."

"I guess that was a possibility."

Gramm opened his fake folder. "Mr. Peterson, we have found the body of Clara Schmidt in the barn. It appears as if she was murdered a decade ago."

Gordy shrugged. "Sues never mentioned a Clara Schmidt. All I know is it's getting late, and I don't want to miss fresh oyster night at the Lazy Moose."

Behind the one-way glass, Preston began to laugh.

"What's so funny?" Milo shrugged. "The man clearly loves his fresh Minnesota oysters."

Gramm stood up. "We will want to talk to you and your wife again, Mr. Peterson."

Zelinska handed him her card. "Call me in the future."

15

"So, it appears that our victim was making nasty phone calls all over the place," Gramm said as the group reassembled in his office. "Do we think she invited her murderer to the farm?"

"What game was she playing?" White wondered.

"I would like to get these 'stir the pot' interviews about Clara Schmidt being dead over with before the weekend. Before we go, let's review the suspects."

"Always helpful," Milo muttered.

White went first. "Arial knew Clara. Her fingerprints were in the farmhouse. And, by her own admission, she got a call from Anna on Saturday threatening her big-money deal. That's a clear motive."

Gramm picked up the thread. "Susan and Gordy Peterson. They get a phone call and go to the farmhouse to meet Anna, and we have an eyewitness putting them there around the time Anna was killed. Motive: Again, money. We already stirred the pot with them without a reaction to Clara being dead."

"Milo? Who's your best guess?" White asked.

"We have Bear, Pendergast, or Rafferty." Milo counted them on his fingers.

Gramm shook his head. "Money is a motive, but no opportunity for Bear."

"He said he arrived on Tuesday. I can check that," Preston added.

"Do it," Gramm said. "But let's interview him today, anyway."

"Rafferty's motive is not as direct—save the company's reputation?" White said. "Yet bird man says he ran out of the farmhouse close to the time Anna was murdered. Rafferty still gets an interview."

"Do we have a motive for Pendergast?" Gramm asked.

"Not really," White said. "But he knew Clara and his fingerprints were in the farmhouse."

"Let's keep him in the frame. Meanwhile, let's lunch on the fly so we can start our weekend. Remember, we want to make dropping the info about 'dead Clara' friendly, as if we are giving people some new information out of the goodness of our hearts. Preston and I will take Bear and Pendergast. Robin, you and Milo stir the pot with Rafferty and Jenkins."

"Milo? I seem to have drawn the short straw," White protested.

"I'm average height," Milo shot back.

Gramm nodded, "I hear you, Robin. Normally, you and I would partner, but the last time Milo and Preston went out together, they ended up with the Crow Wing County Bomb Squad and another dead body."

White rolled her eyes and motioned for Milo to follow her out to the motor pool garage.

"Hey, Keisha, I'm taking number 71," White yelled to an older uniformed woman carrying a clipboard.

"Sgt. White, Interceptor 71," she repeated. "Have a fun afternoon."

White laughed. "She always says that."

"I always have fun afternoons," Milo said. "That's how I roll."

White gave him a side eye. "Get in the car. Jenkins first," White said as they both buckled into their seats. "I know we have thought of her as a ditz, but she got pretty heated yesterday. Maybe we saw the real Arial."

"She's not a ditz, just different," Milo said in Arial's defense.

"Look at you—all soft and fuzzy," White mocked while starting the car.

On the way to Arial's office, White told Milo his job was to come up with a lunch place that would satisfy them both.

"Easy peasy," Milo said. "I'm so flexible this shouldn't be tough."

Arial Jenkins was sitting at her desk when she saw the police Interceptor park in front of the realty office. After her last clash with Sgt. White, Arial's first instinct was to rush out the back. Ed Dammers, who had the desk nearest the window, stopped her retreat by yelling, "Hey, Arial, your police detail is here again."

"Thanks, Ed, glad you could alert the whole office," Arial sneered.

"All part of the service," Ed said.

White and Milo walked in and up to Arial's desk. "Good afternoon, Arial," White said, sitting down on one of the client chairs as Milo stood.

Arial's neck bobbed in her peacock fashion. "It was. I have a closing in an hour. What can I do for you?"

"Nothing. We just wanted to keep you up to date with the investigation," White said. "We found Clara Schmidt."

"Clara?"

"We found her body."

Arial sat down. "She's dead?"

"Yes, murder, an old one. We know you're concerned about the property and your clients. This might be another complication."

"Complication. That's all you people ever bring me."

"Well, in this case, the complication is we found the body in that padlocked barn. Did Wally Schmidt Junior ever mention that barn?"

"Remember, I never talked to Wally Schmidt Junior." Arial shook her head, causing her curls to beat the sides of her face. "I only talked to Susan Peterson. Of course, now you tell me Ted Bear inherits, so now I talk to him."

"Did Susan Peterson or Rafferty ever mention Clara Schmidt?" Milo asked.

"No, no, no!" Her volume was increasing. "What was she doing dying in that barn? It was padlocked."

Once again, White did a quick clearing of her ears to get the latest Arialism out of her brain. "We don't think she went there to die. She was murdered and placed there. No fault of her own."

"People trespass at will these days," Arial grumbled.

"Arial!" White exclaimed. "Focus! Clara Schmidt, wife of Wally Schmidt Jr., was murdered, and her body placed in the barn before it was padlocked. Has anyone ever mentioned Clara Schmidt to you in any context?"

Arial looked around the office. All eyes were on her. "You just did at an embarrassingly loud volume."

"Besides me!"

Arial shook her head.

"Anything else we should know?" White asked in a softer tone.

"Nothing, except the hearing."

"Monday, Judge Hoffer, ten o'clock?"

"Yes."

"Thank you. See you then," White said, rising to leave.

"Really? Why would you care?" Arial asked.

"I'm a police sergeant. This is my case. It's my job to be there," White chided. "See you Monday."

On the way out, White said to Milo, "Our pot stirring didn't get much of a reaction from Arial."

"You do push each other's buttons," Milo said.

"Yeah, next time, make sure I'm not armed when interviewing Arial. I might not be able to control myself."

"You know, you get more like Gramm every day," Milo joked.

"That's not funny, Milo."

§

Gramm and Preston called Ted Bear, who said he was at the Duluth Playhouse enjoying a rehearsal of *Into The Woods*. They found him relaxed in the back of the theater, sitting sideways in a seat with his legs slung across the armrest.

"Mr. Bear," Gramm said, "we have a few more questions and some information for you."

He crossed his arms and huffed. "Do you have to do this to me now? This is where Anna and I met. I can close my eyes, let the sounds and smells of the theater enfold me, comforting me in its magic, taking my pain away."

"Yes, we have to do it now. Put the magic in your bag of personal whatevers."

Preston turned away, bit her lip, then suggested they move the interview to the lobby.

Bear unfolded himself from the theater seats and casually threw a red sweater over his shoulders to join Gramm and Preston into the chilly lobby.

The Duluth Playhouse was one of three theaters in the renovated Art Déco NorShor Movie House. The plush lobby offered several luxurious lounge areas. Bear guided them to the nearest seating arrangement.

Gramm, who was getting hungry, got right to the point. "Mr. Bear, we found your fingerprints in the farmhouse where your wife died. Care to explain?"

Bear shrugged. "They have to be old. I was in that house before Anna and I left for the West Coast."

Gramm began stirring the pot. "Remember, we asked you about Anna's stepmother, Clara Schmidt? Is there anything you can tell us about her? Anything that you didn't think of before."

"Oh, my? You think she's back here, lurking, don't you?"

"Well, we are going to modify that a bit." Preston zeroed in on Bear's face and body language as Gramm had instructed. "We found Clara Schmidt's body in the family barn. She's been dead for a number of years."

Bear's eyes widened. "Zounds!"

Zounds? Preston wondered. *Never heard that before. May never hear that again.*

Bear pulled his sweater over his head, hiding his face for a bit. "Kinda cold out here," he said, rubbing his arms. "Zounds, again. It must be kismet. Lieutenant, this red sweater was Anna's, made by Clara. Both souls are watching over me. It's a great solace to me."

"Can you remember anything else about Clara?" Gramm asked.

"Anna liked her. Like I said, Clara had been her role model, running away from Anna's father." Bear thought for a second. "But I guess she didn't, did she?"

"No, Mr. Bear, she didn't."

§

Robin turned off Superior Street on to 27th Avenue West, causing Milo to question her motive. "I'm hungry. You haven't decided, so I have. Duluth Grill," she said simply.

"Oh, okay. I thought you were heading for one of those trendy breweries with IPAs and limited food."

"I take it you don't like IPAs and limited food?"

"Well, the limited food speaks for itself, and an IPA is weak beer. There, I said it."

Robin parked in the Duluth Grill's parking lot. "I don't know if you're correct or not. Remember, I don't drink."

"I like this place," Milo said, getting out of the car.

"We're not going to run into any of your 'friends' here, are we?" asked White, using air quotes to bracket "friends."

"What do you mean by 'friends?'" asked Milo, mirroring White's air quotes.

"Wait staff and owners who gush over you or give you a hard time and waste mine."

"I don't even know who works here."

White pushed open the door, and she and Milo entered to a shout of "Hey, Milo!" coming from one of the booths.

The cook leaned out of the ordering window and yelled, "Milo! How's it going?"

Milo waved.

White stopped and stared at him.

Milo defended himself. "I know people. I didn't know they would be here,"

While they waited, White tried to set up an interview with Rafferty, but the NTSB and insurance problems tied him up all day. "Not a great way to end the week."

"So far, there is no connection between Rafferty and Clara. If he's our murderer, his motive is money, and using the scissors was pure chance," Milo said.

"We can ask Mr. Honeybuns about Clara on Monday." As their food arrived, so did a call from Saul Feinberg, Duluth's attorney to the poor. "Feinberg," Milo said to White.

"This should be interesting." He slid the green button on his phone. "Saul, you're on speaker with Robin. We're at the Duluth Grill. I'm having a chicken melt. Robin is having a fast Cobb salad. What can I do for you?"

"Milo, I don't care about your lunch. Your question about inheritance on Tuesday was about the Schmidt Farm off Martin Road. Right?"

"Maybe. Why?"

"I'm trying to get some background. I'm now representing a party with an interest in the probate hearing on Monday."

"Who's your client?"

"I'd rather not say."

"Okay. I don't know a thing about that farm," Milo lied.

Feinberg sighed. "Leo Lehto, brother to…"

"Clara Schmidt," Milo finished the sentence. "Preston and I found her in the barn."

"Wait, a minute. When you say, 'found her in the barn,' what does that mean?" Feinberg asked.

Milo gave him the quick version of Wally, Anna, and Clara Schmidt. "I've been told that Wally divorced Clara several years after she disappeared. I don't know if that's true or if it affects any claim your client may have."

"It is true, Milo, and it does affect my client's claim. The courts take a dim view of murdering your wife and then divorcing her just to cut her relatives out of any inheritance."

"We can't prove Wally killed her, yet," Milo said.

"Oh, come on, she was killed with a shotgun. You just talked about a booby trap tied to a…wait for it…shotgun registered to Wally."

"Could just be a series of coincidences," Milo said. "She could have been walking in the barn with a shotgun to hunt wildebeests or hamsters. She could have slipped, fell into the pit surrounded by tires, and accidentally shot herself. The shotgun flies in the air, comes to rest on a barn support with two trip wires connected to the triggers. Sheer coincidence."

"I find the hunting of hamsters with a shotgun to be repugnant."

"Wildebeests don't count?"

"Seeing as how I don't really know what that is, I'm not going to upset wildebeest hunters," Feinberg said.

"Gnus," White said.

"Wait a minute, Saul, I think Robin just sneezed."

"I didn't sneeze. Wildebeests are also known as gnus."

Milo thought about complicating things further by asking what she would call many gnus, but he wanted to eat his food. "See you on Monday, Saul," he said, hanging up.

"So, is Feinberg joining the probate hearing?" White asked.

"He is representing Clara Schmidt's brother."

"Too bad for him, Wally divorced Clara," White said.

"Divorcing her doesn't cut her heirs out if he killed her first. Saul will press that button early and often."

§

Gramm and Preston agreed to skip lunch, interview Bill Pendergast, and then knock off early. Grace greeted them, and showed them into the living room. "Bill's in the back with the dog. I'll go get him. Would you like some water or coffee?"

Both declined.

Bill came in with a mug of coffee and expressed surprise that he was being interviewed again. "I don't know what more I can tell you about Anna." Bill sat back on the couch. Gramm and Preston took side chairs.

"This time it's not about Anna. We're trying to get more information on Anna's stepmother, Clara." Gramm said.

Grace appeared in the doorway. "Why? She left years ago."

Bill sat up. "Is she a suspect?"

Preston zeroed in on Bill, watching for his reactions.

"Well, she was until we found her dead body in the padlocked barn," Gramm said.

"Really? Another murder?" Bill was visibly shaken. He looked at Grace. "We both knew her."

Grace came in and sat next to her husband.

"I thought she was a nice lady. Anna liked her," Bill said. Preston noticed Bill's hands were shaking.

"First Anna, then Clara? Why?" Grace asked.

"Clara never disappeared. She was murdered years ago, and her body was stuffed in the barn."

"Anna's father did it," Bill stated flatly. "Wally was a dangerous man. Anna always thought he killed her real mom."

Grace grabbed Bill's arm. "This is terrible. What else can happen on that farm?"

"We have a problem we just need to clear up. Bill, how did your fingerprints get in the farmhouse?"

"Mine?" Bill blurted.

Gramm nodded. Preston watched.

"Gotta be from years ago? Do fingerprints last that long?"

"These prints were recent, according to the medical examiner," Gramm lied.

"Let me look," Bill began to flip through his phone.

"He keeps his appointments on that phone," Grace explained. "He's so busy. I sometimes have to update it for him."

"Oh, here it is. It was spur of the moment. Last week I saw that 'for sale' sign and thought maybe we might want to make a bid. We could build a lot of houses on that land. My father-in-law would love it."

"But why go into the house?"

"It's the trend these days to leave the original structure in place as we build the modern houses around it. Of course, we remodel the older house, bring it up to code, and put in modern amenities. It's just the outside that retains the original look. Those properties often go for more money than the new ones."

"Where did you go once you were inside the house?" Preston asked.

"All over. I spent most of the time checking out the basement. That place is a complete gut job full of rot, termites, anything that would make the remodel more expensive."

Gramm and Preston thanked the couple and made their way to their car. "Preston, what did you see?"

"Ted was smooth, but he covered his face when he put on his sweater. Bill was shook."

"Text Robin and Milo. See if they know anything earth-shaking before we knock off for the weekend." Gramm sat back, watching Preston's finger fly over her phone's virtual keyboard. The answer came back almost immediately.

"Robin says KJ was not available, NTSB interviews. Arial Jenkins was only upset with us, as usual."

"So, nothing."

"Pretty much. You will be happy to know I'm taking it easy this weekend," Preston smiled.

Gramm turned to Preston, "Before we go, let's chat."

"Did I do something wrong?"

Gramm stared straight ahead. "In my career, I've been to three police funerals. Everyone dresses up in formal blues. Sometimes there is a funeral procession. The force hurts for days, sometimes weeks…sometimes forever."

Preston stared at Gramm's aging, jowly face in profile and remained quiet.

"In a polite ceremony people say things like 'gone but not forgotten,' 'a life well lived,' 'left the world a better place.' In the end, they put up a plaque with the officer's name on the *In Memoriam* wall. But dead is dead!" Gramm paused and looked Preston in the eyes. "I never want to go through that again and I sure as hell do not want your name on one of those plaques!"

Preston's heart raced. Her brain had frozen. "I never thought…"

"You will be a hell of a cop. You just have to live long enough for that to happen. You have an entire police force at your disposal. Use it. Don't go running alone into barns or chasing suspects on a motorcycle. Be safe. Call for backup. For me, if not for you."

"I will," Preston whispered.

§

Being a cop, Sgt. Robin White was used to being awakened in the middle of the night, but this was a first. The desk called to tell her that Birdman, Bernie Waite, needed to talk to her ASAP.

"He wouldn't tell me what it was about," Desk Sergeant Higgins said. "He wants you to call him. Said it was urgent."

Robin sighed. "It's three in the morning!"

"I know, Sergeant."

Robin hung up. She began fumbling with her phone, trying to find Waite's number. She had a system of cataloging numbers on her phone by case, but the early hour made the system blurry. Finding Bernie under *Farm Witnesses,* she rang his number.

"Hello? Hello? Yes, Sgt. White?" Bernie was out of breath.

"Yes, Mr. Waite."

"You said to call. I'm calling! It's the house! It's on fire—burning to the ground!"

"The farmhouse?"

"Yes, the farmhouse. Not my house. Why would I call you about my house?"

"Did you call the fire department?"

"No, but somebody did. The noise. Sirens, horns, clanging! The trucks pulled up about fifteen minutes ago. I wanted to run over there, but the wife said no. I'm up in my bird watching roost with my Swarovskis. Oh gosh! The roof just caved in! Well, that's a goner."

"Thank you, Mr. Waite. We'll be in contact."

"I hope the birds won't be scared off for long."

Robin hung up. She debated her next move. Should she wait for morning or wake the others tonight? "I've never had a crime scene burn down before. Oh, hell, I'm up. I should share that experience." She called the desk back, requesting a conference call between herself, Gramm, Preston, and Rathkey. Ten minutes later, her phone rang with the conference call.

She could hear Preston yawning and Milo talking to his cats, something about revealing how they got into the bedroom.

Gramm spoke first. "What the hell is going on?"

"Our Anna Schmidt crime scene is burning down," White said. "The bird man called me. I'm calling you."

"Why am I on this call?" Milo protested. "I'm not a fireman."

"Because you found Anna Schmidt," White said.

Gramm jumped in. "You wanted to smoke out the killer. Well, you did. But I'm tired. Is there a compelling reason for this call to continue? We can talk tomorrow."

Everyone agreed.

16

Arial Jenkins awoke early and padded to the kitchen to make herself coffee and toast. Before Saturday showings and open houses, her morning ritual included thirty minutes of the Channel Ten morning report. The lead this morning was a fire on the Schmidt Farm off Martin Road. Arial stared at the smoking ruin of the Schmidt farmhouse.

The news moved on to some city council hubbub. Arial refocused on her toast and contemplated what she should do about the fire, if anything. A phone call interrupted her pondering.

"Arial Jenkins," she said.

"Ms. Jenkins, it's Sgt. White, my call this morning is to inform you of…"

"The fire at the farmhouse. I know. I just saw the rubble on the news. Did you people burn my farmhouse?"

"It's not likely we caused the fire, Ms. Jenkins."

"Then who did?"

"Where were you last night?"

"Me? I would not burn down my own farmhouse."

"It's not yours, Ms. Jenkins," White corrected.

"It might as well be. I'm in charge of it until that judge holds his hearing Monday morning. I'm glad I had that attorney insure the place."

"*You* had it insured? Why?"

"Because I am good at my job, Sergeant White. The farm is tied up in probate and Walter Schmidt Junior, being dead, isn't making any payments on home and farm insurance. I had the executor, Wilson David take out a liability policy. It has a small payout in case of loss, like the fire."

"Who gets the benefit?" White asked.

"Whoever gets the farm, gets the payout minus the premiums I paid. I take care of my clients."

"Let's get back to my question about where you were last night."

"I was here, at home."

"Can anyone corroborate that?"

"My cats!"

"Not admissible in court."

"Look, I was being sarcastic. Everyone thinks a woman living alone has cats."

White petted her cat, Biskane.

§

Gramm called Milo just as he and the Lakesong cats were ambling toward Saturday morning's do-it-yourself breakfast. Milo had not informed the cats there would be no beloved

Martha bacon. He paused in the gallery to take Gramm's call. The cats, confused by the unexpected halt in progress, gathered at his feet. Jet meowed as if his heart were breaking. Annie, being more aggressive, batted at Milo's leg.

"Milo, our crime scene is rubble," Gramm accused. "Good plan."

"Thanks for the atta-boy. Where are Robin and Kate?" Milo asked, stifling a yawn.

"Robin is out on her bike. Preston is at an outdoor, baby-goat yoga class."

"Baby-goat yoga?"

"Don't ask. Milo, this isn't an atta-boy. Somebody burned our crime scene to the ground. Why?"

"I think the debate is over. The use of Clara's scissors as the murder weapon was not a spur-of-the-moment choice. I bet our murderer also planted other evidence in the farmhouse to throw suspicion on Clara."

"So, they burned down our crime scene to get rid of planted evidence? Kinda stupid, if you ask me. Forensics has everything."

"I agree it's stupid. A stupid killer should be easier to catch."

"Let's hope." Gramm almost broke into a smile. "I gotta be in court on Monday, Milo, so you and Preston get to go through all the evidence and photos taken from the farmhouse before it became ashes. Oh, and just so you know, Handy was the forensics guy taking pictures."

"Handy? The squirrely guy who shoots eight thousand pictures?" Milo asked.

"Yeah, him. I will get Handy to deliver all of his pictures to you Monday morning. He will even stay and narrate each one."

"Look, I gotta go. The cats are clawing me, and I have weekend plans," Milo said.

"Biking or goat yogaing?" Gramm asked.

"Neither. A lawn party."

"I worry about you, Milo. Lawn party?"

"Well, it's not just a lawn party. It's a lawn party and house demolition."

"I don't wanna know."

"Mary Alice is knocking down the White Whale. We're going to sit on the lawn, sip champagne, and watch a large, yellow wrecking ball slam into the side of the Bonner house."

"I think I do wanna know. That sounds…"

"A lot better than goat yoga?"

"But not as good as cheering for a seven-year-old soccer striker. No goats, bikes, or wrecking balls—just orange slices and juice boxes on a cool fall day."

"Would the kiddies like a bottle of champagne?"

"Optics, Milo! Optics!" Gramm hung up.

Milo looked down at his feet. Jet was lying on his back, pretending to have passed out from a lack of bacon.

"You don't even eat the bacon!" Milo chided.

Annie, who eats the bacon, gave him a nasty meow.

Milo stood up. "Sorry, fur balls, Martha's gone, and I don't cook bacon."

§

Harold "Handy" Schimanski was combining the contents of three cans of dog food for his mixed terrier, Loki, when his cell phone lit up. *M. Holden Forensics. The boss!* Handy thought. Always eager to work, Handy picked up the device with anticipation.

"Handy here," he said.

"Handy, I'm giving you a heads-up," Holden informed him. "Monday morning, a police consultant named Milo Rathkey..."

"I know Milo," Handy interrupted.

"Good. Monday morning, you bring all the Schmidt Farm photos to Milo. He wants to go through them. Be prepared to stay. For some reason, he wants you there while he reviews them."

"Is he looking for anything specific?" Handy asked, putting down the dog food bowl.

"I asked Lieutenant Gramm. All he said was, with Milo, it could be anything."

"I won't let you down. I'll prepare. I'll be ready," Handy said.

"I knew you would," Holden said.

"Should I print them out?"

Knowing Handy probably took at least a thousand pictures, she visualized the budget line item for photo paper magically tripling. Holden told him to hold off on the printing. "I think Milo can look at them on the computer. If he needs a few printed out, he'll tell you."

"Got it."

"Enjoy the rest of your weekend," Holden said as she hung up.

Handy looked at the now empty dog food bowl. Loki, who always wolfed down his food, looked eager to receive more. "Sorry, Loki," Handy said, "the vet said you were getting pudgy."

Loki nosed his empty bowl against the cupboard, flipping it with a clang.

Handy grabbed the nearby leash. "Come on, Loki, time to get in our steps."

Loki was a food-and-nap pet. Walks were not on his schedule. What ensued was a battle of wills between master and dog, ending with Handy lifting Loki and carrying him outside to take care of personal business.

"Loki, you can sleep. I got an important assignment in the office today," Handy said to the dog. "A famous consultant wants me to present my evidence. I must organize and prepare for the presentation."

Loki nosed a fuzzy, black rug over to his favorite spot near the kitchen heating grate and laid down. The look on his face seemed to say, "Sure, knock yourself out. I'll be napping."

§

Milo poured a cup of coffee while staring out the morning room window at a few fall leaves blowing across the back lawn. Sitting, he nodded to Agnes and Sutherland, blinked, and sipped his coffee.

"Are you taking the Mary Alice shuttle with us later this morning?" Sutherland asked.

Milo stared at Sutherland as if he were speaking a foreign language. His thoughts were on last night's fire,

"Where are you, Milo?" Sutherland questioned. "Remember the Mary Alice party, and the shuttle bus leaving from Lakesong to the soon to be demolished home? Are you joining us?"

"Why would we need a shuttle bus?" Milo questioned.

"It's not just for us," Sutherland said.

"All the guests are parking their cars here at Lakesong, and the shuttle will take them to the party," Agnes explained.

"Why are they parking here?" Milo was confused.

"Because she asked, and we are good neighbors. Demolition is messy and dangerous for cars. Flying debris and all that," Sutherland said.

"I was not informed about flying debris," Milo complained. "Flying debris could take the shine off of my nose."

"Mary Alice also said to be prepared to duck," Agnes laughed.

"Why didn't I know any of this?" Milo asked. "Did you know any of this?" he demanded of Agnes.

Agnes took a sip of her morning coffee. "Mary Alice asked if I could make Lakesong's side-lawn parking lot available for her house breaking brunch. I said sure, but I needed to run it past you two. In her Mary Alice way, she pronounced, 'Agnes, you also own Lakesong. You don't have to run it past anybody.' So, I didn't."

"No argument here!" Sutherland agreed.

"So, Sutherland, famous GQ adviser to the stars, are my jeans and a t-shirt okay for a house demolition?" Milo asked.

"More importantly, helmets and protective eyewear. It's going to be dusty," Sutherland said.

"Don't worry about anything. We will have costumes. Mary Alice told me Peggy is taking care of everything."

"Costumes? Are we talking Spiderman? Am I going to have to change my clothes on Mary Alice's front lawn?" Milo asked. "Because if I do, I'm wearing my good skivvies."

"Too much information," Sutherland cautioned.

"Skivvies?" Agnes asked.

"Naval term for underwear," Milo informed her.

Agnes waved him off. "TMI indeed."

§

Even though Amy Gramm assured Ernie they had everything they needed, he still went out for extra juice boxes. Charlie, his granddaughter, was the striker today. He made the case to Amy that there would be a lot of running on this unusually warm day. Once out, he took a quick detour past the smoldering ruins of the farmhouse. Given the recent history of the farm, he wanted to make sure no more bodies turned up.

Several fire department personnel were still on the scene, including Fire Marshal Paul Kutka.

He waved at Kutka and got the come on over signal. "What do you know?"

"Ernie, nice of you to join us on this lovely Saturday morning. Nothing better to do?"

Gramm surveyed the charred wood and debris. Smoke was still billowing up from several places. "Looks like you got here in time to save the dirt."

"Funny, but true. These old wooden places flare up in seconds given the slightest nudge," Kutka said. "Someone intentionally set this fire."

"So, this place got nudged?"

"Yes, but not by a pro. It looks to us that someone poured gasoline around the perimeter of the house and set it ablaze. A rookie move—clearly arson."

"So, our fire starter didn't care about hiding the fact it was arson."

"Not at all. So, answer me a question," Kutka asked.

"Shoot."

"This place has had how many murders?"

"Two we know about," Gramm said. Then thinking of Walter Schmidt's first wife, he added, "Maybe three."

"Three murders, that plane crash, and now arson. Quite the place."

Gramm shrugged. "Something in the water?" His phone vibrated. It was an Amy text. *I know you stopped by that farm. Meet us at the soccer game. The juice boxes are for halftime. Don't dawdle.*

Gramm laughed. "It's my wife. She knows me too well."

§

Lakesong's weekend should have been quiet, free of the bang and whir of construction. However, Sutherland had offered to pay double time if the crew worked Saturdays. As Agnes climbed up to the second floor, the pounding and sawing noises increased in volume. Today, the carpenters were enclosing the new room over Lakesong's garage.

Agnes inched her way onto the plywood subfloor of the newly built hallway. Peering into the room, she watched one of the lake-facing floor-to-ceiling windows being installed.

Outside, another crew was working on the balcony supports. She wondered if it was smart to be working the balcony and windows on the same wall at the same time.

A gruff voice startled her.

"He shouldn't be here, and neither should you."

Agnes jumped and turned in the direction of the rebuke. She spotted Darian, Martha's youngest sib, standing between the gruff foreman and herself. "I'm Agnes McKnight, and he's with me." She held out her hand to Darian to show they were together.

"You're responsible for him. Both of you stay back here!" the worker said. "Also, if you're in here, put on a hard hat. They're outside in the blue truck."

"Kinda of a grouch, but he's right. Hard hats for both of us next time. Here, get in front of me so you can see better," Agnes said as they exchanged places. "So, what do you think?"

"I like that you can see the lake."

"We're putting a deck out there, too."

They stood scrunched to the side of the opening, watching and listening to the progress. She thought about Darian's past pronouncement about the house. Agnes was happy and excited, but wondered if he had any more feelings about the house. She debated whether or not to question him. Curiosity got the better of her. "I'm glad you like the windows, Darian. What does the house think?"

Darian cocked his head to the side and looked up at Agnes, unsure about the question.

"I ask only because you told us once that the house was happy because it was filled with people again. I want to make sure she likes what we're doing."

"I think so. The house is back," Darian said. "It feels whole again."

"Back? Whole?"

"Yes, ma'am." Darian shrugged. "I don't know. Something was lost and now it's back. I don't know what it means."

The house is back? Something was lost?

17

Milo stared into his large gentleman's closet, which was slowly being populated with what he once called fancy duds. His ordinary clothes, which he brought with him a year and a half ago in a black plastic bag, were periodically being dropped off at a men's shelter. His style remained the same—kakis and comfortable shirts—but the quality and fit were a tad better. Part of him didn't want to let his old clothes go, but hanging on to them when someone else could use them seemed selfish.

The immense closet featured a slidable ladder to access the upper reaches, where a series of small storage areas waited to be filled. Milo had stored his gun in one, and the key to a telescope mechanism on Martha's Lakesong cottage in another. One cubicle had never been opened, at least not by Milo. Today, he had the irresistible urge to open it.

Milo slid the ladder to the back of the closet and tugged on the sticky door. He jutted his head forward and squinted to see what the dark cubical held. "Well, thank you, John. I assume you bought this for a costume party—hope it was fun. Mine will be."

He reached in and pulled out a straw hat, the type men used to wear to lawn parties in the 1920s. Climbing back down, he centered it on his head to show Jet, who meowed and walked away.

"Well, I think it's perfect for the occasion," Milo yelled after him. He changed his Saturday jeans and T-shirt for new brown slacks and a rust-colored dress shirt. The natty straw hat was the perfect complement.

Milo checked the time on his phone. He was late!

"Anybody still here?" he shouted as he rushed into the gallery. There was no answer. Milo sped through the gallery doors, descended the terrace steps, and followed the path that led between the tennis courts and the basketball court.

Having reached the field, he adroitly dodged the cars that were making their way to the roped-off area. Outside Lakesong's side gate, Fred was directing people to one of two shuttle buses. Milo stepped onto the closest one and slid in behind Saul Feinberg and his date, Kimberly McKenna.

"Kim, you're in town!" Milo exclaimed. Kimberly, a successful lawyer from Minneapolis, visited Duluth only occasionally.

She turned and smiled. "I wouldn't miss a demolition lawn party. Who knows when there will be another? Love your skimmer, by the way."

"Skimmer?"

"Your straw hat."

"Thank you. It's a gift from Sutherland's father."

"Did it come with the will?" Feinberg asked.

"No, he gave it to me today. I think he knew I was going to a wrecking ball lawn party and thought it would be perfect for the occasion."

"Milo," Feinberg said softly, "John McKnight has been dead for almost two years."

"What's your point?"

Feinberg shrugged. "No point really."

The three continued their banter while other passengers filled the bus. Creedence Durant, Milo's financial advisor, squeezed into the seat next to Milo. "I brought my Morning Star flag, the symbol of hope and renewal for the Northern Cheyenne of Montana. I thought it would help cleanse the land."

McKenna gave Feinberg an accusing look. "Did you bring a symbol of anything?"

"Or a straw hat," Milo chimed in.

The bus began to move. All the passengers cheered. The trip down London Road was short. As the bus pulled into Mary Alice's drive, people caught sight of the festivities. The side lawn had sprouted a long table with champagne bottles, glasses, and platters of hors d'oeuvres. The yellow wrecking ball, dressed in colorful banners, flowers, and balloons, stood at the ready by the front of the house. Guests were urged to find a comfortable place on one of the many lawn chairs and bleachers set out to observe the destruction.

Mary Alice, reprising her role as the ultimate hostess, greeted each guest as they disembarked from the bus. This was the Mary Alice that Milo first met at her late husband's ill-fated New Year's Eve party so long ago.

Milo stepped off the bus, took Mary Alice's hand, and offered a slight bow. "Milo Rathkey. Your neighbor."

Mary Alice batted her eyelashes. "So good of you to come, Mr. Rathkey. Wonderful chapeau."

"It's an old family recipe."

"A chapeau is your hat, Milo."

"My skimmer? This was a present given to me today by the late John McKnight," he informed her.

"John, a dear man, must have given it to you to bestow upon me, I'm sure." She smiled.

Milo, once again falling victim to the beautiful blue eyes, removed the prized straw hat and gently placed it on Mary Alice's waiting head.

She smiled. "You're so easy."

"One of my many charms."

"Move along Rathkey," Creedence said from behind him. "You're holding up the line."

Mary Alice laughed.

Milo grabbed a glass of champagne off the tray of a passing waiter dressed in a tux and yellow hardhat. Holding his flute up for an imaginary toast to the late James Bonner, Milo caught sight of the yellow decorated wrecking ball through the bubbles. Milo smiled. It was so Mary Alice.

Mary Alice's son, Richard, walked up and greeted Milo. He was a much happier young man than the angry, nervous kid Milo met a couple of years ago. "Welcome to my mother's destruction luncheon."

"Are you okay with this?" Milo asked.

"I think it's outstanding. To paraphrase my mother, this was my father's house. We were only housed here." Lifting his glass to the ballooned wrecking ball, Richard shouted, "Let the new times roll!"

Richard introduced the attractive young lady at his side as Mandy. Mandy drank her champagne and looked bored. She did not impress Milo, who hoped this newest girlfriend would not last long.

Sutherland and Agnes came from the back of the house where they had been touring the property. Milo began expounding on the missing straw hat Sutherland's dad had given him that morning, which Mary Alice had usurped.

"I saw it. Looks more fashionable on her," Sutherland said.

Agnes laughed. "A burlap sack looks more fashionable on her."

The group spotted Martha and two of her sibs, Jamal and Darian, and moved to where they were standing. "They're going to smash that ball into that house?" Darian shouted. "So cool!"

Jamal nodded. "Very cool."

As they found their seats, Agnes said to Sutherland, "I forgot to tell you, I have a Darian report."

"About?"

"Darian and I were sneaking a peek at the new room over the garage, and I asked him about the mood of the house. He said the house was back. Something that was lost is back."

Sutherland looked at her. "What does he mean?"

"I've been thinking about it. Tee mentioned the other day the garage had been two stories—something about how the ventilation was installed. Maybe that's it."

Sutherland thought for a second. "Now that you mention it, that flat roof on the garage never went with the gabled peaks of the rest of the house."

"We can check the old blueprints. But if there was a room, where did it go?"

Sutherland smiled. "Looking at your face, I think we have another Lakesong mystery to solve."

Kimberly McKenna paused on her way to the lawn chairs to bend down and run her hand over the grass. She pulled out a four-leaf clover and showed it to Feinberg. "This can be our good luck contribution for this place."

"Nice," Feinberg said.

"That covers Irish good luck. Do you have any Jewish good luck?" she asked.

"I brought a pound of pastrami in my jacket," he joked.

"Good, we may get hungry later."

"Knowing Mary Alice's parties, these hors d'oeuvres are not the only food being served. Hunger will not be a problem," Feinberg stated.

Once all the passengers were off the bus, and Mary Alice finished greeting each guest, she made her way to the front of the gathering. Grabbing a microphone, she announced that Peggy and her crew were handing out costumes—white jumpsuits, matching hardhats, and goggles to deal with the expected dust. "Small chunks of odious debris might take flight and try to harm us. Oh, and we also have umbrellas."

Laughter and chatter were heard as the champagne flowed and hors d'oeuvres were consumed. It was already a joyous event.

The costumed guests in hardhats and goggles settled into the chairs and bleachers as Mary Alice began the official part of the ceremony. "Close friends and neighbors, thank you all for coming to this rather unusual event. As you know, other than the birth of my wonderful son, Richard, this house holds some dark memories. I have decided it's time to let the sun and joy shine through."

A smattering of applause grew to a standing ovation.

Mary Alice walked over to the wrecking ball vehicle, kicked off her street shoes, and stepped into a baby blue jumpsuit with matching work boots. To the shock of the audience, she climbed into the cab. "I've been taking lessons from Reg, my wrecker operator. Can I have a round of applause for Reg?"

Reg was clad in his regular attire—no baby blue. He stood, stroked his long, brown beard, and nodded toward the crowd, which responded with cheers and whistles.

Mary Alice adjusted her matching baby blue hard hat and goggles and fired up the machine. It sputtered and roared to life with a puff of black smoke coming from its exhaust pipe.

Even with the wireless mic Mary Alice was using, she had to shout over the noise of the machine. "This is the tricky part. We have been working on my timing."

The machine swiveled back, throwing the wrecking ball behind it. Then Mary Alice brought it forward. The ball whipped through the air and came crashing into the side of the gleaming white concrete. There was crumbling, but nothing fell. Getting the go-ahead from Reg, Mary Alice flung the ball into the concrete wall one more time. This hit punctured a hole, exposing wire and rebar. The personal irreversible damage to James' mausoleum had begun.

There was wild cheering as Mary Alice, taking Reg's hand, gracefully descended the cab of the machine and took a long bow. She picked up her shoes and joined the party in the chair and bleacher area. Sitting down next to Milo, she took his hand as they watched the experts continue the destruction.

"Is there anything you don't do well?" he asked.

Opening a bright-yellow umbrella, she smiled, "I work at it."

Each blow on the structure brought joy to Mary Alice's heart. An earth-shaking boom filled the air—causing most people to jump as a large section of the second floor fell to the ground sending up a dust cloud. Two water tanks employed to keep the dust down sent a refreshing mist of water the audience's way from time to time.

Emotionally satisfied that the White Whale would soon lie in rubble, Mary Alice announced that lunch was being served at her temporary home, the Hawthorn Estate, next to Lakesong. People began to shed their jumpsuits, hardhats, goggles, and umbrellas to begin reboarding the buses. Mary Alice was the last to board the bus. She looked back and smiled at the dust cloud and rubble. This was a good day.

§

Baby-goat yoga was fun, but because of her wrist, Preston spent most of her time petting the babies and feeding them snacks. After lunch, she decided to do some internet research on Ted Bear. What she unearthed couldn't wait for Monday, or should it? Preston was in a quandary.

If I let them know now, how do I do it? A text message or a conference call? Will the desk sergeant bother them just for me? Robin did it for the fire. I'm not Robin, and this isn't a fire, but it's pretty hot. Oh, why not? Maybe I'll have more than the weekend free if Lt. Gramm fires me.

"Cunningham," the desk sergeant said, answering the hotline.

In her best, *I'm in charge* voice, she began, "This is Officer Kate Preston. I need a conference call set up with Lieutenant Gramm, Sergeant White, and Consultant Rathkey." She held her breath and waited to be assigned to traffic detail.

"What did you say your name is, officer?"

"Preston, Kate Preston."

She heard him typing her name. "Preston…homicide?"

Stifling her urge to cheer and giggle, she responded with a simple yes.

"Hang on," he said. "Who did you want to connect with?"

"Lt. Gramm, Sgt. White, and Consultant Rathkey."

Several minutes later, the phone came to life with three brief beeps. Gramm spoke first. "Okay, Preston, what's this about?"

Inside, Preston was quaking. *I created a conference call… on a Saturday. Who do I think I am?* Outside, she was calm. "Sorry about the interruption, but I thought that a text on a Saturday might get overlooked. I have two pieces of information on Ted Bear. I thought everyone should know before Monday."

"Make it quick," Gramm said, stepping away from the cheering soccer parents.

"I found a photo of Bear and Priscilla Xi looking more than chummy at a party in Hollywood. It was on one of those Hollywood news websites from two weeks ago. The website called them an item."

"For us old people, who is this Xi woman?" Gramm asked.

"A hot A-list actress," White answered. "She's been in a number of superhero films that have killed at the box office."

"Can we see the picture?" Gramm asked.

"I emailed it to everyone," Preston said.

"Chummy is one description," Milo admitted, looking at the dimly lit photo of Ted Bear and the actress all over each other.

"It's Hollywood," White said. "That's how they say hello."

"What else?" Gramm asked.

"Bear lied. He did not fly in on Tuesday when he showed up at our office. He flew into Duluth three days earlier, on Saturday. He was here at the time of the murder."

Gramm sighed. "Marriage in trouble, lied, prints in the farmhouse. Ted Bear is moving up the suspect's list. He had motive before, now he may have opportunity."

"My prints were in the farmhouse, doesn't mean I killed her," Milo said.

"Where were you the day she died?" Gramm asked.

"Report to Interview Room B," White added. "Wait for us."

"Do we need to move on this?" Gramm asked.

"It seems to me," White said, "he doesn't know that we know. I think we can wait until Monday."

"He thinks he's his wife's heir. He'll stick around for the money," Milo said.

"Good work, Preston," Gramm said as he and Milo hung up.

"And just like that, they're gone," White said. "Good job, Kate. See you on Monday."

Kate smiled as she hung up, and this time didn't stifle her urge to squeal, giggle, and dance.

§

"Mary Alice certainly knows how to take a mundane event and turn it into a remarkable and delicious afternoon," Sutherland said as he headed toward the family room and Gopher football.

"Not so fast there, Bobo." Agnes said, stopping Sutherland in his tracks. "We have blueprints on the dining room table waiting for our enjoyment. We have a Lakesong mystery to solve."

Sutherland checked his watch. "I have thirty minutes. Let's knock this out. What a day!"

The blueprints, both old and not so old, were rolled up on the large dining room table. "We only need the garage part. You hold on to one end. I'll hold on to the other," Agnes suggested.

"No need. I have official Lakesong trolls for that," Sutherland said, moving to the large buffet.

"Lakesong trolls?" Agnes asked.

Sutherland opened a drawer and removed eight small but heavy, bearded trolls. "My father's cousin Lucy gave

237

these to my mother, who thought they were hideous. They only came out when Lucy was visiting. After Lucy died, they stayed in the drawer until I found a use for them. Now you know their use too."

Agnes was amused as Sutherland placed a troll in each corner of the blueprint. "Blueprint holders!"

Agnes applauded as she looked closely at one troll. It was an ugly thing with a snarling expression. "Your mother was right. These are hideous."

Sutherland looked at the oldest blueprint which showed Lakesong as it was built. His finger moved to the garage. "Oh, my," he exclaimed. "Darian was right."

"Ron Bello is at the front door," the intercom announced.

Sutherland looked at his phone to see Bello standing by the front doors. "Hi, Ron."

"Can Milo come out to play?" Bello asked.

Keeping his finger on the microphone button, Sutherland said, "It's that Bello kid from down the street wanting to play with Milo."

"Buzz him in. Milo's not here, but he can play with the ugly trolls," Agnes said, as she placed the last troll and rushed over to Sutherland to see what he said "Oh, my" about. The blueprint revealed a second story above the garage. Its roofline matched the rest of the house. "I have to show these to Tee. I want to match that roofline," Agnes said.

"Why was it removed?" Sutherland asked.

"Why was what removed?" a booming voice asked.

Both Sutherland and Agnes flinched, twisting to see the smiling face of Ron Bello.

"Sorry, didn't mean to surprise you," Bello said.

"Hey, Ron," Sutherland said. "We forgot we buzzed you in. We got caught up with another Lakesong mystery. This time, it's about an old room over the garage."

"I'm supposed to be interviewing Milo."

"He's still at Mary Alice's party," Agnes said.

"Mary Alice Bonner had a party?"

"A demolish her house party," Agnes said.

"Complete with a wrecking ball and everything," Sutherland added.

"Why was I not invited?" Bello kiddingly complained. "I never get invited to the good parties."

"Does Mary Alice even know you're in town?" Sutherland asked.

Bello laughed. "I was invited, but I had an interview scheduled. Gotta grab those interviews when I can."

"Milo is probably still at Mary Alice's temporary house, which is only next door." Sutherland pointed in the direction of the Hawthorn House.

Bello shook his head. "You do realize there are acres of land between this house and *next door?*"

Sutherland shrugged. "Well, yes. It's a healthy walk, but it's still the next door."

Bello saw the blueprints laid out on the table. "Looking for more treasure? Are you running out of Scotch?" Bello asked, referring to the bottles of Scotch Sutherland and Milo found in an old smuggler's tunnel under Lakesong's grounds more than a year ago.

"We're still working on the first bottle, Ron."

"The first bottle? How many bottles are there?"

"I am sworn to secrecy," Sutherland laughed.

"Can you divulge what you're tearing down?"

"We're not tearing anything down. We're replacing a room over the garage. It's part of our remodel," Agnes said. "Only we've discovered…look."

Bello leaned in. "I see. There was a room there. What happened to it?"

"We don't know. Why would someone remove a room over a garage?" Agnes said.

"Maybe a fire?" Bello guessed. "Has anyone written a history of Lakesong?"

"I have been told bits and pieces, but nothing about a fire at Lakesong or that missing room. As far as I know, no one has ever written anything,"

"Sutherland, I catalogued all the books in this house," Agnes said, "including some diaries. I only gave them a cursory look. I'll go back and check them. Maybe some of them deal with this house."

"Those diaries in the vault?" Sutherland asked.

"Yes. Let's go down there and check."

Sutherland looked at his watch. "Kickoff time, Gophers versus Wolverines, maybe at halftime."

18

The denseness of the early morning ground fog forced Sutherland to sweep his foot in search of the box of Ilene's pastries. They were not in their usual place. He refused to believe that Ilene would skip the Lakesong precious Sunday morning delivery. Having tapped his way over the brick porch, he began to search the steps cautiously from end to end. After five steps, his foot hit an obstacle. Success! His goat cheese filled, honey fig muffin and Milo's cream puffs were safe in a box on the bottom step. He would discuss the delivery box placement with Ilene on Monday.

Martha had Sundays off, except for poker nights when she made the snacks. Breakfast was not included in those snacks, but she had timed the large coffee urn to brew at seven o'clock. By the time Sutherland returned with the pastries, the coffee was perfectly brewed.

Yesterday, Agnes had thought better of wasting a beautiful Saturday afternoon in the basement. She went biking with friends while Sutherland enjoyed his football game. This foggy morning screamed 'vault diving.' She arrived at breakfast dressed in her musty, dusty gear: a UMD sweatshirt, old jeans, and tennis shoes. She yawned while pouring a cup of coffee from the urn, then forked the fattest, sugary cinnamon bun onto a plate and joined Sutherland.

"I hear a soft clowder of cats," Sutherland said. Both he and Agnes were silent and listening. Sure enough, the soft meow of a cat could be heard in the distance. "Milo must be on his way."

Several minutes later, Milo and the two cats paraded into the room. Milo poured his coffee and grabbed two cream puffs from the pastry box. Annie left him on his own. Jet pounced on imaginary prey.

"I think the cats are sweet to escort you to breakfast on Sunday morning, even though they must know there's no Martha and no bacon," Agnes said.

"I think they feel I would get lost without their guidance," Milo said. "And who knows, I might. It's a big house."

"I checked my catalogue of diaries," Agnes said to Sutherland. "None of them were written by people who lived in Lakesong, as far as I know."

"Why are you interested in diaries?" Milo asked.

Sutherland explained the mystery of the missing room over the garage, giving Darian credit for revealing it.

"Next time I buy lottery tickets, I'm taking Darian with me," Milo said.

"That's the spirit, Milo. Exploit the young man's gift."

"Besides, you are already wealthy," Agnes said.

"Old habits," Milo admitted.

"Since the diaries are a wash, let's look for something else." Agnes nudged Sutherland.

"You could check those metal boxes," Milo said, reaching for a third cream puff.

"Those cream puffs could add up," Sutherland admonished.

"I'm going swimming later today. All is good," Milo responded.

"What metal boxes?" Agnes questioned with annoyance.

"They're on the east wall, by the dragons fighting the really scary birds, not to be confused with the wolves and snakes fighting the really scary birds."

"Hanging from the wall?" Agnes was in a mischievous mood.

"Cute. On the east wall, there are two compartments that have these metal boxes in them. They look like the kind that lawyers used to store wills and deeds. I found them when Sutherland and I were looking for the smuggler's tunnel."

"A tunnel that Milo did not believe was there," Sutherland chirped.

Agnes turned to him. "Sutherland, you're having fun with this, aren't you? Now, Milo, have you ever looked in these boxes?"

"No, we were looking for a tunnel."

Sutherland began to speak, but he closed his mouth after a quick look from Agnes.

"Are you doing anything this morning, Milo?" Agnes asked.

"Swimming off three cream puffs. I thought we covered that."

"I understand that it's best to wait several hours after eating before going into the water, so you could…"

"That's a myth," Sutherland exclaimed.

Once again, he received a look from Agnes. "Ignore the man behind the goat-cheese-filled, honey-fig muffin. I think you should show us where these metal boxes are stored."

"I can do that. This is a good day for a treasure hunt," Milo said, looking at the fog covering the back lawn. "Then a swim. Hope it thunders. Love doing the backstroke, watching the storm through the glass ceiling."

§

Grace Pendergast left her coffee untouched on the kitchen table, stood up, and began to pace. "I wish you hadn't left your fingerprints all over that house, Bill! You work too hard trying to please Daddy. He should have been the one checking out that property. I love you and worry about you, Bill. I don't want to lose you."

Bill looked up from his Sunday breakfast. "Lose me? To what? I was just doing my job. You're overreacting for no reason."

"Bill, I'm not overreacting," Grace snapped. "You know bad things can happen."

Bill stood and put his arms around his wife. "I'm sorry. That was a stupid thing to say. I love you and worry about you and your dad. Your dad is not getting any younger. It's easier for me to check out properties with tough terrain, like broken steps. It'll all be fine. I promise."

Grace broke out of his embrace, turning to face him. "You say that, but you can't control bad things. Anna coming back here was bad. Her leaving a long time ago was bad. It hurt us, both of us." Tears streamed down her cheeks.

"Please don't." Bill walked over, wiping her tears and holding her again. "You're making yourself upset. The bad thing this time happened to her, not us. I love you. You love me. We're fine. We control our lives, not Anna. She's gone forever, now."

Grace put her head on Bill's chest and began her breathing routine to calm herself: in for five, hold for five, out for five.

"When you finish your breathing, let's plan places we want to go in Hawaii—Sunday fun day."

§

"Priscilla? Yes, I saw the picture. It's no problem for me." Ted Bear was sitting by the pool at his hotel. "Where are you? I'm only hearing every other word." He looked at his phone to check his signal strength. It was strong.

Ted waited for Priscilla to move to a better reception area. "That's better," he said. "The picture is no problem because my wife is dead. That's right, dead. Someone killed her a few days ago."

Ted paused while Priscilla talked.

"No, I did not kill her. Why would you even think that?" Another pause, longer this time.

"Well, yes, I was going to ask her for a… Okay, I do come into a lot of money, but…"

The more Priscilla talked, the more Ted realized he was being dumped. He was no longer the latest boy toy; he was now a bad boy entangled in a murder and Pricilla wanted none of that kind of publicity. So much for true love.

The phone went dead. Priscilla's director was calling.

§

Agnes and Milo gazed at Sutherland's ever-growing electric train layout, which had expanded another two feet into the anteroom in front of the vault door. Milo inspected a recent addition, a platform with barrels.

Sutherland, eager to show off his latest toy, rushed ahead to turn on the entire board and guide the barrel car to the platform. They all watched a miniature man load the miniature barrels onto a miniature flatbed train. The train then made one loop around the track, only to stop again at the same platform, where the miniature barrels were offloaded.

Milo feigned unconsciousness. "What's the point?" he asked Sutherland.

"When you're nine, it's really cool."

"I was nine once. Kind of meaningless if you ask me," Milo said.

"It's an electric train, not the topic for an existential discussion," Sutherland retorted, shutting down the board, and re-stacking the miniature barrels.

Agnes punched in the code to open the vault door.

Milo nudged Sutherland. "She has the code."

"I had to give it to her. We're married."

Agnes turned to look at them. "No, you didn't. Every code in this house is the same, 26643. They all spell Annie."

"Can we trust her?" Milo asked.

Sutherland pondered a while. "Hope so."

"Hey, if you two are done, let's get to work," Agnes admonished.

"Such a slave driver," Milo complained. He led them to the winged dragon carving along the east wall.

Agnes ran her hand along the carvings. "We have to find out who did these carvings. Look at this battle. Dragons versus strange birds."

"I think they're buzzards," Milo countered.

"Eagles," Sutherland said. "I'm rooting for the eagles. I always liked the eagles."

"Why hide this art in a vault in the basement?" Agnes asked.

"Well, before we solve that mystery, here are the boxes," Milo said, opening a cabinet in the middle of the battle scene.

Agnes reached in and removed one of three gray metal boxes. "Sutherland, Milo, we each get our own box. Let's take them to the old table in the anteroom and discover what we have found, if anything."

The tops of the boxes swung up on small, metal hinges. Inside each box were letters and legal papers, some still in their envelopes, some unopened. They dumped the contents, sat down, and began unearthing the mundane history of families, long dead, who had ties to their present-day home.

"Mine are financial papers, including mortgage papers about someone named Shellum who bought the house in the early twenties. Last century's twenties," Agnes announced. She wrote that name and date down on a legal pad she brought with her.

Sutherland held up several thick envelopes. "My box has documents in connection with a land dispute over what is now Patterson Park—you know, the one that goes by the road under the bridge. Nothing about the house."

Milo had been perusing the last box. "Have any of you ever heard of someone named Mildred Dowd?"

Both Agnes and Sutherland looked at each other and then shook their heads.

"She seems to be a relative of a Gorman family that owned Lakesong around 1910. There are a lot of letters in here."

"I'm creating a chronology of Lakesong," Agnes stated. "So far I have Gorman, 1910, and Shellum, 1923."

The three split up the letters chronologically and began reading through the box of personal correspondence.

"My letters are between Mildred Dowd's mother, Florence, who lived in Chicago, and a woman named Ethel Gorman, who lived in Lakesong," Agnes said.

"My letters show your Florence and Ethel were sisters," Sutherland said. "Florence begins her letters, *Sister Dear.* Milo's young Mildred, it seems, was sick. They keep calling it consumption. Doctors wanted her in a cool place with fresh air, so they sent her to her aunt, Ethel Gorman, who owned Lakesong."

"Wasn't consumption a catch-all for a variety of lung diseases?" Agnes asked.

"Consumption, fresh air, rest," Sutherland said. "Sounds like TB."

"Oh my," Agnes said.

"Any mention of our mystery room?" Sutherland asked.

"Not directly," Milo said, "but I have this letter from Florence Dowd to her daughter, Mildred."

I am so happy that you are getting stronger. Chicago is sweltering, but I've read the winds in Duluth have been blowing in from the lake for the past two weeks, keeping the city cool. That's exactly what you need, dear girl.

You mention your isolation bedroom has a small window that looks onto the lake. I am glad, but don't spend too much time out of bed. The doctors say rest. If you grow stronger this fall, Aunt Ethel wrote they could take you out on the back lawn for an hour or two.

I smiled at your idea of tearing down the east wall of your room and replacing it with a wall of windows. My prayers are that you could.

"It goes on with other things, but I think we are talking about your missing room. What other room in Lakesong has only a small window looking out on the lake?" Milo asked.

Sutherland turned to Agnes. "Refresh my memory. Was it your idea or mine to rebuild the room with a wall of windows overlooking the lake?"

"I think we both came up with it, or did the house suggest it? Are we remodeling Lakesong for its ghosts?" Agnes wondered.

"A wall of windows makes sense," Milo said, "but I'd sleep with a light on if I were you two."

Agnes held up her hand. "Stop it! Lakesong does not scare people."

"That letter still doesn't answer the question of why they got rid of that room. Did Mildred die?" Sutherland asked.

"That's grim," Agnes complained. She took out her phone to do some research. "Why do I have five bars in this sealed room?"

Sutherland pointed to a device with an antenna on the ceiling. "Dad put in a Wi-Fi amplifier."

Agnes called up her search engine and typed the name Mildred Dowd. "She didn't die!"

"Well, she had to at some point," Sutherland said, garnering him a high five from Milo.

"Here's Mildred Dowd's engagement announcement in the Duluth Evening Herald. She's marrying a young man named Terrance Dudley Shellum. According to this write up, the two will live on the Lakesong estate following the death of Mildred's Aunt Ethel the year earlier."

"So, Ethel had no other heirs?" Sutherland asked.

"Apparently not," Agnes said.

"I think you two are missing the phrase *isolation bedroom*," Milo said. "I think Milly—I hope I can call her Milly—came down with TB as a young girl. They farmed her out to her aunt here at Lakesong, where she recovered. I bet they tore down the isolation bedroom to keep from infecting other people."

"Kinda extreme," Sutherland said. "Oh, and you may not call Mildred, Milly. She thinks you're impertinent."

"I am," Milo said, taking his phone out of his pocket and calling Medical Examiner Doc Smith.

"Milo, it's Sunday. No bodies on Sunday."

"No body, just a question."

Smith sighed. "Go ahead."

"During the turn of the last century, if someone had tuberculosis, would the room they lived in be torn down after they either died or recovered?"

"That would be extreme, but not unheard of. TB germs can live several months after leaving the body if in a dark place. Tear down the room, let in the sunlight."

"Thanks, Doc."

"Milo, your questions are always entertaining." Smith hung up.

"The short answer is yes," Milo said. "If you had the money, tearing down the room would make sense to people in the early nineteen hundreds. I've solved your mystery. I'm going swimming."

"I'm finding out more about Mildred Dowd," Agnes announced.

"Just don't call her Milly," Milo kidded, "or your husband will chide you."

§

Sutherland left the Sunday night poker game $2.35 cents richer, but he seemed to be missing a wife when he arrived back home. Agnes was not in their Lakesong apartment, nor was she downstairs in the gallery, family room, or kitchen. On a whim, he went up to the second floor. He found Agnes sipping a glass of wine. She was sitting on a folding chair, staring at the lake through the new floor-to-ceiling windows in their new room over the garage.

"Hey there," Sutherland said, sitting in a second chair opened beside her. "What's up?"

"She lived to be eighty-eight," Agnes said, reaching down for the wine bottle and a second glass. She poured Sutherland a full glass and handed it to him.

"Mildred?"

"Milly. Yes. She had three children, two boys and a girl."

"You've been doing your research."

Agnes turned to him. "I can almost feel her, a weak, young girl all alone in a room half this size with only a tiny window."

"But she got better. As you say, she married, had children, lived a full life," Sutherland said.

Agnes gave him a sad smile. "But when she was here, in this space, she didn't know any of that was going to happen. She didn't know if she was going to live until the end of the month. How scary that must have been."

Sutherland put his arm around her shoulders, and she laid her head back. "This is an old house. It has many stories to tell—some sad."

She looked up at him. "Hopefully, we will add more to the happy."

"We are the next chapter in the history of this house. A strange chapter with the addition of Milo, but a happy chapter for me. How about you?"

"Oh, yes!"

The fog had lifted. The rain clouds had passed, leaving the lake dark and smooth, reflecting the light of a full harvest moon. "These windows were a wonderful idea, no matter who thought of them."

As Agnes topped off their wineglasses, she pronounced, "I love you, my husband, but you must tell me one thing about which our entire relationship depends."

"What is that?"

"Did you win or lose tonight?"

"I won $2.35."

"Just two thirty-five?"

"That's a lot in our game."

"Do better next time. I have plans."

"Yes, dear."

19

Judge Randall Hoffer was accustomed to uncrowded courtrooms and perfunctory proceedings. He had just turned sixty, a number he preferred to forget. The estate of Walter Schmidt Junior had many claimants, some of whom were deceased. Looking at the crowded table of attorneys and their clients, he joked, "Well, this is different. Who represents Mr. Schmidt Junior?"

"I do, Your Honor, Wilson David."

"I have the filings in front of me. Mr. David, could you summarize your client's last wishes?"

"He left his entire estate, farmhouse, two barns, a silo, and a considerable amount of land to his daughter, Anna Schmidt. At the time of the creation of the will, he had not heard from her for more than six years." The attorney checked his notes. "Anna Schmidt hadn't been seen for almost seven years, so there was the possibility the court would declare her legally dead. If that happened, his cousin, Susan Peterson, would inherit the entire estate."

"Was Anna Schmidt located?"

"She was identified, in a way, Your Honor."

Judge Hoffer remained silent, waiting for the attorney to clarify. That didn't happen. The judge looked up, grimaced, and, while scratching the side of his neck much like a dog, asked, "Identified? Counselor, what do you mean?"

"She was found to be deceased in the Schmidt farmhouse a week ago Sunday. Murdered, Your Honor," David explained.

Michelle Zielinska stood. "Your Honor, I would like to point out that my client, Susan Peterson, is one of two people mentioned by Mr. Schmidt. Sadly, the other person, Anna Schmidt, is now deceased. I feel my client should be the beneficiary of Mr. Schmidt's will, per his wishes."

Judge Hoffer waved her off. "We aren't there yet, Ms.?"

"Zielinska, Your Honor."

"Mr. David, was Anna Schmidt's body hiding in that farmhouse for seven years?"

"No, Your Honor."

The judge waited for more. When it didn't come, he ordered, "Explain, please!"

"She was murdered a week ago Sunday," Wilson David said.

"Is there a representative of the Duluth Police Department here today?" the judge asked.

Lt. Gramm rose, "Lt. Ernie Gramm, Your Honor, Duluth Homicide."

"Thank you, Lieutenant. Can you summarize your investigation into the death of Anna Schmidt?"

"One of our consultants found her body in her family farmhouse on Sunday last week. She had been stabbed several times. Medical Examiner Doctor Cyril Smith pronounced her dead. At this time, the case is ongoing."

"When did Doctor Smith say she died?"

"Sometime that Saturday evening or early Sunday morning."

"So, she was alive when her father died?"

"Correct, Your Honor."

"Does Anna Schmidt have heirs?"

A youngish lawyer stood up, adjusted his tie, and said, "My client, Theodore Bear, is the husband of Anna Schmidt and therefore the sole beneficiary of her estate."

"And you are?"

"Sorry, Your Honor. Nathan Sharpe of Haney, Jenson, and Hempft. We represent Anna Schmidt's husband, Theordore Bear."

Michelle Zielinska stood again. "Your Honor, I maintain that as Anna Schmidt was still missing when the will was written and read, my client…"

"Sit down, Ms. Zielinska," Judge Hoffer ordered. "I understand your client's claim."

"I would simply point out that the Court was due to rule on my client's petition to have Anna Schmidt declared legally dead."

The judge scratched his neck again. "Except her actual death, occurring when it did, superseded that ruling." He turned toward the bailiff and said, "I don't expect to have to say that again, ever."

The bailiff nodded.

The judge continued. "Now, I am told there is yet another claimant to the estate."

Saul Feinberg stood up. "Yes, Your Honor."

"Ah, Mr. Feinberg, I was so hoping you were here simply to observe."

Sgt. White leaned over to Gramm and whispered, "Why do none of these judges like Feinberg?"

"He has a tendency to turn easy cases on their heads," Gramm whispered back.

"I represent Leo Lehto of Oulu, Finland. He is the brother of Walter Schmidt Junior's second wife, Clara Lehto Schmidt."

Zielinska rose again. "Your Honor, if it please the court, I would like to point out that Mr. Schmidt had divorced Clara Schmidt and did not name her in his will."

"Because he shot her!" Feinberg blurted. "Last week, the police found Clara Schmidt's body in a barn on the Schmidt property. Prior to the divorce, her husband murdered her and left her body to rot in that barn."

"There is no proof, Your Honor, that her husband pulled that trigger," Zielinska charged.

Judge Hoffer held up his hand before anyone could speak again and said to Gramm, "Lieutenant, are you familiar with the finding of Clara Schmidt's body?"

"I am Your Honor."

"Have you classified it as a homicide?"

"We have, Your Honor."

"Who committed that homicide?"

"We have determined that Clara Schmidt was killed by a blast from a shotgun. I received a call this morning from the medical examiner telling me that the fingerprints on a shotgun found in the barn where we found Clara Schmidt's body were those of Walter Schmidt Junior. We feel confident that he killed his wife eight years ago."

"I object, Your Honor," Zielinska shouted. "There are a number of problems with that conjecture. One, there is no way to trace a shotgun to the pellets. Two, Anna Schmidt could have killed Clara Schmidt using a shotgun with her father's fingerprint on it."

"Your Honor, Walter Schmidt Junior loaded his own shotgun shells. We found the equipment, shells, and pellets in the farmhouse. The pellets found in Clara Schmidt's remains were identical to the ones on the loading bench," Gramm added.

"Lieutenant, are you going to be investigating the death of Clara Schmidt any further?"

"It's an open case, Your Honor, but given the time and the deaths of most of the principals in this case, I doubt we will ever be able to reach a definitive conclusion."

"Lieutenant, are there anymore murders the court has to know about?"

"Thankfully, no, Your Honor."

"Is Mr. Bear in the courtroom?"

Bear stood up. "I am Your Honor."

"Mr. Bear, you were married to Anna Schmidt. Is that correct?"

"It is Your Honor."

"I am told she had been missing for almost seven years. Where was she all that time?"

"We were both in California pursuing acting careers. I have had meaningful parts in…"

"Mr. Bear," said Judge Hoffer curtly. "I am not interested in your acting career. I am interested in knowing why your wife returned to Duluth."

"She read in the paper that Mr. David was looking for her because of her father's will. She came back to collect her inheritance."

"Thank you, Mr. Bear. Is Susan Peterson in the courtroom?"

"I am Your Honor," Susan stood. Gordy began to stand too, but Zielinska motioned him down.

"How often did you see your cousin, Walter Schmidt Junior?"

"How often?"

"Yes, weekly, monthly, yearly, once in a blue moon. It's a simple question."

"Well, um…" Susan appeared to be struggling. "I contacted him a couple of years ago."

"Did he respond to that contact?"

"He declined my invitation to a family reunion."

Zielinska interrupted. "Your Honor, my client is one of only two people named in the will. Clearly, she was important to Mr. Schmidt."

"Mr. David."

Wilson David stood.

"When you wrote Mr. Schmidt's will, was it your opinion that he was leaving his estate to both his daughter and his cousin, Ms. Peterson?"

The attorney fumbled with a handful of notes he had pulled out of his pocket and took several minutes to find the right one. "No, Your Honor. He left his estate to his daughter, and if she couldn't be found, then to his cousin."

"Ms. Peterson, given that we now know Anna Schmidt was alive when her father died, I reject your claim on the Schmidt estate based on the terms of the will."

"YOUR HONOR!" Zielinska shouted.

The judge grimaced. "Tone it down, Ms. Zielinska."

"Sorry, Your Honor. I feel we haven't made our full case. For instance, the circumstances of the death of Clara Schmidt are still cloudy. There is no direct proof that she was murdered by her husband. Lieutenant Gramm has conceded as much here in court."

"Let me stop you there." The judge held up his hand. "Given that Anna Schmidt was clearly alive at the time of Walter Schmidt Junior's death, I have just ruled Anna inherits by the terms of the will. The death of Clara Schmidt does not matter here. That does lead us to the next issue to be decided at this hearing: Does Anna Schmidt's heir inherit the estate, or does the heir to Clara Schmidt also have a legitimate claim?"

"Your Honor," Zielinska interrupted.

"This is making me weary." The judge began scratching his neck again.

"I wish he'd get some itching cream. I'm starting to itch myself," White whispered to Gramm. "What's wrong with him?"

"No clue," Gramm shrugged. "Probate is not our usual beat."

Zielinska continued. "Your ruling has extremely disappointed my client, and I must inform the court of our intention to appeal."

"Thank you, Ms. Zielinska. I shall not sleep until that appeal is adjudicated. Now, Mr. Feinberg, as to your client,

Mr. Lehto, if Clara Schmidt was murdered by her husband, do you believe her heirs, under Minnesota law, have some claim on the estate?"

"Yes, Your Honor."

"So, here's the problem. The police are confident that Walter Schmidt Junior killed his wife but have no proof. To save time and resources, I would recommend you and Attorney Sharpe urge your clients to come to some mutual agreement as to the splitting of the estate. If you cannot do that, your clients will be at the mercy of my court to decide the final inheritance."

§

"Goddamnit! I'll be damned if I am going to let that pixied, whitewashed blond bimbo cut me out of my inheritance," Susan screamed in the hallway outside the courtroom. Both her husband and her lawyer were trying to quiet her down.

Gramm and White stood off to the side but within earshot, just in case she said something incriminating. This was not the unflappable legal assistant they had come to know.

Gordy attempted to collect her and lead her out the door. She shook him loose. "You…you said we were going to be rich. You knew how to work the system. HA! So far, the system has worked you!" Susan turned her wrath on the gathering of people watching this spectacle. "Anybody here want to buy a BlowVee? My idiot husband thinks it's the latest thing in hair cutting. No? Come on people, buy two or three. We have an entire storage unit full of them! Arrggghhh! Why can't I ever win? Why?"

Gordy's shoulders slumped. He stepped back.

Michelle Zielinska, who was not only Susan's lawyer but also her boss, grabbed her by the shoulders and moved her face inches from the screaming woman. "Susan, we are leaving the courthouse. We are leaving it now!"

Zielinska grabbed one arm while nodding at Gordy to grab the other. The two dragged Susan out the front doors. White moved forward and heard the lawyer tell the husband to call Susan's doctor.

"She has her little benzos in her purse," Gordy said.

Zielinska stopped. "Then, for God's sake, give one to her!"

"She took one this morning."

Susan began screaming again, attracting a larger audience outside the courthouse.

"Give her another!"

Gordy reached into his wife's purse, took out a pill bottle, tapped out one white pill, and forced it into his wife's mouth. "Swallow!" he ordered.

She swallowed the pill and slowly became much calmer as she was guided to the attorney's nearby car.

"She took that well," Gramm said to White.

White was on the phone. "Mr. Bear, when did your wife cut her hair short?" She looked at Gramm as she got the answer.

"Yes?"

"According to Teddy Bear, Anna got her haircut into a pixie-do two weeks ago."

"And Susan Peterson just described Anna as a pixied, whitewashed, blond bimbo."

"Of course, if we believe her, she did say she saw Anna's dead body," White admitted.

"I don't know. A hair style is something you usually describe about a living person. When people describe a cadaver, they rarely mention the hairstyle."

§

Over the summer, Kayla had made changes to her look. She still had the stringy, dirty-blond hair, and red lipstick. Her ever-present jean jacket had been taken as evidence after the mugging, so she switched to a yoga jacket and pants. She also added color. Today's colors were a bright turquoise jacket with black pants and matching turquoise piping. Kayla considered it actively professional and reflective of her calmer, brighter self.

Since the murder last winter of his friend and partner, Alex Sithens, Vincent van Dyke had been barely able to sustain his sign business by reorders from longtime customers. His accounts were about to dip into the red. He had always avoided dealing with people—that was Alex's job—and he desperately needed a salesperson to run the front of the store.

Kayla opened the door and saw Van Dyke sitting behind the counter in back of the showroom. He stood up. His usual mop of coiled, red-copper curls had been tamed. The sides and back of his head were shaved. He felt naked but wanted to make a good impression on Kayla. It was a good investment. He wouldn't have to get another haircut for a year.

As she approached, his mouth began to dry up. He still found her beautiful. Towering over the young woman, Van

Dyke hesitantly offered an ink-stained hand. "I...I...I'm Vincent. I design and create signs. I don't sell." Vincent, who almost never looked anyone in the eye, couldn't stop staring at Kayla.

Kayla smiled. "Here's my resume again if you have questions."

Vincent took the single sheet of paper as a customer walked in. His head turned toward the backroom. His breathing became labored. He squeezed his eyes shut and muttered, "Can I...I...help you?" Vincent's voice shook.

A heavy-set and white-bearded middle-aged man in a red flannel shirt and jeans marched to the counter. "I just bought a tree farm up the shore. In a month, I'm going to start selling Christmas trees from an empty car not too far from here. I need a sign."

"Umm...umm." Vincent knew he should be asking questions, but all he could do was flip through a thick book of signs, pretending to be looking for something.

The lack of conversation was getting uncomfortable— even for Kayla. "You'd be good at selling Christmas trees with your white beard and all," Kayla said. She spun the book away from Vincent and asked the tree farmer, "What did you have in mind?"

Vincent shrunk back to his chair, relieved to let Kayla do the talking.

"I just need a board that says *trees* in like red and green paint."

"Well, you could do that, but I've been in business for a while, and I know for a fact a painted, wooden, slapped-together sign screams *temporary and cheap*."

"The lot is temporary. Only for Christmas, and cheap fits my budget exactly." The bushy guy bristled.

Kayla nodded and smiled. "I get that, but do you plan on coming back next year? Isn't it your plan to have this be the first of many years to come? Your sign should say, 'Bert's Trees is Here to Stay.' Getting a tree at Bert's from a person who looks like Santa will become a fun family tradition. Right?"

"Max. My name is Max. But you know, I like Bert. *Max's Trees* is hard to say. My mouth moves too much. Max's trees. Max's trees. Don't like it. Never thought of that Santa angle either. All my people will wear a white beard. That's good."

Kayla and Max flipped through the book and, in the end, settled on two backlit signs with professional lettering that could be used for many years. Max also added five Santa tallboys that would annoyingly wave at the customers for two months annually.

As the man was paying, Vincent managed to ask if he was going to be selling in the old Friendly Al's lot. Max nodded.

"We are familiar with that property," Vincent said.

After Max left, Kayla handed the book back to Vincent. "So, I made a healthy sale. Do I have the job?"

"Yes. I'm going to the back room to mockup those signs."

"Ah, boss? Don't I have to fill out paperwork, and I also want to know how much I get paid?"

Vincent began opening desk drawers looking for the new-hire paperwork.

"Boss?"

"Yes?"

"Maybe I can help you find that paperwork."

"Please. I have no clue."

She marched around the counter to an old gray file cabinet, pulled open the top drawer, and found everything needed. The money negotiation took less time, and Kayla was quite pleased with the result—base salary plus commissions. Much better than selling candles and soaps.

§

Milo and Preston crowded around a single desk with a large computer screen. As they looked through the forensic pictures, Handy hovered nearby.

"Thanks for helping us out here, Handy," Preston said.

"I'm yours for the day," he beamed. "I organized the pictures by rooms. I can do it differently if that doesn't work for you."

"Thanks, Handy," Milo said.

A picture of the kitchen came up the first of hundreds of pictures showing the body, the table, each appliance, the floor, even the walls. "You certainly are thorough, Handy," Milo congratulated the man.

Milo said he wanted to see the room where the attack began.

"It's a sewing room," Handy said.

"Shouldn't we look at the staircase, too?" Preston asked. "There was some blood on the wall leading down the stairs."

"I'm not looking for what we know. I'm looking for what we don't know."

Preston tilted her head and looked at Milo in confusion.

"I think someone burned down that house hoping to destroy fake evidence. Evidence they planted to further blame

Clara Schmidt for Anna's murder. It was bad luck for them we found Clara's body."

Milo stared at a picture of the sewing table. "A sewing machine, thread, scraps of cloth—looks normal to me."

"Yes and no."

"What's yes and no?" Milo asked.

"What you named is normal for a sewing table, but the red yarn doesn't belong there. It's kind of eerie."

"What do you mean?"

"All of Clara's sewing things are here, but none of her knitting things. I think she knitted elsewhere. When Lt. Gramm and I interviewed Ted Bear, he had a red sweater. He made a big deal about it. He said Clara always knitted things in red."

Milo looked at the monitor more closely. "Handy?"

"Yes?" The man came closer to Milo.

"Is that a sales slip? Zoom in on that."

"Sure."

"Kinda blurry. Did you take a close-up of just the sales slip?"

"No, not the sales slip."

Milo slumped.

"I don't bother taking closeups of items the forensics team bags and tags."

Milo unslumped, "We have that sales receipt?"

"Oh, yes."

Milo looked at Preston. "We need to make a trip to the evidence locker."

20

Court had been interesting, but no one had jumped up to confess. Gramm was eager to return to his office. He was hungry. The office rumors had the burritos reappearing in the vending machine, and he wanted to beat Milo to them. White, never a fan of vending machine food, had ordered a delivery of loaded chili and a grilled cheese while still on the road.

When Gramm and White arrived in the bullpen, Milo looked up from his feast of two vending machine burritos. "About time you two came to work."

Gramm's eyebrows knitted in an unfriendly fashion. "Those had better not be the last two of their kind."

"Not a problem," Milo said. "The guy loaded two rows of burritos."

"Oh, happy day," White mocked.

Milo lifted a clear plastic evidence bag and waved it in the air. "Gotta little gift here."

Gramm yanked it out of his hand. "What am I looking at?"

Preston walked in, having taken her lunch out of the refrigerator. "It's a receipt for a skein of yarn—red yarn, the kind Clara Schmidt used to use."

"Look at the date," Milo ordered.

Gramm looked closely at the receipt. "The day of the murder."

"Maybe Anna Schmidt was taking up knitting?" White questioned.

"Maybe we go to Yarn Harbor and see if they remember who bought it," Milo suggested.

"Winter's coming, Milo. People are knitting things," White said. "I doubt they are going to remember one red skein purchase."

"There may be cameras. It's worth a shot," Gramm argued, "*after* lunch."

White flipped through the many pictures provided by Handy and stopped at a wider shot of the kitchen. "We have another store to go to."

"Do tell," Gramm said.

"Roger Lund's furniture store."

"Why would we bother Roger Lund?" Gramm asked.

White handed him the picture. "Look at this table. If it's newish like Ms. Jenkins said, the fingerprints on it would be recent. Ted Bear said his fingerprints had to be old, but we know he was in town in time to kill his wife and touch that table. It would be nice to get solid physical evidence against him."

"It's a table. How is Roger going to know when it sold?" Gramm asked.

"I think this is worth a shot, too," White said, echoing Gramm's earlier statement about the yarn store.

"Okay, Milo and Preston do yarn——carefully. Robin and I will do furniture, but first, vending machine burritos."

White's phone buzzed. "Good, my chili is here."

§

Kirkland Rafferty Jr., debated with himself all morning. His foot was still booted, and he had orders to limit any weight bearing. He was unsure, but he needed to know. His father's reputation and his future were riding on it.

He drove to the Schmidt Farm. There was no police presence, no guard. He parked near the old barn and silo, the one he clipped with his plane. Swinging his torso so both feet touched the ground, KJ pushed himself up and out of his car and limped to the barn doors.

Pulling one door slightly open, he peeked inside. The barn was empty except for an old milking machine hanging on the far wall and a couple of rusting pitchforks lying on the floor. The silo was empty. Disappointed, KJ got back into his car and drove up the road to the new barn.

He once again maneuvered himself out of the car with one bad foot and one bad shoulder. As he stood, he avoided looking at the charred remains of the farmhouse. Not a fond memory. Sidestepping a broken padlock and chain as best he could, KJ leaned his good shoulder into the sliding barn door. He shined a flashlight inside.

271

Hundreds—maybe even a thousand—old tires had been neatly stacked up along the back and sides of the barn. KJ smiled as he estimated the cubic feet of the barn and did the math in his head.

I think that's all of them! he thought. *They're all here. None of them were buried, just stacked. I'm safe.*

He left the barn door open and limped to his car.

Kirkland drove away from the farm and, out of curiosity, drove to one of the nearby subdivisions. It was a forest of three-bedroom homes with attached garages. The sign on the stone gates at the entrance proclaimed this to be Martin's Landing. He stopped by the community green space to check the address of the house nearest to the entrance. That's usually one of the first houses built. He put the address into his phone. It was constructed twenty-five years ago, the same time his father and Walter Schmidt Jr. schemed to bury tires on the farm.

If I had only known the tires were in that barn, none of the rest would have happened, Kirkland thought while calling Arial Jenkins.

"Mr. Rafferty, glad to hear from you," Arial said. "We've taken a giant step in probate. The farm should be a free and clear sale in about…"

"I don't want it."

Arial was taken aback. "But we had a deal!"

"It's taken too long. I'm out."

Arial looked at her phone. Rafferty had hung up on her. *What a flake!* Normally, Arial's stomach would ache at this point, but she knew others would want that land. In fact, she was now free to seek a higher price, which, of course, would lead to a higher commission for her.

§

Preston parked the police car in front of the small brick building that housed Yarn Harbor. Two large glass windows on either side of the front door displayed hundreds of multi-colored balls of yarn. *Yards of Yarn,* Milo thought, and played with that phrase in his mind all the way inside.

"An avid knitter could go comatose from overload in here," Preston said. She looked at the shelves filled with skeins of yarn—every color, size, and texture.

"I will try to control myself," Milo said.

Preston walked over to several white angora hats and petted them softly. "I had a hat like this when I was a little girl. I still have it. My grandmother knitted angora hats for all of her granddaughters."

Milo had made his way to the counter. He showed the receipt to the clerk. "We're from the Duluth Police Department. We need to know who bought this yarn."

The clerk, an older woman who wore her glasses down on her nose, looked at the receipt. "By golly, no luck. They paid cash."

Milo looked around and saw a round ball attached to the ceiling. "Is that a camera?" he asked.

She looked up, squinting her eyes. "Oh, gosh, yes, it is. I always forget about that." She looked at the receipt again and invited them into the back room. "Do you happen to know how these things work? The owner isn't in town, and I've never worked it."

Milo said he did and sat down at the computer. Preston joined him and together they shuttled the video back to the date and time on the receipt. "Look at that!" he exclaimed.

The two were looking at a gloved figure in a black hoodie, walking up to the counter with one red skein of yarn. The person pulled a bill out of their pocket, paid for the yarn, pocketed the change, and left, disappearing behind shelves of yarn. There was never a clear shot of the face.

"That could be anyone, male or female," Milo said.

"What if that's Anna Schmidt?"

"Could be," Milo said. "Or it could be my Aunt Shirley's second son Bernie." This was disappointing. Milo sent a still of the video to a nearby printer.

After thanking the clerk, Milo and Preston left the shop. As she started the car, Preston asked, "Do you even have an Aunt Shirley?"

"Not that I know of."

"If you are going to make up an Aunt Shirley, why do you have to name her fictitious second child?"

"Anything worth doing is worth overdoing."

§

A couple of years ago, furniture store owner Roger Lund was one of many suspects in the death of James Bonner. Bonner, real estate cheat and Mary Alice's husband, had been trying to bankrupt and extort Lund out of business.

The block had changed significantly. Lund's Fine Furniture sported a new sign. A coffee shop had replaced the garish X-rated bookstore, and the empty store next to that was now a CBD shop. On the other side of Roger Lund's furniture store, parents were bringing their children to the Tumble Bumble, a place where kids could bounce and climb. The entire block was becoming a happy, thriving destination.

"Things have changed for the better," Gramm said to White as he parked the Ford Interceptor.

The furniture store was still as empty of customers as it was when they first entered it almost two years ago. Roger Lund came running up to them. "Lieutenant Gramm and Sergeant White, it's been a long time," Roger said, a grin stretched across his face.

"Still in business, I see, Mr. Lund," Gramm said.

"And thriving." Roger followed their gaze to the back of the store. "Not many customers today, but our business model has changed, thanks to Mrs. Bonner."

"Really?" White questioned.

"Yes, Mrs. Bonner is not her husband. Come over to the counter. I'll show you," Roger urged.

They followed him to the check-out counter, which used to support a tired old cash register and a sliding credit card reader. A wide computer screen had taken the place of the cash register. "Seventy-five percent of the furniture I sell never makes it to this showroom. It's all online."

"How does Mrs. Bonner come into play?" White asked.

"She felt sorry for how her husband treated me and my family. She ordered some expensive pieces from me—nothing I had ever handled before. Much too upscale, but I was able to find them, order and deliver them with a personal touch. She spread the word. Some of her friends called me and wanted me to do the same thing. I may still be in the west end, but now I do a lot of business along Millionaire Row."

"We'll have to pass that on to Milo," Gramm said to White, sarcastically before turning back to Lund. "Mr. Lund, we were wondering if you could help us date a table."

White showed him a blowup of the Schmidt kitchen table.

Lund looked at it. Handy had taken a picture of the underside of the table because that's what Handy does. Roger copied down some numbers and entered them into his computer.

"My father always said, you can buy furniture that lasts a lifetime, or twenty years, ten years, or the cheap stuff that lasts only five years if you're lucky Sometimes that's all some families can afford. Here it is, or at least something very similar." Roger smiled. "This is definitely a five-year table."

"When was it first manufactured?" Gramm asked.

"That's hard to say exactly, but the fact that it's still standing says to me it was made in the last five years."

"Do you handle this table?"

"No."

"Where could someone buy this table?" Gramm asked.

"Furniture Fantasy up on the Miller Trunk. They sell the really cheap stuff. Maybe they can give you a more exact date of manufacture. Like I said, some people can't afford to buy better. There's a place for everyone."

Gramm thanked him, and he and White left. Once back in the car, Gramm asked, "Shall we continue our furniture hunt?"

"Absolutely."

§

By midafternoon, Milo was back in Lakesong mixing a vodka gimlet. Author Ron Bello had poured himself two fingers of the Macallan single malt whiskey and began getting his digital recorder ready to capture his long sought after interview with Milo. "I am told by Sutherland that you have more of this golden liquid."

"I can neither confirm nor deny," Milo said. "Let's go to the gallery. I can gaze longingly at the lake hoping an ore boat will crash through the door, ending the interview."

Bello selected chairs away from the windows. "Just in case," he cautioned. "So," Bello said, pushing record, "let's begin."

"It all began in a log cabin on the Minnesota prairie. I was a precocious child, full of the wonderment of life," Milo said snidely. "My only childhood friend was a three-legged dog."

Bello thought he would go along. "The dog's name?"

"I don't know. He never told me. Dogs don't talk, Ron."

"Let's move ahead a bit. Who found the bodies at the Hawthorn Estate?"

"Really? I have some great coming of age stories. Just me and Scooter and that kid from Milwaukee who always gets shot at the end."

"End of what?"

"The movie. I'm saving some time here and moving from your still unwritten book to the subsequent movie. I'm being played by Chris Helmsworth."

"It's Hemsworth! Hemsworth! Why do you always put an L in there?"

277

"It should be Helmsworth. Not my fault the guy doesn't know how to pronounce his name."

"I'm told he's on another project, but the casting director has snagged Steve Buscemi. Cooperate or you will be played by Gary Busey."

Milo sipped his gimlet. "Okay, okay, Mary Alice Bonner and Agnes Larson McKnight found the bodies of Faythe Cummings and Alex Sithens."

"Why?"

"Why what?"

"Why would that unlikely pair find two bodies?"

"Mary Alice was remodeling her house, which, by the way, she just tore down."

"The remodel was that bad?"

"It's a process—first remodel, then raze."

"Could be a new show on that house channel, Tear Down My House."

"She served champagne, hors d'oeuvres, and swung the first wrecking ball herself."

Not knowing if this was the truth or more of the three-legged dog on the prairie nonsense, Bello tried to keep Milo's fantasies to a minimum. "I would expect nothing less. Can we please move on?"

Milo explained that Mary Alice was going to hold her New Year's Eve party at the Hawthorn estate but found dead bodies instead. He tried to make his narrative as dull as possible and kept the spotlight on others.

§

Furniture Fantasy had several couples milling around, one looking at couches, the other living room recliners. Gramm asked a young man with horn-rimmed glasses if he could see the manager. The man pointed to his name tag, which read Gary Idazoric Manager.

Idazoric, expecting a complaint, barked, "All sales are final. You were told that when you checked out. It's also on our receipts."

"We don't want to return anything," Gramm said, showing his badge and Handy's picture. "Do you sell this table?"

"Sorry, yes, we sell a lot of these."

"For how long?"

"We've sold this table for as long as I've worked here. It's a staple. I can check. Let me type in those numbers on the product tag and find out more."

As he typed in the model number from the underside of the table, he asked why they cared.

Gramm explained it may be an important detail in a current case. "There was an incident at a farm on Martin Road. We need to know when the farmer bought this table."

Idazoric stopped typing. "Farmer? On Martin Road? Old guy? Crazy?"

"Could be."

"My first day closing, three years ago, if we're talking about the same guy. He was my last customer of a very long day. He wanted this table, the one in your picture. I tried to sell him a better table, like I was trained to do. He went nuts. He screamed at me and said if I didn't ring up the blankety-blank sale right now, he would get an axe out of his car and cut off

279

my hands. I mean, that's nuts. The other salespeople had left. I was alone with this hand chopping nut job."

"Did you sell him that table?"

"Do you see any axe scars? Yes, I sold him that table… as fast as I could. As I rung him up, he entertained me with a nightmare about how he chopped up his other table and his wife. Unforgettable!"

"If it was the same guy, there was no axe. He shot her."

The young man didn't quite know what to do with that information. "Maybe I should have called 911."

"Where did you deliver the table?"

"Martin Road. Let me check for a name." The manager clicked a multitude of keys, many more than Gramm thought necessary. Minutes went by. Finally, the man looked up. "It says deliver 9-23 to Schmidt Farm off Martin Road. That's all he would tell me, and frankly, I didn't care. I just wanted him out of the store."

On the way to the car, Gramm said, "There's your solid evidence. That table was bought three years ago. All those prints are new, not old."

§

Later that evening, Gramm, White, and Rathkey got a text from Preston. *We finally got Anna Schmidt's phone records.*

And? Gramm texted back.

We have a surprise.

21

Everyone assembled en masse in Gramm's office Tuesday morning. White arrived with an extra sweater and a London Fog Tea Latte. She defended her choice of tea as medicinal—scratchy throat. Milo couldn't resist entertaining himself and the group, musing about how they got a London Fog raincoat into the cup. Preston was impressed that Milo even knew about London Fog raincoats. Gramm just wanted to start the day.

"PRESTON!" Gramm shouted.

She flinched.

"Begin before I am forced to shoot Milo, compounding our paperwork and probably forcing me into early retirement."

White laughed. "I'm thinking department commendation, not early retirement."

Milo began to retort when Gramm reared his head and bellowed, "Preston, for the love of God, phone record—now!"

Preston sprang up and handed out collated copies of Anna Schmidt's phone records. "I have marked the most called number. That, as it turns out, is her agent in California. She also calls her husband, Ted Bear, but in the past month, those calls have become irregular and short. In the days before her death, she called Arial Jenkins, Kirkland Rafferty Junior, and Susan Peterson."

"Not Bill or Grace Pendergast?" White asked.

"Those are texts, second page," Preston said. "Again, most of those texts were to her agent. She blamed her lack of work on the agent. The agent accused Anna of missing auditions or showing up unprepared."

Anna's recent texts to her husband were angry and threatening. Anna references the picture of Bear with Priscilla Xi. That picture was causing trouble between them. Bear defended himself, texting the arrangement was strictly business, and the picture was great publicity for him.

"This is good. Is this the surprise you promised?" White asked.

Preston grinned. "Oh, no. Next page. Second to the last text."

They all turned a page and read a text from Anna on the Friday before she died. *Oh, where have you been, Billy Boy, Billy Boy? Oh, where have you been, lovely Billy? I have been away too long—am back where I belong. I'm a young thing that needs her former lover. Love Anna.*

Pendergast texted back. *Farm 8AM Sunday.*

The last text from Anna Sunday morning, the day she was murdered, was much more straightforward. *Billy Boy, Upstairs. The door is open. You know the way.*

Gramm leaned back in his chair. "Wow! Quite an invite. Pendergast never mentioned these texts. In fact, if my memory is correct, he told us he had no contact with Anna since she came home."

"My eyeballs have steamed. I'm waiting for them to clear," Milo said.

"Pretty direct," Preston agreed.

"Well, let's get Bear in here, and also Bill Pendergast," Gramm ordered.

§

Ted Bear radiated outrage: back straight, head tilted, chin lifted, lips pursed. As he took a seat in Interview Room B, he demanded to know why he was there. As if on cue, he folded his arms. "This is harassment."

"Did you get that line from one of your plays?" White responded as she began the recording.

Bear remained in his angry-man character.

White slid a picture of the Schmidt Farm kitchen table over to Bear. "Do you recognize this table?"

He strained his eyes to look down at the picture and scoffed, "You dragged me here to identify furniture?"

Gramm picked up the questioning. "You told us you haven't been in the Schmidt farmhouse since you and your wife left for California seven years ago."

"Correct."

Gramm smiled. "But, you see, there's a problem with that. Your fingerprints were on this kitchen table."

"From seven years ago!" Bear barked.

"This table wasn't there seven years ago, Mr. Bear," White charged. "Your wife's father bought it three years ago."

"We want a straight answer!" Gramm shouted. "When were you in that farmhouse?"

Bear's eyes shifted from Gramm to White, then back to Gramm. His tilted chin descended to human level. "Anna broke my heart. She summoned me to the farmhouse on Saturday." The gray eyes began to water. "She wanted a divorce."

White thought this was either Academy Award-winning stuff or the truth. "Did you meet with her?" White asked.

"I had to. She was hysterical about the picture of me and Pricilla. I explained it all to her about how it was staged and planted for publicity for Anna and me. For our future."

"Did you stay the night?" White asked.

"No. Anna said she needed space."

"Tell me more about that picture," Gramm ordered.

"Our agents got paparazzi to snap the picture of Priscilla Xi and me having a drink together. It was perfectly innocent. I didn't do anything wrong, but Anna used it to create some drama in our lives. She loved playing a role, and this time it was the wronged wife. We were fine. We had our big scene. It was over except there will never be anymore scenes." His tears began to fall as he held his arms tight around himself.

Oh Lord, White thought.

Gramm slid the texts between Anna and Bill Pendergast across the table. "Your wife sent these texts to her old boyfriend the day before she died, and on the morning she died."

Bear stopped the crying and the hugging to read them and then burst out laughing.

White and Gramm glanced at the guard, not sure of Bear's next move.

"We laughed about this. She was going to get the lovesick beau, Billy, to sell her farm for her at no charge. She said he would do anything for her. Poor sap."

"What about this second text, suggesting that the poor sap come join her upstairs in her bedroom?" Gramm asked.

Bear was silent, then met Gramm's eyes. No laughter or tears. "Bait and switch. Getting Pendergast to sell the farm at no cost to her was the endgame. Classic Anna."

"What if it wasn't a game, Mr. Bear?" Gramm asked. "What if she cheated on you?"

"She didn't. We were good when I left."

White leaned forward. "I don't think so. I see it this way, Mr. Bear. You can't sleep. You arrive at the farm early Sunday morning just as your wife's lover is leaving. Who's the sap now? You confront her, grab a convenient weapon, and you stab your wife to death!"

"Sergeant, you too have a flair for the dramatic. That needs a rewrite. I wouldn't kill her. I'd kill him. She was my muse. He was a pesky mosquito. But, of course, I didn't kill either." Bear stood up, ran his hand through his hair, and rolled his shoulders forward and back. "If that's all, I have a business call I'm late for."

Gramm let him go.

White, Gramm, and Milo met up in Gramm's office. "What do we think?" Gramm asked.

"Acting is lying, and he's really good at it," White said.

"But if he's telling the truth, our victim led Pendergast upstairs with the promise it would lead somewhere," Gramm said. "Male hormones are tricky. In my career, I've seen that rage, and it isn't pretty. How well do we know Bill Pendergast?"

§

Bill Pendergast sat in Interview Room A impatiently checking his watch. His father-in-law was allowing him to take the lead on the Schmidt Farm deal. Plus, he was still playing catchup on their other Martin Road development. His life was on overload. He didn't have time for police stations. The detectives said they had new evidence that needed clarification. He brought an attorney, hoping to speed things along.

"Just answer their questions, it will be fine," attorney Harold Walters said.

Milo and Preston took their customary seats behind the one-way glass while Gramm and White walked into the interview room. "Mr. Walters, we meet again," Gramm said, remembering the attorney from the James Bonner murder case.

"Aren't you a real estate lawyer?" White asked Walters, as she began the recording.

"I am, but my client asked that I accompany him to this interview."

Pendergast defended his choice of lawyers. "We are putting together a significant real estate development deal and Mr. Walters' firm is representing us. We were meeting this morning when you called, and I asked him to come along."

"Fine," Gramm said. He opened his usually fake folder, but this time he had filled it with a print-out of Anna

Schmidt's calls and messages. The texts sent to Bill Pendergast were on top.

"Mr. Pendergast, do you remember getting this message?" Gramm said, handing the paper over to him.

Pendergast twitched when he read it. "What is this?"

"It's a text from Anna Schmidt to you on the day before she died," Gramm said.

"Do you recognize it?" White asked.

"No!" Pendergast began to raise his voice. "This is a lie! I never got a text like this!"

"Mr. Pendergast, please. It's a text sent from Anna Schmidt to you," Gramm said.

"It wasn't. I never saw anything like this." Pendergast took his phone from his back pocket and slid it over the table. "Here, check it."

White began scanning the phone for messages. She looked at Gramm and shook her head.

"Of course, you might have simply deleted it," Gramm said. "We will subpoena your phone records to make sure you received it."

"Go ahead. I never got this."

"Let's pretend for a minute that you are telling the truth," White said. "Is this a typical text from Anna—Billy Boy and all that?"

Pendergast took a deep breath. "Billy Boy used to be her pet name for me in high school. Anna was theatrical. She turned everything into a song or a play."

"Were you in love with her?" White asked.

"We were in high school. She was my girlfriend. I…I…"

"When she left town with Ted Bear," Gramm interrupted, "were you upset?"

"Yes, I was. Then I grew up. Anna was beautiful and good for my teenage ego. I do not still have feelings for her."

Gramm read Anna Schmidt's second message, *Billy Boy, Upstairs. The door is open. You know the way.* "Pretty suggestive, Mr. Pendergast. Did you act on that information?"

"I love my wife and have a good life. I'd be a fool to mess it up."

"Were you and Anna Schmidt ever intimate?" White asked.

Pendergast took a deep breath. "We tried to be toward the end of our senior year, but something always interrupted us. So, no, we weren't."

"This message implies Anna was willing to give it another try. Spice up a dull marriage?" White asked.

Bill looked at his lawyer.

Walters asked, "Is my client under arrest?"

"Not at this time."

"Then you are wasting our time."

Pendergast and his lawyer stood up to leave and Gramm didn't stop them.

§

Gramm and White left the interview area, leaving Milo and Preston in the viewing room. Preston noticed Milo was deep in thought.

"You know who did it, don't you?"

Milo looked at her. "Maybe."

"Give me a hint."

"It's not what you see. It's what you don't see."

Preston laughed. "What does that mean?"

"I'm never completely sure about these things. It could be nothing. It could be everything. I like to let my mind lint cook for a while."

"Part of your game?"

"Definitely."

§

"It's got to be Pendergast or Bear, but I'm going to go with Pendergast," Gramm said. "I think we have enough to swear out a warrant."

"Both have motive, opportunity, and means," White said.

"What's the motive for Pendergast?" Preston asked.

"Anna lured him to the house with an implied promise of canoodling," Gramm said. "Then he discovers she was only teasing."

"Again, with the term, canoodle," Preston said. "At least this time I don't have to look it up."

"Milo?" White asked.

"What? I was there when Preston looked it up the first time."

"No. What do you think about Bill Pendergast?" an exasperated White asked.

"I think he's the murderer," Milo said.

"Oh, good," Gramm agreed.

"Or not," Milo added.

"We have a third suspect with a money motive, means, and opportunity," White said.

"Do tell," Gramm said.

"No one guards their business closer than Arial Jenkins. The farm is a multimillion-dollar property. Arial's cut will be substantial—not something she would want to lose. Anna Schmidt was going to have Bill Pendergast sell the property, but that didn't happen because Anna is dead. And let's not forget, Arial knew Clara Schmidt and could have planted evidence." White added.

"Get her in for a formal interview, after lunch," Gramm said. "I still think it's Pendergast or Bear, but Jenkins is a close second."

"I think that makes her third," Milo pointed out.

§

Gustafson's Restaurant on Superior Street was Milo's second favorite eating establishment. Owned by Nick and Nichola Christos, it featured a number of Greek dishes but recently had branched out into French cuisine.

Milo opened the door and took in the mixture of delicious aromas served with the cacophony of voices, shouts, clanking dishes, and laughter. As usual, Nick waved as Milo led the group to their favorite back booth. Nicola was busy at the cash register.

Pat the waitress arrived with her signature pencil tucked behind her ear. "Is this it?"

"Do we need more?" Milo asked. "I'm sure I can find someone outside, and we could pull up a chair to make five."

Pat was unfazed. "Sometimes you people come in like you're a leaking faucet, one drip at a time. I don't want to go through the specials twice just because one of you arrives late."

"Only four and we're all here," White assured her. "What are the specials?"

"We don't have any today. Our delivery guy hit a bus. Everyone is okay, if you were going to ask."

"Wait," Milo said.

White groaned.

"What was the special going to be?"

"Why?" Preston whispered.

"Squid ink over old rocks," Pat said in perfect deadpan. "Now, order your meatloaf sandwich and stop asking questions."

"Pity," Gramm said. "I had my heart set on squid."

"You are not helping!" White admonished.

Pat took her pad from apron pocket and wrote down Milo's usual order: meat loaf sandwich, mashed potatoes and gravy, and green beans. The latter was always ordered but never eaten. She then turned to White. "What'll you have?"

"The avgolemono soup." White thought the Greek chicken soup would be good for her throat. Preston opted for the moussaka, while Gramm went with meat—a souvlaki, a Greek beef kabob with rice pilaf and tzatziki sauce.

"What about our drinks?" Milo asked.

Pat pointed at him. "Diet Coke." She turned to White. "Hot tea with lemon."

Preston said, "Just water."

"And our wild card," Pat said, pointing her pencil at Gramm.

"I'll double dip, water and coffee."

"A pleasure as always," Pat said as she left the table. Minutes later, she came back with four waters and placed them on the table, spilling a little by Milo.

"I see the water's back," White said.

"Pardon me?" Pat asked.

"A couple of months ago you didn't have water because busboy Carl broke a lot of glasses."

"That's former busboy Carl…"

"Nick fired him?" Preston asked.

"Of course not. He's Nick's brother's nephew by marriage. Nick made him a sous-chef."

"A sous-chef? This place has a sous-chef?" White asked.

Pat shrugged. "Nick put him in charge of cutting cucumbers, peppers, onions, and eggplant. The kid watches The Food Network and gave himself the sous-chef title."

Pat left for a second time.

"I love the family updates at this restaurant," Preston said.

Gramm, who thought the updates were a waste of time, tapped his water glass with a knife. "By a show of hands, are we down to three suspects, Pendergast, Bear, and Jenkins?"

"Milo thinks he knows who did it," Preston said.

"Care to share with the group?" Gramm asked.

Milo gave Preston a look. "The mind lint is still linty. Loose lips sink ships."

"Have I rushed ahead again?" Preston asked.

White laughed. "This time, it's not lethal, but you sent Milo back to old Navy days."

Pat arrived with the food, carefully putting the plates in front of each person—except for Milo. Pat plopped his plate in front of him, spilling some of his gravy.

"She loves me," Milo said.

"Damn it, Milo! You and your mind lint. What if the murderer isn't one of our top three? What about Susan Peterson?" Gramm asked.

"She was pretty unhinged outside that courtroom yesterday," White said.

"She also has motive, means, and opportunity," Preston said.

"As does everyone else," Gramm grumbled. "I know I've said this before, but I want a straightforward murder just once where we follow a set of bloody footprints out to the barn…"

"where the perpetrator is wearing a sign that says *I'm the murderer*," White interrupted.

"And is playing a peaceful game of solitaire," Preston added.

"So boring," Milo added.

White looked at an incoming text. "Arial Jenkins says she'll be at the station in an hour."

22

Arial Jenkins had been shown into Interview Room B. She sat and waited for a good fifteen minutes before an officer came in to ask if she wanted water. She accepted and asked how long before the detectives arrived. The officer said he didn't know. Arial took out her phone and began answering emails.

Gramm and White arrived twenty minutes later offering no apology. To make matters worse, White started the recording, and Gramm got straight to business. "Ms. Jenkins…"

Arial ignored Gramm and White and continued her texting.

"Stop! Put your phone down!" White ordered.

Arial looked up. "Why? You kept me sitting here. That's a waste of my time. I don't waste my time. I will send this text, then get to whatever."

Gramm resumed his questioning. "You said you talked with Anna Schmidt on the day before she died."

Arial tossed her red curls. "Again, wasting my time, and again, you're wrong. I said the woman identified herself as Anna Schmidt. I didn't say she *was* Anna Schmidt. I still think that call was a phony."

"It wasn't," Gramm said. "According to the victim's phone records, Anna Schmidt talked to you for ten minutes."

"If you say so," Arial replied dismissively, shutting down her phone and putting it in her purse.

"In that time, did Anna Schmidt tell you she was going to have someone else take over the selling of the property?"

Arial bristled. "Certainly not!"

"But she was. Her husband told us that Anna didn't like you and would not use you to sell her farm. That's a multimillion-dollar sale going up in smoke," Gramm said.

"What's your point?" Arial asked, whipping her red curls.

"Our point is, that's a motive," White said. "We think after that phone call, you rushed out to the farm, confronted Anna, and killed her."

Arial straightened her back and slapped the table. "I do not kill my prospective clients. It's bad for business."

"She wasn't a prospective client. That's the point!" White said.

"Of course, she was. I can't tell you how many people yell at me and threaten to fire me, only to hug me when the sale is complete. To be a realtor means having thick skin, dealing with all types, and getting the deal done. That's what I do. In fact, tonight, at the Radisson, I am hosting an intimate get together to celebrate my deal to sell the Schmidt farm."

That bit of news came as a surprise to Gramm and White. "That was fast."

"The judge urged compromise. I simply helped that along."

"Who's the buyer?" White asked.

"Wouldn't you like to know?"

"This is a murder investigation, Arial. Refuse to answer and you are courting an obstruction charge," White said.

Arial rolled her eyes and sighed. "Hannah Construction, if you must know."

"Isn't that Bill Pendergast's father-in-law?" Gramm asked.

"Maybe."

"This deal," White said, "why Hannah Construction?"

Arial folded her arms. "There should have been multiple developers interested, lots of bidding, bigger money, but you people screwed that up."

White almost laughed. "How did we do that?"

Arial slammed her hands on the table. "You broke into that barn! Found those tires and a second body! Shocker! Developers stopped answering my calls. They don't care about the bodies, but tires on the land would cost money—digging them up—super expensive. Whatever. Hannah was the only one still interested. Bird in the hand."

"What about Kirkland Rafferty Junior?" Gramm asked.

"He's out, but he's still a party to my deal."

"How does that work, out but in?"

"There are many moving parts, and I really object to being here and explaining my business to you."

"Answer the question," White demanded.

"It's a compromise. Everything is a compromise."

White bristled. "Explain, or you're going into a cell for obstruction, and you'll miss little soirée tonight."

"Oh, very well," Arial huffed. "No one is getting what they want."

"That's not true," Gramm said. "You're getting a hefty commission check."

Arial sniffed. "Not as hefty as it was going to be before you opened that horrible barn."

§

Late in the day, Gramm assembled the group in his office. "The DA has agreed that the case against Bill Pendergast is weak, but prosecutable. Pendergast was called to the farm by his former girlfriend; his prints are in the farmhouse; and he would know about Clara Schmidt's sewing room and the scissors."

"I agree," White said.

They all turned toward Milo.

"What bothers me is what we don't see," Milo said.

"Yeah, right!" Gramm said. "While Milo is pretending to know, we obtained an arrest warrant for Bill Pendergast. I say we serve it at Arial Jenkins' little get together. That way, if it's not Bill Pendergast, all of our other suspects will be there."

"This soirée is in a large, public space with lots of variables. Shouldn't we do this in a more private area?" White asked.

"Let's go, read the room, then proceed or not proceed," Gramm said. "At the moment, we don't have anything else."

"Let's get undercover backup." White said.

"Agreed."

§

Arial Jenkins was beaming. The rotating restaurant at the top of the Radisson was the perfect venue for this magical night. The lights of the Duluth harbor and hillside twinkled as the chatter and laughter of her guests filled the room. Prosecco, oysters, shrimp, prosciutto wrapped dates, baked brie bites, and sushi were being devoured.

At the moment Arial perceived a lull, she rang a little silver bell she bought for the occasion. The assembled turned toward the sound. Waving her hands, Arial chirped, "Hello everyone. We will get back to socializing, but I wanted to say just a few itty-bitty words. This has been a complicated and exhausting week for everyone. Let's raise a magical toast to our magical deal," Arial said, holding up her third glass of Prosecco.

They completed their toasts as several servers wound their way through the group, taking dinner and additional drink orders.

"Don't forget to enjoy our beautiful city, as this welcoming venue circulates."

KJ turned to Ted Bear. "I thought we were rotating, not circulating."

"She's had two more Proseccos than you and I. Her room is circulating—or spinning more likely."

Arial asked everyone to find their places around the large, round table. She scampered over to an empty place next to Ted Bear and adjusted the computer to face as many people as possible.

"Let's begin with the man in the computer, Mr. Leo Lehto." A distinguished-looking man with a stylish mustache, white hair, and beard waved.

"Mr. Lehto is zooming to us from Oulu, Finland." Arial giggled a bit. "No really, not our Oulu, Finland's Oulu. Hello Mr. Lehto and welcome."

Mr. Lehto raised his hand again.

Susan Peterson leaned over to her husband, Gordy. "That computer has a place setting. Is he going to eat?"

Gordy just shook his head, thinking Lehto's full head of hair needed a BlowVee.

Arial began introducing her non-digital guests. "For those that haven't met Bill Pendergast yet, he represents Hannah Construction and Development Corporation, which has agreed to purchase the farm. Stand up, Bill," she said, motioning to her right.

Pendergast stood up, nodded to the group, and quickly sat down. Grace smiled at him and grabbed his hand.

Arial continued. "Next to Bill is his lovely wife, Grace, who is also an officer in the Hannah Corporation."

Grace didn't stand, but smiled and raised her hand.

"Next to Grace is Ted Bear, poor Anna Schmidt's husband, who, along with Mr. Lehto, inherits everything. Poor Mr. Bear and wonderful Mr. Finland in the computer have agreed to compromise and split the profits!" Arial giggled again, grabbed another Prosecco, and declared this all to be so much fun. Mr. Lehto waved again and raised his glass. "I made sure Mr. Lehto received several bottles of Prosecco, so he could join us in each toast."

KJ leaned toward Ted Bear. "Shouldn't someone take him off mute?"

"On the other side of Mr. Lehto is Susan Peterson," Arial continued, "and her husband, Gordy. Walter Schmidt Jr. mentioned Susan in his will, but unfortunately for her, the judge ruled her claim to be invalid. So sad." Arial shook her curls for a moment.

"However, because this night is magical, Mr. Bear and Mr. Lehto have generously offered her a ten percent stake in the farm if she agreed to not sue or delay this deal."

"Gordy, could you turn Mr. Lehto so he can see you and Susan? Thank you. Wave."

Arial, glassy eyed by now, pointed to KJ. "Next up, KJ. I'm sorry, that's too familiar. His full name is Kirkland Rafferty Junior, whose lovely name and lovely plane crash started this entire…um…adventure. It seems Mr. Rafferty's father delivered the tires that were found in the Schmidt barn. If you don't know about them at this point, you don't need to. In short, Kirkland's company agreed to pay half the cost of removing the tires, and if there are more tires, well, that's Bill's problem. Right, Bill?" Arial began to laugh.

"I personally would like to thank every single one of you for your compromises that have moved this deal along so quickly. Let's eat, drink, and be merrier." Arial tried to sit down gracefully as several servers arrived with the food.

All was cheerful and chatty throughout dinner. As the desserts were being placed before each guest, Gramm and company entered from the non-revolving elevator in the center of the restaurant.

"Should we just wait for the rotation to bring our group around?" White asked.

"Kinda like waiting for my little cousins on the merry-go-round," Preston quipped. "Where are the undercover people?"

"Some are eating dinner, one is bartending, and two are servers," White said.

"I'd volunteer for the eating gig," Milo offered.

"Since everyone is in place, let's go to them," Gramm said. White sought out the manager and directed that all real servers leave the table until the police were finished. When she returned, they began walking counterclockwise on the inside track.

Arial saw Gramm and White approaching with several uniformed officers. She popped up. "No, no, no! Go away! You are not invited!"

Gramm produced his warrant. "This piece of paper says I am." He brushed past Arial and walked up to Bill Pendergast.

"Me?" Pendergast squeaked.

Gramm began to read him his rights.

Milo stood next to Preston behind Arial. "Figured it out yet?"

Preston turned and stared at him. "Not Bill Pendergast?"

"Nope. Think about the idea that the murderer is sloppy."

"Yeah, so many fingerprints," Preston said. "Didn't wear gloves."

Milo nodded. "Now, reverse your thinking."

Preston thought for a minute. "The reverse of sloppy is neat. The murderer was neat...wore gloves...didn't leave fingerprints."

Milo swept his hand toward the table. "There they are, Preston. Our suspects. Whose fingerprints did we not find?"

Preston looked from one person to the next, stopped, and stared. "Grace Pendergast," she whispered.

"You're getting good at this."

As Gramm was about to put the cuffs on Bill Pendergast, Grace jumped up. "What are you doing? Bill wouldn't hurt anyone!"

"Please sit down, Mrs. Pendergast," White said, getting herself between Grace and her husband.

Milo reached around to grab Arial's bell and rang it to gain everyone's attention. Gramm stopped. Grace stopped. Lehto, still on mute, was obviously talking, but no one heard him.

"That's it?" Milo asked, looking at Grace. "Bill wouldn't hurt anyone. That's all you want to say?"

"It's true. He wouldn't hurt anyone. What do you want me to say?"

"I was kind of hoping you'd confess to murdering Anna Schmidt, because you know, and I know, you did."

Bill Pendergast looked at his wife. "Grace?"

Grace turned to confront Milo. "I didn't murder anyone."

"Milo?" Gramm questioned, his eyebrows arching upward.

"You would know details about Anna's stepmother, especially the scissors. Clever trying to pin the murder on the missing Clara Schmidt. It was your bad luck that we found her body in the barn."

Bill Pendergast stepped away from the table. "Grace?"

Grace stared at Milo. "No, no, Bill. I won. I got you and she wanted you back."

Before anyone could react, Grace grabbed a steak knife from the table. Arial moved to stop her. "The servers will take that, dear," she said, not understanding the situation.

Grace grabbed Arial's arm, pulled her back, and put the knife to her throat. "Don't anyone move. We are going to walk out of here and no one is going to stop me!"

"What is going on?" Arial demanded.

"I think she's taking you hostage," Milo said. "I suggest you not move much."

"Hostage!" Arial yelled. "You're taking me hostage in the Radisson? This is the Radisson! You don't take hostages in the Radisson! It's magical."

"Shut up!" Grace yelled in Arial's ear, bringing the knife closer.

Milo, trying to distract Grace, asked, "What's the end-game, Grace?"

The undercover officers began to move in, but Gramm motioned them back.

Grace was moving backward, dragging Arial.

"Grace, where are you going?" Milo asked.

"Grace?" Bill asked.

"Bill, I won."

White was about to speak, but Gramm held up his hand and shook his head.

Milo repeated, "Where are you going, Grace? Are you going home?"

Grace stopped. Tears streamed down her face. "I won! I want my Bill! I wanna go home."

"Okay, drop the knife, Grace," Milo urged, waving Bill forward toward Grace. "You still have Bill."

The knife fell to the floor. Bill embraced his wife. "I'm here, Grace. I always will be." She lowered her head and started to sob.

Arial took cover behind Gramm. She grabbed another glass of Prosecco and drained it.

White and Preston negotiated each arm behind Grace's back, handcuffed her, and guided her out the door. Bill, their not so prime suspect, followed.

Gramm looked at Milo with outstretched hands as if to say, "*what the hell?*"

"Don't look at me," Milo complained, "it was all Preston."

"Yeah, right. Warn Martha, we need to come over for breakfast," Gramm said and followed White and Preston to the elevator.

"You realize we just let Milo talk her down," White said to Gramm.

He nodded. "I've seen him do it before. He's good."

KJ leaned over and took Lehto's computer off of mute. "You're finally free to talk, my friend."

"Vau, tämä on hauskaa," said Lehto, holding up his glass of Prosecco.

"After-dinner drinks, anyone?" Arial asked.

23

Milo nodded to Jet and Annie, both of whom were standing on his bed demanding he get up. "I have decided to no longer try to figure out how you two get in here. Clearly, you want to keep it your little secret."

Annie gave a meow of derision, as if to say, "We all know you can't let it go."

Jet gently stepped up on Milo's chest and pawed at his face. He didn't care if Milo knew the secret or not. He liked his morning pets. Milo complied, petting him under his chin and behind his ears.

Annie shook her head and jumped from the bed. This was too disgusting for her calico temperament.

By the time Milo had showered, shaved, and dressed, Sutherland and Agnes were about finished with their morning smoothies. Milo nodded to the couple, poured a cup of coffee, and accepted his breakfast from Martha. Annie received her piece of bacon, which she gobbled up in an instant. Jet took his and batted it around the morning room—a typical morning at Lakesong.

"According to my online paper, the police arrested a woman named Grace Pendergast in connection with the murder on Martin Road," Agnes said.

"Really?" Milo questioned. "Nobody tells me anything."

"The paper didn't mention you," Agnes said. "Did you have anything to do with it?"

"Maybe. Martha," he shouted, "Gramm, White, and Preston are coming over this morning."

"I know. You left me a note last night," Martha yelled back.

Milo blinked. "It was late and dark. No telling what I put in that note."

Martha leaned into the room and read, "*Cops coming. Morning. Hide the good china.* I'm keeping this for my memoir."

Annie clawed at Milo's leg for more bacon and was rewarded for her bad behavior.

"You know, Milo, bacon is not good for cats," Sutherland said. "According to the internet, it can cause vomiting, diarrhea, and obesity."

Milo stared at him before responding. "You do realize if Annie was out in the wild, she would be eating a squirrel's head right about now."

"No nitrates in a squirrel," Sutherland retorted.

Milo's response was cut short by the intercom buzzer. Sutherland didn't even look at the phone. He just pressed the *gate open* button and rose from his seat to open the front door.

"I always wondered why he goes to let in the police when they are here to see you," Agnes said.

"Me too, but I don't want to stop him," Milo said. "I'm hungry and trying to forget about cat vomit and diarrhea. Thank you, Sutherland."

The police trio strode in behind Sutherland and took up residence in the empty chairs around the morning room table. Gramm got up to secure a cup of coffee, followed by White and then Preston. After Martha verified their usual breakfast orders, they returned to their seats and the debriefing began.

"So, last night we went to the Radisson Hotel restaurant with a warrant to arrest Bill Pendergast, our main suspect, but it didn't happen," Gramm said to Agnes and Sutherland.

"Pray tell, why not?" Agnes thought she'd play the game.

"Funny you should ask. As we were arresting our main suspect, our for sure murderer, for whom we also had evidence of guilt, our and I emphasize 'our' consultant, instead pointed the finger at his wife, Grace."

"Preposterous," Agnes said.

"That's what I thought. Grace wasn't even a suspect."

"Then what?" Sutherland questioned.

"Grace Pendergast, never on our radar, shocked at being accused, grabbed a steak knife and held it to the throat of realtor Arial Jenkins."

"In the Radisson?" Agnes questioned.

White started to laugh.

"You're not the first to point that out," Preston said.

"Grace Pendergast confessed to everything when we got her to the station. She had read Anna's texts to her husband and took them as a serious threat to her marriage."

"Were they?" Sutherland asked.

Gramm shrugged. "According to Ted Bear, Anna was just playing. She only wanted Bill to sell the farm for no commission. Grace read the texts, thought Anna was stealing Bill. She deleted the texts Anna left on Bill's phone and went to kill her rival. She kept repeating that it wasn't fair, and that she, Grace, had won Bill. Grace also admits to creating the ruse of Clara Schmidt's involvement."

"It was Grace in the black hoodie who bought the yarn," White said. "She also admits to burning down the farmhouse to get rid of it after we found Clara."

"Kinda overkill," Preston said.

Gramm turned to Milo, "So, oh consultant of ours, we found Bill Pendergast's fingerprints in the farmhouse. He had a motive, spurned love, and he had means. Having been in the house numerous times in the past, he knew where the scissors were kept. Why would you think that Bill Pendergast wasn't the murderer?"

"It was the fingerprints," Milo said.

"Of course," Gramm chided, "our killer's nonexistent fingerprints."

Milo turned to Sutherland. "Let's say Sutherland here was going to kill Anna Schmidt…"

"I didn't even know her!" Sutherland said emphatically.

"Should I worry?" Agnes asked. "My husband is off killing complete strangers."

Sutherland took Agnes' hand and kissed it.

"Can I get to the point?" Milo asked.

"Please do," Gramm said.

"So, Sutherland, you arrive at the farmhouse planning to kill Anna Schmidt. What's the first thing you do?"

"Aha, I put on gloves so I do not leave my fingerprints at the scene."

"Exactly! And that my friend, is why I suspected Grace Pendergast."

Gramm was about to question Milo further when Preston said, "It's not what you see..."

"It's what you don't see," White finished the sentence.

"Everyone else left fingerprints and bloody footprints. They might as well have taken a selfie in front of the body. I thought either we had a stupid murderer, or someone smart enough not to leave fingerprints. But first we had to deal with the most likely suspect, Clara Schmidt, whose fingerprints were on the scissors. Finding a dead Clara Schmidt was a lucky accident for us."

"Who's Clara Schmidt?" Sutherland asked.

"The victim's stepmother. Everybody thought she up and left eight years ago," Gramm explained.

"Grace planned to make it appear that Clara had returned and was living in the farmhouse. Originally, we thought Clara's motive was that she wanted the money from the inheritance, and Anna was in the way."

"I think there's a *but* coming," Agnes said.

Preston raised her hand. "I kinda bumped into Clara while avoiding a shotgun blast in a barn."

"I thought she was dead. Who shot at you?" Sutherland asked.

"Walter Schmidt Junior," Preston said.

"But isn't he dead, too?" Agnes asked.

"Well, Clara is the most dead, but Walter is recently dead, but not as recently dead as Anna. Try to keep up," Milo chided.

Gramm sighed. "Why can't we get a simple murder?"

Milo continued with his explanation. "Well, the old murder, Clara's, was found by accident, booby traps, and plane crashes. Kinda boring and predictable. The new murder, Anna's, was clever. I thought, in order to frame Clara, the murderer had to know Clara. Kirkland Rafferty didn't. Susan Peterson might have met her a couple of times. Ted Bear was in the frame. His wife Anna might have talked about her. Bill Pendergast was definitely a suspect because he knew her when he and Anna dated in high school. Arial Jenkins knew her. She knitted in a group with her."

"Like we thought—Pendergast, Bear, or Jenkins," Gramm said.

"Except…"

"You said it last night," White said. "A guy wouldn't know about sewing rooms or where scissors are kept. Not enough to plan a murder around it."

"I object. I know about Agnes' sewing," Sutherland complained.

"Really, dear? Do I sew?" Agnes asked. "If I sew, where do I sew?"

"In the, um, in the bedroom where you take a bath!"

"TMI," Preston said.

"Do I have scissors in there? Big scissors, the kind murderers use?"

"Yes. Definitely. Maybe. I don't have a clue," Sutherland said. "Wait! I lost a button once. It reappeared on my shirt."

"Well dear, I suspect the dry cleaners sewed your button back on. I didn't, but my point is, you didn't know." Agnes smiled.

Gramm returned to Milo, "If Ricky and Lucy are done, can we get back to the murder?"

"Ricky? Lucy?" Preston asked.

"Two miniature schnauzers the Lieutenant had when he was a rookie," White explained.

"I guess we are now in agreement that many men do not notice sewing rooms and scissors," Milo said, looking at Sutherland, who nodded. "So, I'm thinking we are looking for a woman who pre-planned this murder and wore gloves. We have Susan Peterson, but, like I said, I doubt she knew Clara Schmidt. We have Arial Jenkins or Grace Pendergast. Both knew Clara Schmidt and knew about Clara's knitting and sewing. Throwing the murder on Clara was smart. If Preston had not been lonely and needed a friend, we would never have known Clara was dead. We'd still be looking for her, and Grace would have gotten away with murder."

§

The week had been long and trying for Agnes. She hadn't slept well since Mary Alice had told her she was destroying the Bonner house. For Agnes, even thinking about that house brought up memories of death.

She thought a lengthy workout in the pool might prove exhausting enough to help her sleep. The water enveloping her in a warm hug would be comforting.

She had been reading all the correspondence concerning Mildred Dowd, letters she wrote, letters written to her, and letters written about her. Mildred's loneliness was written down over and over. Agnes and her late sister, Barbara, always tried to diminish their loneliness, rarely speaking of it. Instead, they focused on how lucky they were to have each other.

Agnes began her four hundred IM. When finished with her cool down, she drank some water, flipped over, and floated, watching the red and orange leaves fall from the blue sky onto the dome.

She wrapped the towel around herself, threw on a coverup, and left the pool. Straight ahead were the stairs leading to Milo's bedroom. He had offered it to Sutherland and her when they married, but it was old-fashioned, didn't fit their style. This was the only time Agnes thought better of that decision.

Instead of a quick flight of stairs, she now had to trudge through the basement and up the stairs to the kitchen hallway. She stopped and leaned against the wall as she put on her flip flops. The cement floor was cold on her bare feet.

Agnes absently ran her fingers against the wall. She was thinking about last spring's unsuccessful search for a hidden staircase leading up to the third floor at the south end of the manor.

Resuming her trek out of the basement, she began to talk to the house. "I recreated the room over the garage. How about a hint of the location of those stairs?"

Agnes listened. Only the hum of the furnaces. Even though Agnes knew Lakesong liked her, the house didn't talk to her like it talked to Darian. Agnes climbed the stairs in her flip flops to change into warm work clothes and join Martha in the kitchen. It was coffee time.

The basement was now empty of people, silent, except for the furnaces' hum. Minutes later, they too fell silent. There was no one to hear the faint click where Agnes had leaned against the wall. A portion of the brick moved only an inch.

Agnes had gotten her hint.

OLD MURDER, NEW MURDER, WHERE ARE THE COWS?

If you wish to contact the authors, email us at authors@dbelrogg.com or leave a message at www.dbelrogg.com.

If you enjoyed this book, please leave a review on Amazon.

BOOKS BY D.B. ELROGG

GREAT PARTY! SORRY ABOUT THE MURDER

FUN REUNION! MEET, GREET, MURDER

MISSED THE MURDER. WENT TO YOGA

MURDER AGAIN! HAPPY NEW YEAR!

SNAP, ZAP, MURDER

CLUES, CASH, PIECES OF MURDER

OLD MURDER, NEW MURDER, WHERE ARE THE COWS?